MURDER IN THE MILITIA

Readers are encouraged to go to www.MissionPointPress.com to contact the author or to find information on how to buy this book in bulk at a discounted rate.

Published by Mission Point Press
2554 Chandler Lake Rd.
Traverse City, MI 49686
(231) 421-9513
www.MissionPointPress.com

ISBN: 978-1-954786-12-7
LOC: TK

Printed in the United States of America.

This is a work of fiction. Names, places, and incidents are the products of the author's imagination or are used fictitiously. Any resemblance to actual events or locales or persons, living or dead, is entirely coincidental.

MURDER IN THE MILITIA

A MYSTERY BY

STUART SAFFT

MISSION POINT PRESS

Chapter 1

"What happened? You all right?"

"Yeah, fine. Better'n fine, in fact."

"Tell me. What happened?"

"The bastard's dead. That should let us start carrying out the reason we're here in the first place."

"Who? How? What do you mean?"

"Who do you think? You'll see. A nice clean shot, perfectly centered in his forehead."

"Are you sure he's dead? Should I call an ambulance?"

"A bit late for that. Probably gone before he hit the ground."

"But why?"

"'Cause it's the only way we can start actually doing something about what we believe in. Not just talking to each other about them. If we don't, we might as well fold our tents and go back to Utah. But he was equally against our closing up shop and heading back to the mother ship."

"No. There had to be another way."

"Yeah, well, I can't think of none. And no one ever had any other suggestions. Least I never heard any of them."

"My God. What do we do now?"

"Easy. You gotta bury him in the woods. Nice and deep, so no one finds him — and no stray animal decides to dig him up for dinner. Take one of the pickups. He's about three-quarters of a mile along the old logging road that runs from next to the big barn into the woods. You can only drive about a third of the way there. After that you can still make out the old road, but it's way overgrown. You'll have to walk the rest of the way. You'll find him lying right next to the logging road. Pull him far enough from the road so no one can see anything if they're walking back there."

"Shouldn't we have a proper funeral and all? What are you going to tell the police? And our members?"

"No to the funeral. And screw the police. What they don't know won't hurt 'em. Plus, them nosing around here is the last thing we want."

"But, but—"

"Enough buts. Get the damn body buried. And bury the blanket with it. His blood's all over it. And not a word to anyone. I mean anyone — not even any of his wives. And don't let anyone see you burying him. No one knows what happened to him or where he's run off to. End of story. Got it?"

"Yeah, I got it. But I can't believe he's dead."

"Well, believe it or not, you better get him buried. And I mean now, dammit."

"Yes, sir. Yes, sir. I'll get on it right now."

Chapter 2

At dinner that evening, about 30 members filled the sparsely decorated dining room, helping themselves to grilled chicken, rice, green beans and cups of iced tea. In addition to these 30, three women supervised the ten or so children eating in a separate room, and eight men were spread around outside in pairs, armed and ready to prevent any nonmembers from entering the property.

During dinner, a few members asked where Mark Davis was. No one claimed to have any idea. Nonetheless, the members, including Davis' three wives, weren't worried. Since they'd relocated from Utah to Ohio almost three years ago, Davis had periodically gone off for three or four days at a time without telling anyone. Davis never obtained an Ohio driver's license, and the members had no idea how he got around off the property. They never felt comfortable asking him where he had been or how he'd gotten there, and Davis never offered any details or explanation. So, they viewed this as another of his typical mysterious absences.

As was usual in Davis' absence, Aaron Turley, his second in command, would run things until Davis returned. Turley stood six-foot-six, broad-shouldered and muscular. In his late 40s, his brown hair, generously sprinkled with gray, was cut extremely short, looking all the more extreme because of his full, albeit well-kept, beard and mustache. As dinner was ending, Turley stood up and in his loud, deep voice announced to everyone that, since their leader had left again, he, Turley, was in charge until Davis returned.

Following dinner, while the women cleaned up the kitchen and dining room and got the children off to bed, almost all of the men went outside. Sitting on the porch and standing around, most were smoking cigarettes. With it already mid-September, they were enjoying the fresh air, knowing winter wouldn't be long in coming.

Chapter 3

The next morning, Rudy Musser was up well before sunrise. In fact, he hadn't had more than a few hours sleep the entire night. *Jeez, how could he have shot him like that? And why'd he have to pick me to bury him? I can't get the picture of his head with the bullet hole in it out of my mind. It's amazing I didn't throw up while burying him — and that bloody blanket. I wish I could talk to someone, but if word got back I'd likely wind up in the ground next to him. He sure wasn't perfect, but he didn't deserve to die, and he sure as heck didn't deserve to be buried like a bag of garbage. It ain't right. Dammit, I am gonna call the police and get them involved. I wouldn't be able to live with myself if I just went on without doing anything.*

And that's exactly what Musser did. He told a few people that he had a stomachache. Then, when everyone else was at breakfast, he got out of bed, grabbed the burner cellphone he'd had for two years but never before used, went into the bathroom and locked the door.

"9-1-1. What's your emergency?"

"He's dead."

"Sir, who's dead? Are you sure he's dead? Did you check for a pulse? Do you—"

"I said he's dead 'cause he is. End of story."

"Sir, may I have your name and address? Is your address where the body is located?"

"Can't give you my name. They'd kill me like they did him."

"Where is the deceased's body? What's his name?"

"He's six feet under."

"Yes, sir. But what's the address? And his name?"

"Not sure we have an address. But we're at the FRAP farm."

"Frap farm? I'm not familiar with that, sir. Can you tell me where it's located? Is it owned by a family named Frap?"

"No. It's our headquarters. We're the Free Republic of America Patriots. That's where the FRAP name comes from, like initials or a nickname, if you know what I mean. We all live here on the farm. It's out in the country, northeast of downtown."

"OK, that helps. I'm sure our detectives can locate it. What's your name? Who should the detectives ask for when they get there?"

"No way. I already told you I'm not giving you my name. And you better tell your detectives they won't be welcome if they try to enter our property."

"Then why'd you call 9-1-1, sir?"

"'Cause it's the right thing to do. OK, I gotta go now."

"Sir, if you could—," said the 9-1-1 dispatcher, who stopped speaking mid-sentence when she heard the click of the phone call being disconnected.

Chapter 4

"Joe. Ginny. In here. Now," yelled the chief from his doorway to Detectives Joe McFarland and Ginny Harris, whose desks sat all the way at the other end of the large, bull-pen-like room.

"Whaddaya think Grouchy wants this morning?" asked Joe as he and Ginny rapidly walked to the chief's office. Ginny shrugged her shoulders in response.

"Morning, Chief," said Ginny in her cheeriest voice.

"Come in. Shut the door. Sit down. I've been waiting twenty minutes for you two. Hope your jobs didn't force you to get up too early."

"Chief," said Joe, "give us a break. It's all of ten after eight. What time you think we should be here?"

"How about whenever a murder takes place?"

"What murder?" asked Ginny.

"That's what I'd like to tell you about, if you can get your partner to be quiet for a couple of minutes."

"Go for it, Chief," said Joe.

The chief filled the detectives in on the 9-1-1 call received earlier that morning.

"That caller sure as hell wasn't very forthcoming with details," said Joe.

"You got that right," said the chief.

"What do we know about this FARP group?" asked Joe.

"First off, it's FRAP not FARP. They're one of those private militia groups," said Ginny. "Been here a few years now, and have kept a fairly low profile. A lot of anti-government, anti-black or Jew or Muslim sentiment, and, of course, pro-guns and anti-abortion."

"That's right," said the chief. "Militias usually have quite the arsenal, and I'm sure this group's no different. But they've been smart enough not to raise too big a stink. Individual members have been convicted of vandalizing a Jewish cemetery in Dayton, of breaking windows and scribbling graffiti all over an abortion clinic here in Jasper Creek. That kind of thing. But it's always been individual members. No one's been able to prove these acts were organized or ordered by the militia group or its leaders. The group occasionally attends protests and marching around off their property with their guns, but haven't gotten into any shoot-'em-ups. Not yet, anyhow."

"Might I assume you're telling us about this 9-1-1 call for a reason other than making sure we're up on the latest news? Perhaps like dumping this case in our laps."

The chief smirked. "Joe, sometimes you amaze me with how perceptive you are."

"OK, I guess we ought to head on out there. Ginny, you know where they're located?"

"No, but I'm sure it'll only take me a couple of minutes to find out. I know the general area."

"Slow down, cowboys," said the chief. "I like your enthusiasm, but you'd better go a bit slower on this one. See what you can find in our databases and on the Internet first. The more you know before you get there, the better.

I can assure you these folks will not be welcoming you with open arms. You're a part of the repressive government they're fighting against. Let's hope their hostility doesn't include gunshots."

"You really think it could be that extreme?" asked Ginny.

"Don't know, but better safe than sorry. Last thing we need is our own Ruby Ridge or Waco. I'd love to be famous, but not for something like that."

"OK," said Ginny, "we'll do some research before we head out there. You're right, the more we know up front the better."

On that note, the two detectives left the chief's office and returned to their desks.

"Well, this one should be interesting," said Joe. "I know that Ohio's one of the favorites for these nutty white nationalist groups, but this will be my first real and up-close dealings with them."

"Yeah, Ohio's got a lot of great stuff going for it, but being home to a bunch of these groups isn't one of them. OK, let's dig in and get a quick education on militia groups in general — and this FRAP outfit in particular."

The detectives spent the next four hours going through several of their databases and searching the Internet, also speaking with some of the other detectives in the department and with the state Bureau of Criminal Investigation. Joe called fellow law enforcement officers he knew at the FBI and DEA, and Ginny did the same with the U.S. Marshal's Office and the ATF. They worked right through lunch, having asked one of the other detectives who was going out for lunch to bring them back burgers, fries and Diet Cokes.

"OK, Joe. It's 12:30. Let's stop and compare notes."

"Good idea. You first."

"Fair enough. First off, I have their address. Don't know the street number, but it's at the very end of Pickens Road."

"Pickens Road? Never heard of it."

"Not surprised. Not much out there. It's in the far northeast corner of the city. You'd think you were way out in the county. Nothing there but farms and empty land."

"Well, at least you know how to get there. What else?"

"Spoke with someone I've known since high school, but we sort of lost contact with each other years ago. He's now a deputy U.S. marshal in Columbus. His office handles all of southern Ohio. He's been aware of this group since they moved here three years ago; it's either a breakaway group or a branch location of the main group in Utah. The marshals' office hasn't had any official interaction with the group here. They'd typically get involved only if there were a hostage situation or a federal arrest warrant for one of the members, but neither has occurred. 'Yet,' as he emphasized. He's not aware of any details, but he assumes there have been situations with the group in Utah, which is much larger and has been there for years. He'd be happy to put us in touch with someone in the marshal's office out there if we want him to."

"OK. And the ATF?"

"Voicemail. One of their special agents is the niece of the couple who lived next door to us when I was growing up. We became sort of friendly back then. That was a long time ago, but I'm sure she'll remember me and call me back sooner rather than later."

"Hope so. I think you're unforgettable — in a good way, that is."

"I've also been bounced all over the BCI, but have nothing to show for it. Supposedly Ohio's version of the FBI, here to help us local law enforcement folks, but I'm once again underwhelmed. All they could do was point me to several of the arrest and intelligence databases they maintain. I'd already looked at those databases before I called them."

"I understand your frustration, Ginny. But they are often very helpful with some of the forensic work they do. A small city like Jasper Creek couldn't begin to duplicate the skills and staffing they have."

"Agreed. That part of the BCI earns its pay."

"I also had to leave a message at the FBI. Special Agent Franklin, who we worked with before, recommended I talk with ASAC Steve Cohen just down the hall from him in their Cincinnati Field Office. I tried, but had to leave a voicemail. At least I was able to speak with Singleton at the DEA in Youngstown."

"And?"

"Pete knows of them in general, but hasn't had any direct dealings with them. In fact, he said that many of these private militia groups are very anti-drug. With few exceptions, most of the members are totally drug free. They view drugs as one more way the government and its rich co-conspirators weaken and control the public. He did say that the local FBI folks probably have the most info on groups like them. Let's hope Cohen gets back to me soon."

"Joe, checking the Internet and the newspaper archives, I did pick up a few tidbits. This group did, in fact, come from Utah about three years ago. They bought this almost 600-acre farm out of foreclosure proceedings. Guess the former owners couldn't make it as farmers and couldn't find a buyer for the property. The group here started as a geographical expansion of the main group in Utah. The leader here, who came from the Utah group, is a Mark Davis."

"Anything else?"

"Not much. Like the chief said, there've only been cases against individual members of the group, including a house robbery by two members about 18 months ago and a bunch of offenses for illegal weapons. But the group as a whole and its leaders have only been convicted of minor things, like protesting without a permit. That sort of thing. No actual violence."

"Do we know if they've added members from the local population here?"

"No idea."

"Well, Ginny, I'm not sure why I wasted my time searching the Internet. I found about half the items you did and didn't find anything you hadn't found. I could have been equally productive taking a nap."

"Don't beat yourself up too badly, Joe. I'm sure we were looking at the same websites. I was just a little faster than you. Probably results from our age difference."

"Better watch yourself, young lady. OK, what say we

move? We can sit here going over everything we already know and don't know for the rest of the week while we wait for our messages to be returned, or we can drive out there and see for ourselves."

"Works for me. Let me just run down the hall and give the chief a quick update."

"Fine. Meet you in the car in ten."

Chapter 5

"Jeez, Ginny. Are you sure about this? I'm not even sure we're still in Ohio, much less Jasper Creek."

"Hang in there, partner. We should be there soon. You'll need to take a left about three miles ahead. That'll be Pickens, and we just stay on it to the very end."

"Aye, aye, sir. And I'm not believing you just because of your GPS. I have faith that spending your whole life in this major metropolis has made you familiar with every backwater road out here."

"Yup, I'm a living, breathing Jasper Creek road atlas," said Ginny with a smile.

Joe made that left turn a few minutes later. Pickens Road, two nicely paved lanes with a white line painted down the middle between them, weaved through several small hills and valleys. Much of the land was pasture for cattle, and, every few minutes, a small house or barn was seen in the distance. After another five minutes or so, the road suddenly turned into a single-lane, gravel-packed surface. Joe had no choice but to slow down to 20 miles per hour.

Almost ten minutes later, Ginny said, "Joe, I think that's it up ahead. Looks like a fence with two men guarding the gate."

As they got closer, Ginny and Joe could see that was

exactly what it was. Cyclone fencing, about eight feet high, ran perpendicular from the road in both directions as far as one could see. Across the road stood an equally tall gate blocking access to the property, and a large "Private Property — Keep Out" sign on the gate served to correct any lingering confusion. Standing just inside the gate were two men. Both looked to be about 25 years old, dressed identically in camouflage pants, jacket and cap. One was quite tall and the other short, but both were broad-shouldered and appeared to be in excellent physical condition. The short one had long hair, but was clean-shaven, while the tall one had a full beard but a cleanly shaved head. As Joe got closer, both men removed their semi-automatic rifles from their shoulders, holding them in a non-threatening but immediately available position.

Joe slowly drove up to the gate and stopped. He opened his car door and stepped out.

Before Joe could utter a word, the taller of the two men yelled, "Sorry, mister. This is private property. You need to turn around."

"Sorry, but we're—"

"Let's not start a discussion. We really don't care what you are. Why don't you and your girlfriend there just turn around and go?"

"My girlfriend? Oh, you must mean Detective Harris, sitting there in the car. And I'm Detective McFarland, Jasper Creek PD."

"Well, ain't that special. It still don't get you access in here."

"Hold on. We're here to investigate a murder."

"A murder? Don't recall having one of those recently. Who's the victim?"

"Don't know."

"Who did it?"

"Don't know that either."

"So, who told you all these details about this here murder?"

"Don't know that one either. An anonymous caller."

"OK, here comes your final bonus question. Got a warrant?"

"No, we don't. Just want to talk with whoever's in charge."

"Well, I'm betting you're shit out of luck. But just hold on a minute."

The guard pulled a walkie-talkie out of his belt holster, pressing down the call button. "Hey, Aaron. Wallace here at the front gate. Two cops want to talk with you about a murder. They said someone called it in anonymously and didn't give any names or details."

"Have a warrant?"

"Nope."

"Tell 'em to take a flying leap."

"Happy to."

Wallace returned his walkie-talkie to his holster.

"Sorry, but the boss man said what I expected. Has no idea what you're talking about. Even if he did, he doesn't want you on our property. So youse have yourselves a nice day now."

"We'll be back," said Joe. "That's a promise." He got back into the car, made a U-turn and drove slowly back down the gravel road. "This won't be as easy as I thought," he said to Ginny once the gate had vanished from their rearview mirror.

"You got that right, Joe. First thing, we need to get a search warrant."

"No question. Plus, we oughta come back in force. A group will be a lot more intimidating than just us two."

"Yup. And we'd better learn a little more about those Ruby Ridge and Waco disasters. Don't want people referring to 'Ruby Ridge, Waco and Jasper Creek' in the same sentence in the future."

"Well, it's too late to catch anyone at the station now. Tomorrow morning, we need to talk with the chief, hit up one of the attorneys for a search warrant and tap whoever we're going to get backup from. And let's hope we get our call-backs from the ATF and FBI."

"Roger that. What say we pick up some Indian for dinner on the way home?"

"Sounds good to me."

Following dinner, Ginny soaked in a relaxing hot bath while Joe changed into his exercise gear and went out for a run. *Ginny thought I'd never stick with it when I committed to cranking up my exercise program and getting back into shape. Can't say I actually enjoy the exercise, but jogging is a good way to clear the cobwebs out of my head every couple of days. Though I gotta admit, proving to Ginny that I can stick with this is probably my strongest motivation.*

Soaking in the tub, Ginny's thoughts weren't too different than Joe's. *Gotta admit, I'm pleasantly surprised that Joe's sticking with his exercise program. He's still in good shape — six-three, broad-shouldered and very strong. But as he gets older his metabolism's going to slow down, even though I'm sure his appetite won't. Exercising will keep his muscles active and his weight where it should be. Now I've got to start living up to my part of the deal — I did agree I'd jog with him a couple of times a week. But definitely not tonight!*

Chapter 6

"Dammit! You gotta be kidding me. The one thing I told you two was to avoid any kind of standoff. Or did I only dream that I told you that?"

"It wasn't a dream, Chief. That's what you told us, and that's exactly what we did. There was no standoff. We asked to enter the property and talk with the person in charge. They said no. We turned around and left. End of story," said Ginny.

"So, what's your next step?"

"Ginny's going to talk with the prosecutor's office to get a search warrant."

"And then?" asked the chief.

"That's where we'd like your help," said Ginny.

"Doing what exactly?"

"When we next head out there, we'd like to have a little show of force. Nothing threatening, but something that proves we're more than just a pair of local detectives on our own."

"OK. And what specifically do you want me to do?"

"We thought," said Joe, "that you could use some of your contacts and help us get a handful of patrol cars, say from the sheriff's office and a couple of the surrounding towns we have mutual aid agreements with."

"Not so difficult. I can handle that. Just be sure none of

you get carried away with all your power and try to force things."

"You can trust us on that. Also," said Ginny, "a couple of Highway Patrol vehicles could be helpful."

"Shouldn't be a problem. When do you want this posse to be ready, and where should all of you meet? Or rendezvous, as they say in the movies."

"So I have enough time to get that warrant, how about three o'clock? We can all meet on Pickens Road, where the pavement ends and the gravel surface begins. That's a few miles from their gate, so we won't be seen before we're ready."

"OK, get out of here now so I can make a few phone calls."

"We're gone," said Joe. "And thanks."

After they got back to their desks, Ginny called the county prosecutor's office. She was transferred to Barbara Larkin, one of the assistant prosecuting attorneys she'd worked with in the past.

"Hey, Barbara. Ginny Harris. How's it going?"

"Just fine. Fortunately, crime is continuing at a high enough level that my job security is pretty solid. How about you?"

"Also doing well. Joe and I are doing our best to catch enough bad guys to help maintain your job security."

"Appreciate your help. Oh, and hey, I heard that you two finally actually got engaged. Congrats. Sure took you two long enough. Sorry I haven't called to congratulate you, but…."

"No problem. Thanks. But, now to business. We need a search warrant. By mid-afternoon if possible."

"Wow. Thanks for all the lead time. Give me the specifics."

"Probably easier if I just walk over. Got time now?"

"Sure. I might even buy you a cup of coffee if you play your cards right."

"My lucky day. See you in 15."

Ginny told Joe where she was going, then headed out the door, left the station and walked around the corner to Larkin's desk in the prosecutor's offices, located on the second floor of the county courthouse.

Quick hellos, a walk to the small kitchen area for two cups of coffee and back to Larkin's desk. Ginny jumped right in with the details of her request.

"You gotta be kidding."

"What? Why?"

"There's no way a judge, at least a sober honest one, would sign a warrant based on the information you have. Or rather don't have."

"But —"

"Just listen to what you told me. An unknown person reported an unknown murder victim killed by an unknown perp, and the victim's body is in an unknown location."

"Well, yeah, but —"

"Ginny, for all we know or don't know, this could've been a teenager's crank call to 9-1-1. Without something specific, a search warrant isn't warranted — pun intended. I wouldn't feel right even asking a judge to issue one based on how little we know."

"Damn."

"Let me know when you get a few facts, and I'll be happy to run with it."

"Thanks, Barb, but it's not so obvious how to get any facts without the warrant. Talk about a chicken vs. egg situation."

"Guess that's why you and Joe get paid the big bucks."

"OK. Thanks for hearing me out. Hope to be back with a few facts sometime soon."

"Good. I'll be ready. Take care."

"Ditto."

Ginny walked back to the station. She and Joe went to the chief's office, where Ginny filled in both Joe and the chief about the search warrant problem.

"Well, you two should still plan on returning out there this afternoon. I already have support lined up from the sheriff, two neighboring towns and Highway Patrol. HP will also do some aerial surveillance and photographing later this morning. Not sure if they'll be using one of their helicopters or a fixed-wing. You'll have their photos by one or so. They won't show a buried or dumped body, especially with the heavily wooded areas out that way, but they will at least show the perimeter of their whole property, where the gates are and how many guards are at each gate."

"Wow. Pretty impressive, Chief. Thanks for all the arrangements. And so quickly."

"We aim to please. Now, again, no confrontation. Remember, you just want to speak with the boss man.

Maybe all your support will convince them to cooperate, at least with this first request. Just don't try to force it — I mean it."

"Chief, I'll be the perfect gentleman, or diplomat or whatever."

"I know you will, Joe. And it's the 'whatever' that has me worried."

Joe and Ginny spent the rest of the morning planning their approach. They also checked their guns, made sure they had plenty of extra ammunition and that their bulletproof vests were ready to grab.

They walked over to Sancho's Taco Shop at about 11:45 for lunch. As she often did, Ginny tried to picture what the two of them looked like together. Joe at six-foot-three, broad-shouldered and muscular, next to five-foot-five Ginny, thin but surprisingly strong and wiry, agile and fast. *We may look like the odd couple, but it works for us. And that's what matters.*

The detectives were back at their desks a little before one. Sure enough, a large envelope of about thirty photographs had arrived from the Highway Patrol headquarters in Columbus. Ginny and Joe went through the photos one by one. They were surprised at how large the property seemed, how heavily wooded more than half of it was and how large the main house and surrounding buildings were. They also saw that there was a second area of fencing on the north end of the property, with a gate across a side road.

"Joe, did you take a good look at the zoomed-in photos of the two gates?"

"Yes, I did. The amount of detail captured is pretty

amazing. I wonder how high they were when the photos were snapped."

"Did you notice that there are four guards at each gate?"

"Yup. Most likely a doubling of their normal two because of our visit yesterday."

"Probably so. Guess they're not sure about our intentions and want to be ready, just in case."

"Nice to know we made such an impression."

Chapter 7

Wanting to be there when the others started to arrive, Ginny and Joe were at the meeting site by 2:30.

Everyone was there by three o'clock: two Jasper Creek uniformed officers, each in their own car; two deputies, together in one vehicle, from the sheriff's office; two uniformed officers in two cars from nearby Riverside; one officer from Dayton; and two Highway Patrol officers, each in their own vehicle.

Joe and Ginny gathered everyone together. Introductions were made all around, and Joe laid out the objective and operating rules for this action.

"Again, we're not looking for any trouble. We need to be sure not to escalate things. If the exchange gets heated, our primary responsibility is to de-escalate. Have your guns holstered but ready. Be sure your vests are on. Only draw your weapons if they actually aim their guns at us. I'm sure they'll be armed, but we do not react if they're not aiming at us. And we only shoot in self-defense. Is that totally clear to everyone?"

General nods of assent, accompanied by a checking of weapons and gear.

Ginny then spoke up, saying, "We have all of you here to show them we can gather resources if we need them. You are not here to help us force our way in or to threaten them, other than the indirect, unspoken threat of seeing us all. Understood?"

Everyone nodded again or mumbled their agreement, after which they dispersed, got in their vehicles and followed Joe and Ginny down the gravel road toward the gate. The dust thrown up by their caravan was soon spotted by the guards.

As the caravan approached the gate and all the vehicles stopped, Joe and Ginny recognized the two guards from the day before. There were also two additional guards. As Joe and Ginny had expected, the guards were holding their semi-automatic rifles, with the muzzles pointed at the sky.

Like the day before, Joe got out of the car and walked up to the gate.

"You gotta be kidding," said the guard who had seemed to be in charge the day before. "What part of yesterday's message didn't you understand? Or maybe you just forgot. Think bringing all your friends and neighbors with you is going to scare us into letting you in?"

"Good afternoon to you also. We brought our friends with us for the same reason you doubled your manpower here at the gate."

"Could be. I wouldn't know. Someone way above me made that decision. I just do what I'm told." The barrel of the guard's gun dipped down a few degrees as he spoke.

"Understood. Seriously though, we're not looking for any trouble. All I want is to speak with your leader for a few minutes. Happy to do it here or someplace inside, wherever he wants. I'm also willing to leave my gun in my car while he and I are talking. Why don't you be a good boy, call him and tell him what I just said?"

"I don't think he wants to be disturbed. He's pretty busy these days."

"Even so, he might want to talk with me and maybe put this whole thing to bed. Imagine how pissed he might be at the guy who didn't even bother to call him so *he* could make that decision."

The guard thought for a minute, then said, "OK, I'll call him. But I ain't makin' no promises."

"Wouldn't expect you to."

The guard walked about 25 feet away, took his walkie-talkie out of its holster and started a conversation. A few minutes later, he walked back to Joe. "OK, he said he'd come here for a brief talk. Wants me to watch you leave your gun behind, then I gotta frisk you when we let you through the gate."

"Fair enough."

Joe returned to his car, removed his SIG Sauer P226 from his shoulder holster and put it on the seat. He also removed his backup Glock 43 subcompact from his ankle holster and placed it on the seat. After promising a nervous Ginny that he'd be careful, he walked back to the gate. Wallace, the same guard in charge as yesterday, opened the gate and let Joe in. While one of the other guards closed the gate, Wallace thoroughly frisked Joe.

About ten minutes later, three vehicles approached the gate from within the militia group's property. An old, heavily dented, light brown F-150 pickup truck stopped about 75 feet before the gate, an even older Dodge pickup stopped further from the gate and a World War II-era jeep stopped immediately in front of the gate. The F-150 had only a driver; the other two vehicles each carried four men. The F-150 driver remained in his truck, while the eight others all got out of their vehicles and stood facing the gate. Four of them carried shotguns, two had semi-automatic rifles and two held handguns. All the guns were pointed at either the sky or the ground — not threatening, but easily accessible. Wallace walked Joe to the F-150 and Joe got into the passenger side.

Man, this guy sure looks the part. Camouflage clothing and well-kept beard. Seems taller than me, and built like an ox. I sure wouldn't want to get into a fight with him. I'd probably last five seconds. Max. Time to turn the charm on, see how proud I can make the chief.

"Good afternoon, sir. I'm Detective McFarland with the Jasper Creek Police Department. Thanks for agreeing to talk with me." Joe held his hand out, but retracted it when he saw it was being totally ignored.

"OK. Talk. I really don't want to spend all day at this." The man glared at him, his icy blue eyes making Joe uncomfortable.

"Understood. Are you the one in charge here?"

"Yeah, for the time being."

"Can I have your name?"

"Sure. Ain't no secret. Turley. Aaron Turley."

"Thanks. My first name's Joe. You said you're in charge 'for now.' What do you mean?"

"I'm officially number two here. But whenever our leader is away, I take charge 'til he returns."

"Oh, I see. What's your leader's name? How long has he been away? When do you expect him back?"

"Whoa. Hold your horses. Enough with the interrogation. What's this all about anyhow?"

"We got a call. Or actually 9-1-1 got the call."

"So I heard. And?"

"And the caller said that someone was killed out here."

"That's crazy. Who's supposed to have been killed? Who did it? And who called 9-1-1? Been told you don't have answers to any of these questions."

"That's why I've been wanting to talk with you."

"Sounds like some prank call to me. Maybe someone who doesn't like that we set up shop here. No one's been killed here."

"Are you sure? Any of your members missing?"

"Yeah, I'm sure. Everyone's present and accounted for. Anything else before we end this pleasant little tea party?"

"We'd like to check for ourselves that no one's missing."

"Bet you would. Perfect opportunity to search every corner of the place. Probably also want to talk with our members, getting their names and all while you're at it." Red veins stood out now around the blue of Turley's eyes.

"Well, we —"

"Ain't gonna happen. That's all great info for you to have if and when you decide to attack us."

"Attack you? Why would you think we'd want to do that?"

"Lotsa reasons. Look what happened at Ruby Ridge. And Waco. Nobody ever thought those massacres would happen either. Attacking and maybe killing us could be a great way for one of your damn politicians to win a few points with the dumb sheep following after them. You might even get a big fat promotion out of it."

"Well, I don't see an attack ever happening here. While we're talking, how 'bout you give me a five-minute education on your organization? Its history, what you're trying to accomplish, and so on." *Here we go*, Joe thought to himself. *Let's see what comes out of these floodgates.*

"Sure, happy to. 'Specially if it then gets you to get the hell outta here. Be nice to have one more person out there that doesn't have a totally wrong impression of us. We really ain't servants of the devil. In fact, we fight the devil every day." A gleam came into Turley's eyes as he spoke, different from the cold hostility he'd projected toward Joe so far.

"Go for it. I'm all ears."

"History's pretty straightforward. Free Republic of American Patriots was formed more than 20 years ago. In Utah, not too far from Salt Lake City."

"For what purpose?"

"Our founders saw what was happening."

"What exactly did they see?"

"In short, damn near everything. The government went from serving the people to trying to run our lives. Forget about the 'of, for and by the people' stuff. The government started acting like they knew what was best for us. They want to do away with our Second Amendment right to have guns. And abortions? Sure, the more the merrier. Religious beliefs — forget about 'em, just do what we tell you to do. Be sure to treat everyone equal, except of course for white Christian males, who get screwed over so the government can give unfair help to blacks and Jews and women, and who knows who else. Oh, and, as if we don't already have enough of them, let's let a zillion more immigrants in. Anyone who wants to come here — just open the gates. And, once they're here, why not let 'em all become citizens? So what if they don't speak English or understand and live by our customs? Hell, they don't even eat the same foods we do."

"Wow, that's quite a list. Anything else?"

"Yeah, there's more. A lot more. But that's a good enough start for now."

"People seem to think you and all these other private militias are really white nationalist groups. Sorta like a modern-day Ku Klux Klan."

"Well that's bull. It's the crap they read in their newspapers and see on TV. It's what the politicians say without knowing any of the facts."

"Are you sure?"

"Can't speak for all the groups out there, but I'm sure about us. If by 'nationalist,' you mean we love and support our country, hell yes, then we're guilty of being nationalists. And the white part. We're not prejudiced against people of other colors. We just don't want the government screwing us to help them get ahead."

Right. "So, what're your objectives? And how do you go about achieving them?"

"We want government to get back to how it used to be — how it should be. People say we should make it happen through the ballot box, but that's bull. Damn near everyone who runs for office is corrupt and only interested in themselves — having power, making money and, above all, getting re-elected. It's too late to make the changes needed just by voting."

"So, what's the plan?"

"For now, we're focused on getting more people to listen to us, to see that what we're saying is right and to join us, or at least support our efforts."

"And then?"

"Well, we got some thoughts, but we're not ready to talk about 'em yet."

"Do they involve violence?"

"Hope not, but they may have to."

Uh huh. "Well, thank you. That was quite informative. One other question: How'd you wind up coming to Jasper Creek from Utah?"

"Our mother organization is still in Utah. Realizing we had to eventually spread all across the country to be effective, we decided to start what we call subsidiary chapters throughout the US. We moved here about three years ago. So far, this is the only subsidiary chapter."

"Why here?"

"As I'm sure you know, Ohio has been home to several militia groups for years. Plus, Ohio's open-carry gun laws don't interfere with our efforts. It's also a good base location to expand to the Northeast and Midwest."

"How many members do you have here? Are they all transfers from Utah?"

"Nice try, but our numbers are confidential information. I will say that most of us are from Utah, but we do have some folks who've joined since we moved here. I can also tell you most of our members are men, but we do have some women and children, a few of which were born here on the farm."

"Understood. Can you—"

"No, I can't. School's over for today. Time for you to leave so we can get back to work."

"OK, but how do we follow up on that 9-1-1 call?"

"Good question. No idea, but luckily that's not my problem, now is it?"

At that point, Turley waved his hand towards Wallace, who immediately went over to the truck and opened Joe's door.

Joe thanked Turley for his cooperation, got out and followed Wallace to the gate. A minute later Joe was back in his car, giving Ginny a quick summary of his conversation while simultaneously making a U-turn and leading the other law enforcement officers away from the farm.

"Jeez, Joe. Sounds just like the nutcases you hear about. Women and children — I wonder how many?"

"No idea, Ginny. We better figure out a way to get into that compound."

Joe stopped where all the officers had met earlier. Everyone got out of their cars and gathered around. Joe gave them a summary of his conversation with Turley, thanked everyone for their help and said they'd be in touch if and when they had to do this again.

Back at the station, Joe gave a detailed summary to both the chief and Ginny. All three agreed they had to figure out how to follow up on the 9-1-1 call but, as the chief emphasized, in a way that continued to avoid any confrontation which might lead to a serious standoff or worse.

"Chief," said Joe, "based on what I heard out there, these are a bunch of nutcakes. Feel like the whole world's against them and they're the ones to fix everything. Would be kinda funny, except for all their guns."

"And," added Ginny, "they may not like the comparison, but I do think they're the modern-day Ku Klux Klan that Joe mentioned to them. Seems like they're prejudiced against most every group of people not exactly like them. Pretty damn scary."

"Yes, they are. So far, we haven't had any serious problems with this particular group, but that can change at a minute's notice."

"Well, in any event, we still have a possible murder out there to look into."

"Yes, you do," said the chief.

The detectives returned to their desks. Joe wrote up his notes on the afternoon, after which he and Ginny headed home. Following dinner, they both sat on the couch watching an old movie on TV. Things gradually developed from hugging to kissing to more passionate kissing, and the detectives wound up in the bedroom without ever seeing the end of the movie.

Chapter 8

"OK, let me tell you why I called you all together. I want to fill you in on our visitors yesterday. I don't think it's anything to worry about, but I know how the rumor mill works around here."

"Thanks, Aaron," said Abigail Davis, the first and oldest wife of Mark Davis. "We appreciate your keeping us informed. And, yes, the rumor mill has been working overtime."

Turley gave the group an abbreviated summary of the two attempted visits by the police, also describing his discussion the previous afternoon with Joe. "I'm sure there's nothing to worry about, but we all need to be on high alert. Just in case. We sure as hell haven't had any murders here, so I don't know what this is about. Could have been a prank call to 9-1-1. Or it's a police trick, an excuse to be let in here and get to know more about us."

"Can't argue with that, Aaron," said Abigail. "Other than Mark being off on one of his mysterious trips, there's no one missing from here. Like you asked, I checked attendance during breakfast and no one's AWOL."

"Thanks, Abigail. Now, any of you others seen or know something the rest of us don't? Now's the time to fill us all in." After a minute of waiting, during which no one spoke up, Turley continued, "OK, then. That's it. Business as usual, but with two minor modifications. As the unofficial leaders of our group, I want you to fill all the others in on what we just talked about. Not the younger children, of course. And be sure to do it in a way that doesn't get anyone upset or spooked. Also, Wallace, I want you to double up our exterior security for the next few days. Keep the four guards at each gate, and let's double the number roaming around the buildings and property. Any questions? OK, then. That's it. Thanks."

Shit. Now what do I do? Musser took his position guarding the food shed out back, but couldn't keep his mind off of his dilemma. *I couldn't say a damn thing in that meeting. I'd either be killed for saying what I know, or I'd be killed after they realized I must have been the one to call the police. Of all the people here, why'd I have to be the lucky one chosen to bury Mark? I couldn't even look at Abigail during the meeting. She and his other wives just think he's off on another short trip. Sooner or later they're gonna get tired of waiting for him to return. Then they'll realize there really may have been a murder. Of their husband! Jeez! What the hell do I do now?*

As Musser was having this conversation with himself, Ginny and Joe were asking themselves the same fundamental question.

"Joe, what the hell do we do now? We sure as hell can't storm the damn place."

"Good question, partner. Wish I had an equally good answer. One possible move could be to contact their parent organization in Utah. Maybe the leader there knows something about I-don't-know-what."

"Sure can't hurt. I've got one other thought. You said they had a few members who've joined since they came from Utah. I wonder if we can find some of these new members. They might not be fully indoctrinated yet, and may be more willing to talk to us. Even better if we could find a couple of ex-members who dropped out and stayed here in the area. If they dropped out, they're clearly not super-believers and may be willing, or even happy, to talk with us."

"Good ideas, Ginny. But how do we find these people — if they exist?"

"Let's start with the uniformed guys who patrol that part of town. They might know. Worst case, they can check with their local contacts — their informants as well as local ministers, teachers and so on. If some of these local joiners or droppers-out exist, these local folks would know it."

"Good for you, Ginny. Why don't you get that started with your buddy, O'Grady? I'll bring the chief up-to-date in the meantime."

"Deal."

While Ginny was downstairs explaining her request to Desk Sergeant O'Grady, Joe brought the chief up to date about the next steps he and Ginny were planning.

"Sounds logical to me. But don't even dream about us paying for you and Ginny to take a nice vacation trip out West. Besides the Tabernacle Choir in Salt Lake, I'm sure you'd enjoy the Grand Canyon. And why not swing by Hoover Dam and Las Vegas while you're out that way?"

"Very funny. Not to worry, Chief. I was thinking of using the telephone, not the department's private jet."

"That's good. Because I think our jet's booked solid for the next few weeks."

"But we might actually travel to the furthest reaches of Jasper Creek if we get any leads from the uniformed guys."

"No problem. I'm pretty sure our budget can handle that. But seriously, Joe, I am pleased that you two have a few next steps. And, best I can tell, none of them are likely to start a war with the militia group. Keep me informed."

"For sure."

While Joe was back at his desk waiting for Ginny to return, he started searching online to see if he could identify which police department or sheriff's office in Utah he should call to get information on — and maybe even an introduction to — the militia's headquarters group out there.

Ginny returned a short while later. She told Joe that O'Grady would contact the two officers who patrolled that corner of the city; they should hear back within 24 hours or so. Joe filled Ginny in on his session with the chief and happily turned over to her the task of searching for the right law enforcement agency out in Utah.

Fifteen minutes later, Ginny had the information.

"OK, Joe, I've got what you need. Their headquarters out there is like the compound here. They're on a farm, or I guess a ranch, but much larger than the local one. It's in the middle of nowhere, between Salt Lake City and Provo, two of the largest cities in Utah. But it's way out on unincorporated county land, and counties are pretty large out there. The sheriff's office responsible for policing in the area is headquartered 40 miles from their ranch."

"Great. Do you have a name and phone number for me to call?"

"Of course, Your Highness. I was just getting ready to tell you. The Utah Department of Public Safety seems to have several groups that might be useful. But the best place to call is probably their Statewide Information & Analysis Center. Located in Salt Lake City. It collects and analyzes information from all the law enforcement agencies in the state. Seems like the perfect place for one-stop shopping. A lot better than you calling a dozen different agencies."

"Sounds right to me. It's at least the place to start."

Ginny gave Joe the name of the center's leader and the office's phone number.

"Thanks, Ginny. I just better wait until it's a little later. Our crazy system of time zones. They're two hours behind us."

Chapter 9

"Good morning. I'd like to speak with Captain Brooks, please."

"May I say who's calling?"

"Sure. Detective McFarland with the Jasper Creek Police Department, here in Ohio."

"OK. Please hold, Detective."

Less than a minute later, a voice came on the line. "Captain Brooks."

"Good morning, Captain. I'm Joe McFarland, a detective with the Jasper Creek Police Department in Ohio."

"Good morning, Detective. What can I do for you?"

"We're trying to gather some information on the Free Republic of American Patriots, a private militia group headquartered in Utah. Not too far from Salt Lake City, I believe."

"Yes, we're well aware of them. What kind of information are you looking for?"

Joe described the problems he and Ginny were facing, explaining how he hoped communicating with the main group in Utah might help open things up.

"Joe.... OK if I call you Joe? My first name is Noah."

"Sure, Noah. Joe is fine."

"You probably made the right choice in contacting us. Our charter is to gather, analyze and disseminate to law enforcement all the information from our many state and local agencies, as well as info from the FBI, Homeland Security and other federal agencies with offices in Utah."

"Perfect. What can you tell me about that particular militia group?"

"Let's see. They formed here more than 15 years ago. All the standard beefs about how repressive the government is, both federal and state, and the supposedly unfair way white males and Christians are treated by the government. Not to mention the standard Second Amendment issues and, of course, their racist, anti-immigrant and hardcore anti-abortion views."

"Sounds just like their so-called subsidiary operation here in Ohio."

"Yeah, and pretty much like several other groups we're blessed with here in Utah."

"Any serious criminal incidents?"

"A few, but, fortunately, nothing too recent. There've been quite a few relatively minor incidents over the years — several gun law violations, fights at protest rallies, blocking roadways for a few days, that sort of thing. But also a few more serious crimes. Minor damage from a pipe bomb set off in front of a black church in Provo. Death threats, thank heaven not acted upon, to a few of our political leaders. Nothing in the past couple of years, but we're keeping our eyes on them just in case, or more likely for when, things heat up again. We folks here in Utah are pretty tolerant of others. Live and let live kind of attitude. But only so long as your way of living doesn't interfere with mine. Once it does, look out."

"I can understand that. Any chance I could talk with

their leader? By phone preferably, but in person if need be."

"Extremely doubtful. We, of course, know who he is, name's Orrin Heaton, but he won't speak with you. Not only do you and I work for the repressive government, we're the ones actually enforcing their repressive policies."

"That's what I expected. But figured it was worth an ask."

"Yup. We're running a special today — no charge for questions."

"Noah, what can you tell me about them sending a group to set up the operation here in Ohio?"

"I do know they did that about three years ago. For years, they've been talking about becoming a national organization. But until that move, they remained a Utah, or you could even say a north-central Utah, organization. Most of their activities were in the Salt Lake City and Provo area. So, they finally sent a group to set up in your neck of the woods. As I'm sure you know, Ohio, like Utah, is a favorite location for these militia screwballs."

"Yeah, well aware of it. That's a contest we're not so pleased to be winning."

"Can't blame you for that."

"What can you tell me about the individuals who made the move to Ohio?"

"I can probably put together a list of most who went. Give me a couple of days and I'll fax it to you."

"That would be great," said Joe, after which he gave Brooks his fax number.

"I do recall that six or so went first, presumably to get

the lay of the land, check out the real estate and buy a piece. Most likely, out in the country away from everything. Like their location here.

"Then around nine months, maybe a year later, a couple of dozen others headed east. Mostly men, but also four or five women, and even a few kids. I saw pictures of their caravan. Mostly old, falling-apart cars and trucks. Less sure, but I think a few others then gradually left here and joined your group over the past couple of years. Don't know how it's going in Ohio, but, best we know, no one's moved back here from Ohio since they started the expansion."

"Appreciate the info, and look forward to you sending the names. But just to keep us moving, any names come to mind now? Even a few would let us start researching while we're waiting for your more complete list."

"Umm. Lemme think for a minute. Well, of course, there's Mark Davis. He was among the first group to head out. We believe he is, or at least was three years ago, the leader of the Ohio group. His number one wife, Abigail, went with him, and his second wife too. I can't remember her name."

"I thought polygamy was made illegal in Utah years ago?"

"Well, yeah, it was. Pretty much. But it's a complicated story. In any event, members in this group play it smart. They only legally marry one woman, then in several cases they and their wife also live with one or more other women. But they never legally marry these other women, so technically there's no polygamy."

"Pretty sneaky."

"These folks know exactly how to go up to the line but not cross it."

"Point taken."

"In any event, we believe Davis led the work on buying the property in Ohio, setting things up, and then, when they were ready, calling for more members to move there from here. Things were pretty simple and straightforward between him and his uncle."

"His uncle?"

"Oh, yeah, sorry. Forgot to mention that Davis is a nephew of Heaton, the leader here in Utah. Davis' mother, a member of the group out here for years, is Heaton's sister."

"Like you say, that should help simplify things between the two locations."

"For sure. Can't recall other names, but we'll get them to you as quickly as we can. Any other questions?"

"One more, but I hope it doesn't offend you."

"Very little left that can offend me these days. Go ahead, give it a shot."

"Uh, OK. I'm guessing you're Mormon, right?"

"Right you are. But no big prize for correctly guessing. More than half the folks living out here are."

"Are most of the militia members Mormon?"

"Now that's a more difficult question. Most likely very few are active members or true believers in the main branch of the religion, The Church of Jesus Christ of Latter-day Saints. In fact, the Church leadership, on a number of occasions, has clearly told its members not to participate in armed resistance to political, police or military authorities. And definitely not try to justify actions like that based on our scriptures and beliefs."

"Sounds pretty clear to me."

"It is, but there's a big 'but.'"

"Oh?"

"Like many religions, ours has seen the splintering off of several branches. You could call them subgroups or denominations or even rebel groups. Some stick pretty close to our beliefs, but others are far different. Some of them even seem to just use the veil of Mormonism to try to justify or hide their real motives. So, given all this, it's hard to know how many Mormons are in militia groups. It's even hard, or more like impossible, to tell who is and who isn't a real Mormon anymore."

"Interesting. Didn't realize I was asking such a difficult question. But I get what you're saying and I appreciate your explaining it all."

"Happy to. Anything else?"

"No. That's it for now, Noah. Look forward to the list. And trust I can call you again when I've got more questions?"

"No problem. Good luck. Take care."

"Will do. And thanks again."

"Glad to help all we can."

Joe hung up and filled Ginny in on the call.

"Good thing we found him. Seems like he has a wealth of info."

"Yes, it does. But we didn't find him, you did, Ginny. Well done."

"Did I do well enough for you to buy me lunch?"

"Sounds only fair to me. Let's go."

And the detectives were off for their normal lunch at Sancho's Taco Shop.

Chapter 10

Back from lunch a little after one, the two detectives spent about two hours going through their notes and trying to add to their list of next steps.

"Clearly," said Ginny, "the key is getting inside that compound, or at least getting info from someone who is or recently was a member."

"Full agreement. Hopefully talking with the two officers who patrol that part of town, or the list of names we should get in a few days from Utah, will give us what we need."

"True. But I'm not very comfortable with our whole action plan being built on something that starts with the word 'hopefully.'"

"Can't argue with that, Ginny. If you have any suggestions, I'm in a most receptive mood. I'm plumb out of ideas."

"Let's hope we come up with something before the chief asks for an update. Not sure if I'm more concerned about not progressing with the case or having the chief all over us."

"Difficult choice. Both are pretty bad. Let's keep working this. Maybe one of us will have a brainstorm."

Neither did, but Ginny's phone rang at about 3:30.

"Hey, Grady. What's up?"

"You're gonna be meeting with the two officers covering the area around that militia group."

"Oh?"

"Yeah. Hope I didn't overstep, but I scheduled you for early Sunday morning. They switch shifts at eight. They agreed to meet you and Joe around 7:45 so you guys can talk with both of them together."

"Definitely worth getting up early for. Where do we meet them?"

"There's a Total gas station out that way. Intersection of 72 and Beaver Dam. Has a few tables and chairs off in one corner, so you four can enjoy some tea and crumpets while you talk. Place should be deserted that early on a Sunday."

"Fantastic. Although some of us may go for coffee instead of tea. Thanks for setting it up. What're their names?"

"Richard Patterson and Nancy Williams. Solid folks. Both on the force more than four years."

"Great. Thanks, Grady. I think I remember meeting Williams. Let them both know we'll be there Sunday morning, and coffee, or tea if they prefer, and crumpets will be on us."

"Will do. Hope they'll be able to help you."

Ginny filled Joe in, after which they both brought the chief up to date.

In view of their early Sunday morning meeting, Ginny and Joe felt no guilt when they left the station a bit early.

Chapter 11

Joe and Ginny were up bright and early Sunday morning. Knowing they'd be having more coffee during their meeting, they limited themselves to one and a half cups each before they left home.

With large cups of coffee in front of them, Ginny and Joe were sitting at the rearmost of the three tables in the Total station by 7:30. Patterson arrived about 7:35 and Williams a few minutes later. After introductions, and Ginny and Williams recollecting having met shortly after Williams joined the department, Joe walked the officers back to the cashier and paid for two large coffees and four pre-wrapped donuts.

Realizing Patterson had been one of the officers who accompanied them to the compound that past Thursday, Joe thanked him again for his assistance.

Back at the table, Ginny started right in. "Appreciate you both agreeing to meet this morning."

"No problem," said Patterson. "I'm wrapping up my shift and Nance is about to start. A brief overlap here lets you get us both together. Two for the price of one sorta thing."

"We're glad to try and help. But the sarge didn't tell us anything other than you're looking for information about the Free Republic of American Patriots."

"Yes, we are. As you know, last Wednesday, 9-1-1 got an anonymous call about a murder out on their farm, or ranch, or whatever it is. The caller, a male, wouldn't give any specific info."

"Yeah, I was notified about the call, but was told not to respond as detectives were going to follow up. Was with you guys on Thursday when you had a bunch of escorts out there. We call it their compound. Nance and I talked about it. We both concluded it was probably another crank call."

"Another?" said Joe. "Get many of them?"

"One every few months," said Williams. "A lot of folks aren't happy about this group settling here, so they try to do whatever they can to make their lives miserable. Guess they're hoping it'll lead to the group packing up and moving someplace else."

"Yeah. But fat chance of that," said Patterson.

"What kind of info are you looking for?" asked Williams.

"Ideally, we'd love to hear what you may have heard about the possible murder. But, given your silence on the matter, we assume you've heard nothing."

"That's correct," said Patterson.

"So, the next best thing would be a way into the compound, but we're not holding out much hope in that regard. What we are hoping is that you know of one or more members, or former members, of the group who we could talk to. Maybe they joined, quickly became unhappy with something and left the group. Or maybe you have a CI who's still in the group. A confidential informant on the inside would be a home run."

"Well, we may be able to help you some. We know of

three people who joined the group but left after a few months, totally disillusioned."

"Yeah," said Patterson. "And I know one who's still a member. Pretty willing to talk in general about what goes on in there."

"Tell us more," said Joe.

"The three who quit," said Williams, "are two brothers plus the wife of one of them. The three of them joined together, probably almost a year ago now, and then quit three or four months ago."

"Why'd they quit?"

"Couple of reasons. First off, they envisioned a nice democratic-type place where everyone was equal and decisions were made by the whole group. Didn't take them long to realize that a few at the top made all the decisions, and all the others just did what they're told."

"And secondly?" asked Joe.

"They were true, maybe naively so, believers in the Second Amendment and gun rights. Also believed that abortion was murder. The militia talked about these things a lot, but didn't actually ever do much to further their beliefs. Sort of all show and no go — which is great for us cops, but not so much for them."

"Did they have any problem in quitting?"

"No, not really. A couple of the big shots tried to talk them into staying, but that was it. There was no force or threats. The members are there 'cause they want to be. It's not like they've been kidnapped. Brainwashed maybe, but not kidnapped."

"And you think we could talk with these three?"

"Don't see why not. They're not hiding or anything. And they're not shy about spouting their opinions. They don't hate the group, they just say it turned out to not be for them. Their families have lived here for many years, so these three are now back in the local community as if they'd never left."

"If you guys could arrange for us to meet with them, it'd be super."

"No problem."

"And what about the one who's still inside the group?"

"No idea. I'll have to ask him," said Patterson.

"How are you able to communicate with him?" asked Ginny.

"Simple. He's one of about a half dozen who work at regular jobs in the community. They live at the compound, but leave every weekday morning to go to work."

"Just like us regular folks," said Ginny.

"Yup. It's all part of how the group finances itself."

"Interesting. Tell us more," said Joe.

"The group has several wealthy members. They contribute a fair amount of the total needed. The parent group in Utah also provides some financial support. Then there's this small group of men who work regular jobs off the property and turn over their entire paycheck in exchange for room and board. Most of those who remain in the compound also generate some cash. Men mostly do farming, while the women grow vegetables and bake pies and breads, all of which they sell at a few stands around town."

"Makes sense. Embarrassed to admit I never thought about how these groups financed themselves," said Joe.

"Well now you know. They clearly have expenses — food except for what they grow, cloth for the women to sew into clothing, shoes, coats and so on. Plus farming supplies and equipment, guns and ammo, gas, car and truck repairs, phones and computers and so on. They even pay property taxes."

"Interesting. But back to the topic at hand. How'd you get a CI, and how do you communicate with him?"

"Getting him was easy. Caught three of them robbing a house. Actually, the other two were robbing the house. He was sitting in their car, waiting for them to return so he could drive them back to their compound.

"It became clear pretty quickly that he'd happily snitch rather than be arrested and probably convicted. I checked with the sarge and cut the deal. And, of course, once he snitched the first time, I owned him. Worked with the prosecutor to drop all the charges against him, claiming they didn't have sufficient evidence to convict. Fortunately, the two other robbers confessed, so my CI's snitching never became known outside of the sarge and a few in the prosecutor's office."

"How do you and he arrange meetings?"

"Whenever either of us wants a meet, we send a coded text which indicates the time and place. As he drives by himself to and from work every day, a short detour and quick stop is pretty easy to pull off. So far, best he can tell, no one has any idea of this arrangement."

"Think you could set it up for us to meet him?"

"Happy to try. But no idea. I'd want to meet with him first and get his OK. Last thing I want is to spook him with you and wind up losing him as a source."

"Understood. Appreciate you giving it a try."

"OK then, think we're set. I'll try to arrange for the two brothers and the wife to meet with you, and Rich will see whether his CI agrees to meet."

The two detectives thanked the two officers and said their good-byes. Patterson headed home, Williams started her shift and the two detectives also headed home.

"Well, that went as well as could be expected."

"Sure did," said Joe. "Definitely worth getting up early on a Sunday morning."

"Agreed. Let's hope they're able to arrange the meetings. Now I say we get home and take a nap before we have lunch."

"Ginny, you really do come up with some great ideas."

The detectives drove home, napped and had lunch, after which they, and a cold six-pack, spent two hours in the small backyard. Sitting in the warm sun while a cool breeze was blowing felt good.

"Joe, not too bad a life we have. This sun feels great."

"Sure does, even more so when you realize winter will be here in all its glory before too long."

"Very true."

"Amazing when you think how fate worked to get us together here."

Ginny nodded. She was born and grew up in Jasper Creek, in fact never having lived anyplace else. Without a college degree, she worked her way up from a police department clerk to a beat cop, then all the way to detective. And, almost that whole time, she did it alone. Her parents were gone, and her marriage to her high school sweetheart right after high school fell apart soon after

Ginny put on the police uniform, which threatened her husband's sense of manliness.

Joe grew up in Chicago never having heard of Jasper Creek, much less ever thinking he'd wind up living there. After high school and community college in Chicago, he joined the Chicago Police Department. Following a military tour in Bosnia, he returned to the Chicago police force and worked his way up to detective. Four years later, a drunk driver killed his wife and young son. Joe wound up depressed and heavily dependent on alcohol. After several warnings, he was terminated from the police department. He eventually moved to rural Jasper Creek — where he knew no one — to make a clean start. He finally got thoroughly bored doing nothing and joined the Jasper Creek Police Department. He managed to alienate everyone they tried to partner him with, until they put him and Ginny together. It wasn't clear whether they were two well-fitting misfits, or just two lonely people without any close family, but they immediately clicked. They'd remained effective partners on the job while graduating to also living together and planning to get married.

"Ginny, it all makes me realize we ought to stop screwing around and get to it."

"Huh? To what?"

"We've been talking about buying a new house forever. If we're waiting for that house to walk up to our front door and ring the bell, we've got a pretty long wait."

"Joe, are you really serious? Are you really ready?"

"Yup. We know we're getting married, even though we haven't picked a date or any of that stuff. And we did agree to sell what was my house and buy one that will be our house."

"Oh, Joe," said Ginny as she jumped up from her chair, dropped into Joe's lap and gave him a huge hug.

"So, how do we proceed? We've got a few ideas of what we want and don't want, but we still have a few biggies undecided. Like where — Jasper Creek or not? In town or more in the country? Ranch or two-story? Size of property? Number of bedrooms and bathrooms? Just to name a few."

"I know. Maybe it's time to hire a realtor."

"Should we use — I don't remember her name — the lady who sold your condo for you? We were pretty happy with her work."

"Yes, we were. But I think she was more of a specialist in apartments and condos. Not sure how good she'd be at helping us with our big mansion on our huge estate."

"So how do we find someone?"

"I think we need to first decide on Jasper Creek or one of the neighboring towns. Doesn't have to be JC for me, but I don't want a long commute every day."

"Agreed," said Joe.

"Once we pick the town, I can do some Internet research for agents. Then, like with my condo, we'll pick a few and interview them."

"Works for me. What say we commit, especially now before it gets dark too early, to taking a detour every day we can on the way home to a different town or section of town to help us pick which one we'll honor by becoming residents?"

"Good idea. We can also use the weekends if we need

to. Living here my whole life, I can immediately eliminate a bunch of areas and pick a few that I think could be contenders. And I'll start doing Internet searches on a few of the nearby towns — looking up population and demographics, schools, taxes, shopping and restaurants and so on."

"Sounds like a plan."

"Think it matters to the department whether or not we live in town?"

"No. Heck, some of the guys live in JC and others live in surrounding towns. Just shouldn't be too far away in case of an emergency."

"And, like we said, not too long a commute. What would you say we start with — up to 30 minutes?"

"Sure. We can always widen the search if we have to."

"OK, I'm excited. In fact, despite enjoying sitting here, I want to get started. I'm heading in and hopping on the Internet."

"Go for it. I'm just going to sit here and enjoy life for a few. Join you shortly."

Joe joined Ginny about twenty minutes later. Ginny already had a local map printed, on which she had drawn a raggedy circle estimating the boundaries of a 30-minute drive to and from the station house.

Joe pulled up a chair next to Ginny and helped, or more accurately watched, Ginny research Jasper Creek and five nearby towns. *OK. This is for real now. Thought I'd be spooked, but I'm not. Guess that means I'm ready for the next big step. Sell this place and buy our new house, then we gotta get on with wedding plans. We can't keep letting the job get in the way, thinking we'll get to the wedding as soon as whatever big case we're working on gets solved. So glad Ginny and I visited Lori and Adam's graves when we were in Chicago. I'll never stop loving them or getting over their being killed by that damn drunk driver, but I feel like I have their blessing to move ahead with my life with Ginny. Guess you could say I'm both the unluckiest and* luckiest *man in the world.*

Chapter 12

Monday morning was totally unproductive for the detectives. They managed to look busy, but actually accomplished nothing other than waiting — for names from Brooks of the Utah Statewide Information & Analysis Center, for possible meetings with the ex-members of the Ohio group and with Patterson's confidential informant and for return calls from the ATF and FBI. They were still waiting when lunchtime finally arrived.

About 30 minutes after they got back to their desks following lunch, Ginny's phone rang.

"Detective Harris, Jasper Creek Police Department. How may I be of help?"

"By saying 'hello.'"

"Excuse me?"

"Ginny, it's me, Kathy Rogers. Long time no see."

"Hey, Kathy. Great to hear from you. Thanks for returning my call."

After a few minutes of chatting, bringing each other up to date from when they were friendly years ago, Ginny steered the call towards her reason for calling Rogers.

"Yeah, I'm positive, Ginny. We're a small, tight group here and anything going on within the ATF, unless it's top secret, national security stuff, is shared with the entire team here. We're definitely aware of that group. There've been a few incidents — illegal weapons, carrying in prohibited buildings. That kind of thing, but nothing over the top."

"I believe you. Just surprised."

"I guess they know the laws and mostly obey them regarding firearms and explosives, at least out in the open. Which could simply mean they're hiding their real activities — no record doesn't necessarily mean they're law-abiding. Also, not much regarding alcohol and tobacco, but I assume these are of less interest to you."

"You got that right."

A few more minutes of personal chatting, including a promise from Rogers that she and her husband would get together with Ginny and Joe for dinner "soon," and the call ended.

Shortly before Ginny finished her call, Joe's phone rang. It was ASAC Steve Cohen calling from the FBI's field office in Cincinnati.

"Thanks for calling me back."

"Happy to. Sorry it took a few days, but we were in the middle of wrapping up a large case. Your voicemail message said that you got my name from SA Franklin. What can I do for you?"

Joe gave Cohen a summary of the case he and Ginny were struggling with, stating his hope that the FBI might have information or contacts that could be helpful.

"Hang on a minute. Let me see if I can grab one of my guys, Mel Kalinski. He's our agent most focused on white supremacist, white nationalist militia-type groups."

Two minutes later, Cohen was back on the phone introducing Joe and Kalinski to each other. Joe gave Kalinski a five-minute recap of what was going on, also summing up the kind of help Joe and Ginny were hoping for.

"Happy to help all I can."

"Great," said Joe.

"I suggest I first give you an overview of the situation in general with these private militia groups, then we can focus specifically on the Free Republic nuts."

"Appreciate that. My partner and I can come to Cincinnati most any time, whatever works best for you."

"Hang on, let me check my calendar." Then a minute later, "Boy, you guys sure are lucky."

"Good to know. But why?"

"My family and I are leaving here late Wednesday morning. Going to spend a long weekend with my sister and her family outside Cleveland, darn near right on the lake. We'll almost be going through Jasper Creek. How about I make it to your place, say around one o'clock? My wife and kids can wander around downtown while we spend some quality time talking about militias."

"Works for us. Just have to forewarn you — our coffee sucks."

"Not a problem. I've drunk bad coffee for so long, I don't think I'd recognize what a good cup tastes like."

Joe gave Kalinski their address and told him where to park. A sincere thank you, followed by good-byes, and the call ended.

Joe filled Ginny in on the call.

"That's great. And the teacher comes to the students. Not bad."

As they had agreed, Joe and Ginny took a detour on their way home to begin their house-location investigation.

Chapter 13

Tuesday morning provided a step forward with the case.

Arriving at their desks, Joe found a three-page fax on his chair.

"OK, Ginny. We got the fax from Brooks. Why don't you grab us a couple of coffees while I make a copy of this?" said Joe as he waved the fax in the air.

"Sounds like an effective plan to me," said Ginny as she turned and headed to the coffee machine.

Five minutes later, Ginny and Joe were deeply engrossed in their copies of the fax.

"Brooks came through as promised, Joe. Nice when someone actually does what they say they'll do."

"Amen to that. I like the way he started with a summary of their moves here from Utah. In waves, as he calls them. Looks like we have a bunch of names to work through. What say you take the Internet and I'll search all the standard databases?"

"Deal."

And that's how the two detectives spent the rest of their morning. With 16 male names and four female names, the search was slow and tedious.

Three hours later, Ginny said, "OK, Joe. Let's see what we have so far. I hope you found some juicy stuff, 'cause I didn't find much. In fact, most of these people are ghosts."

"Ghosts?"

"Yeah, ghosts. They didn't drop off the grid. Most of them were never on it. Other than what are probably their birth certificates, almost all of which are from Utah, there's nothing. No driver's licenses, no credit cards, no ownership or rental of houses or apartments or cars, no state or federal tax returns — not even social security numbers, no speeding or parking tickets, no nothing. This, of course, isn't the case for the few who work regular jobs off their compound."

"I feel a little better about not having found anything. A few disturbances, like fights and protests, but nothing really serious. They do seem to be mostly invisible."

"Agreed. And, interestingly, except for the house robbery that led to Patterson developing his CI and those few other individual crimes, virtually nothing since they came here. Seems like most of whatever trouble some of them may have gotten into happened in Utah."

The detectives developed a list of whatever Utah and Ohio legal proceedings they could find for each individual and printed out whatever detail they had for each occurrence, including the date of each infraction, along with the date that the person left Utah for Ohio. The detectives also carefully noted the details of the three waves of members who moved east. The initial eight people, including Davis and two of his wives, came first to check out the area and then purchase the large farm. Shortly after the purchase, the main wave, consisting of 20 males, six females (including Davis' third wife) and five children, came. Finally, an additional seven people left Utah for Ohio in two small groups about six months later. This total of 46 Utah transplants, plus a few local joiners in Ohio, resulted in a total of about 50 current members in Ohio.

"Interesting how so few of them have driver's licenses," said Joe.

"Yeah, but maybe they don't have that many cars and trucks. Plus a few of the newer arrivals may still be using their Utah licenses."

"True. And perhaps some of them even drive off their property without licenses on occasion."

"What? I'd be shocked," said Ginny, putting on her best fake-shocked expression.

"If nothing else, having these names and knowing which ones have licenses might be useful when we talk to Williams' and Patterson's contacts and CI."

"For sure."

Ginny no sooner finished her sentence than her phone rang. It was Nancy Williams.

"Yes, Detective, that's right. The couple and the brother are fine meeting with you two. As they all work during the day, they'd prefer early evening, like six or so. They said any night this week would be fine. They also said they could meet over the weekend if six o'clock is too late for you."

"No, six would be fine. How about tomorrow evening? Where should we meet them?"

"They suggested the Eatons' house. Their names are Vicki and Carl Eaton, and Carl's brother, Daryl Eaton, will be there as well."

"Great. Appreciate you setting this up so quickly."

"No problem."

Williams gave Ginny the address, and the call ended after thanks and good-byes.

The detectives again did a bit of house-location checking on the way home.

Chapter 14

t about ten to six that next evening, Ginny pulled into the Eatons' driveway and turned off the engine.

"Cute little house. Small, but well kept."

"Yeah, and the small lawn around the house looks freshly mowed. Wonder how much of the surrounding pastureland belongs to them."

"No idea. Let's head on in."

Ginny and Joe got out of Ginny's car and walked along the short gravel path to the front door. The house, with muted-yellow vinyl siding, appeared to be a single level bungalow type. Based on its size, there was probably one, or a maximum of two, bedrooms. Ginny knocked on the door, and it was opened about 15 seconds later.

"Hi, you must be the detectives. I'm Vicki Eaton. Please come in." Eaton was a tall, thin, attractive woman, probably in her mid-20s.

Ginny introduced herself and Joe, then the two detectives followed Eaton into the house. The front door opened immediately into the living room, a small but neat space, furnished with what was obviously a mixture of hand-me-down furniture and a few inexpensive tables and lamps.

Vicki introduced her husband, Carl, who was sitting in the one recliner in the room, and the two detectives to each other.

The detectives sat on a pink couch while Vicki went to the kitchen to get coffee for all.

"Thank you for agreeing to meet with us," said Ginny.

"Sure. Glad to help if we can. My brother should be here soon. If he's true to form, he'll pull in about 6:10 for our six o'clock meeting. Don't know if he does it intentionally or if it's in his DNA, but he's always five or ten minutes late."

"Not a problem," said Joe. "We're a bit early. We can start before he gets here if need be."

As it turned out, they didn't have to start without Daryl. He arrived just as Vicki was finishing handing out mugs of hot coffee. Daryl said his hellos, went into the kitchen to get a mug for himself and was soon sitting with everyone else in the living room.

"Thanks for meeting us," said Joe. "As I'm sure Officer Williams told you, we're interested in learning more about the Free Republic of America Patriots group. As I'm sure you know, it's not too easy for an outsider to get much info about them."

"Yeah, and at least twice as tough when that outsider is a cop."

"Seems that way."

"What can you tell us about your time with them?" asked Ginny.

"Whaddaya wanna know?" asked Daryl, his voice betraying a slight nervousness.

"How about just walking us through your experience. When and why you joined? What you did while you were a member? Why you decided to leave, and was it difficult to leave?"

Joe added, "I'm sure we'll interrupt with questions as your story triggers them in our minds."

"OK," said Vicki, after first glancing toward her husband, then his brother. "I'll start."

"Great," said Ginny.

"We got nothing to hide or be ashamed about. What we'll tell you won't be no different than what we told the big shots in the militia when we quit."

"OK, let's hear it," said Joe.

"First off, you should know we're from here. In fact, our families go way back. We're the fourth generation living on this property. Our 20 acres of farmland is a lot smaller than back when, but the family had to sell off pieces over the years. The need for money is stronger than the love of the land."

"I can understand that," said Ginny.

"Anyhow, the three of us over the past, I dunno, maybe four or five years started getting more and more unhappy with how this country was changing. People were getting more and more selfish and greedy. Making more money was all that mattered. Don't worry about trying to help others having any kind of difficulty. Seems like it was going downhill across the whole country, not just here."

"Yeah," jumped in Daryl, "and politics wasn't helping. Abortions were becoming more and more common. Like, what the heck, no big deal, we're only killing little harmless babies."

"And," added Carl, sitting upright in his recliner, "the government is clearly moving to tighten up on gun controls, which we all know is just their sneaky way of eventually doing away with the Second Amendment." He thumped a fist on the arm of his chair for emphasis.

"Anyhow," continued Vicki, "we learned some about FRAP — that's the abbreviation we call the group by — and they seemed to be pushing the very things we were feeling. We liked the idea of their egalitarian-kinda organization, where everyone has an equal say in what's going on, where everyone shares their food and other stuff."

"And did that prove to be the case?" asked Joe.

"For the first few months, we thought so. But then we realized it wasn't. We thought that everyone would participate in deciding things, but it didn't work that way. There was a leader and a small group, and they ran the show."

"Hell," said Daryl, "it was worse than I picture the military. We were just little worker bees doing whatever the queen bees told us to do."

"At first, we at least were happy that everyone was sharing everything," said Vicki. "But then we realized that the leaders were taking more, and I mean a lot more, for themselves before the rest of us got to share the leftovers."

"Can you give us some examples?" asked Ginny.

"Sure," Carl answered. "When food was harvested, the leaders first picked out the best stuff for themselves. In terms of housing, they took the best rooms and the best, most comfortable furniture. We had to make or buy clothing for them before anyone else."

"So is that why you all decided to leave the group?"

"That's half the reason," said Carl.

"And the other half?" asked Joe.

"All show, no go."

"Care to explain that a bit?" asked Joe.

"Happy to. Like we said before, abortion and gun rights are things we're very interested in, and we were excited to support a group which seemed to be fighting for exactly the way we thought. Sure, they supported some questionable stuff too — like, white supremacy and anti-government stuff. We couldn't stand their blatant racism. We don't have any problem with immigrants or people of other colors. And the Mormon stuff, the multiple wife stuff. That was all kind of weird."

"And?" prompted Ginny.

"They weren't fighting for the Second Amendment or the rights of the unborn at all," said Carl. "They constantly talked about them internally, and they'd talk about them with outsiders whenever they were asked, but they never actually did anything about them. And I mean nothing. Not even a peaceful march or protest. Nothing except blah, blah, blah. Felt like a bunch of adults playing at being a real militia."

"Any other reasons?" asked Ginny.

"Nope. But ain't those enough?"

"Yes, they are. Can you tell us a bit about how you joined? The process, I mean. And what you did — did you have assigned jobs while you were there? Also, when you decided to leave the group did you have any difficulties?"

"Not too much to say," said Vicki. "We decided to join about a year ago. We drove to their gate and told one of the guards. One of the leaders came out and talked with us, told us we were welcome whenever. We came back home to organize things, including having one of our cousins live here and take care of the place. A week later we arrived with our three suitcases, and, wham, we were full-fledged members."

"Was leaving more difficult?" asked Joe.

"Not at all. Two or three of the big shots talked with us, asking why and trying to get us to change our minds, but there was no real pressure, no threats or anything like that. In fact, we occasionally see a member around town and we chat and everything. We have nothing against the group, we just found it wasn't for us."

"What jobs did you have while you were there?" asked Ginny.

"I split my time about equally taking care of the little kids — meals, bedtime, playing in the afternoons, and baking goods that others sold around town," said Vicki.

"I worked as one of the farmers almost the whole time. We ate most of what we grew. We sold anything extra we had," said Carl.

"I was a bit different. I kept my job at the autobody shop in town. Drove there and back every day. Only change was that after I cashed my paycheck, I turned all the money over to the group," said Daryl. "Feel like an idiot for it now, but at least I got wise fast."

"You guys have been extremely helpful," said Joe. "One more question, then I think we're through."

"Go for it," said Carl, leaning back in his recliner.

"We'd like to get the names of as many members as you can remember. They're not in any trouble whatsoever. We just want to try and meet more of them and talk with them, much like we're talking with you now. Also, the structure of the organization — who are the leaders? Do they each manage different areas? That sort of thing."

Over the next ten minutes or so, the three Eatons came up with almost 25 names, ten or so of which were only first names, and indicated which were in the leadership group and what their roles were. Having left the group three months earlier, they had no idea about anyone currently missing or having been murdered.

The detectives thanked the three for their help and left. They stopped for takeout from one of the local Chinese restaurants and were back in Joe's house, sitting in the kitchen with their Chinese food and two beers each, a little before eight o'clock.

"Boy, that was a weird meeting with those three."

"Whadda you mean?"

"Not sure, Ginny. Just about everything. Didn't expect militia members, even if ex-members, to have a decent house, with the outside, as well as the inside, looking so neat and clean. Plus, Vicki and Carl seemed just like a nice, ordinary couple. Probably in their late 20s or early 30s. She was attractive, well-dressed and her hair neatly combed. Her husband, like Vicki, was tattoo-free, at least as far as I could see, and well dressed."

"True. But I bet you won't say the same thing about his brother."

"No way. Daryl was close to the opposite of the other two. Overweight, unshaven, sloppily wearing old, wrinkled clothing and displaying a shitload of tattoos. All he needed was his camouflage outfit and automatic rifle, and he could be the poster child for these militia groups."

“Agreed. And I was impressed with how well-spoken they were.”

“Yeah. And I bet part of the reason they didn’t fit in well was that, despite being pro-guns and anti-abortion, they didn’t seem to have all the typical racial and other prejudices.”

“Yup. Militia life may not work for you if you’re not full of prejudices and don’t believe in all types of crazy conspiracy theories.”

“OK, then, guess we need to remove joining a militia from our bucket list of important things to do in our lifetime.”

“‘Fraid so.”

Chapter 15

Ginny and Joe got to their desks around 7:45 the next morning. There was already a phone message from Officer Patterson. Joe immediately called him back.

"Morning, Rich. Just got in and saw you called."

"Sorry it's taken so long. But my CI and I have to be careful where and when we get together."

"Understood. What's up?"

"Took some work to convince him, but he's willing to meet. Wants me to be there too, as I'm the one he knows and trusts. Also, only wants one of you. Doesn't care which one, but, like he said, 'I'm not looking to rent the grand ballroom for this meeting.'"

"OK, that'd be me then. When and where? And anything more I ought to know before we meet with him?"

"Wants to meet tomorrow about 5:30. He can tell the folks back at the compound that he joined a few of his co-workers for a beer after work. Of course, as a Mormon, he'll be sipping seltzer while his co-workers knock back a few. Figures he can say that everyone else in his work group was going and it would have looked weird if he didn't join in."

"Makes sense. Did he say where?"

"Yeah. Place we've met at before. Parking lot behind the old Hastings plant on Frederick. Been empty for years, and there are a bunch of nooks and crannies in the lot behind the building where we can all park, then get in one car and talk. I'll arrange to unlock the gate to the lot a few minutes before the meet."

"Works for me."

"One other thing. Really don't want to scare this guy away. So please follow my lead. If I say we should skip that question or whatever, just go with the flow."

"Will do, and not to worry. I've been at this long enough — sometimes I think too long. I know my way around."

"I know. I know. Didn't mean to insult you. Just a bit nervous. Took me quite a while to develop him, and he's my first and only so far."

"Understood, and no offense taken. Thanks for setting this up. See you tomorrow."

"Right."

Joe filled Ginny in.

"We probably should update the chief."

"Yeah, it's been a few days. One thing first. I want to apologize for jumping in and saying I'd be the detective to go with Patterson. Just had a feeling the CI would prefer another male. Still, I should have waited so you and I could discuss it."

"Not a problem, Joe. I think you probably made the right call."

"Well, I feel bad about it anyway. Thanks for being so understanding."

"Like I said, no problem. Just a reminder before we see the chief — we still have no idea how to get on the property and look for a body, but we've got a bunch of things underway and about to be happening."

"You're right. We haven't actually made much of a dent in the case, but at least we're not sitting here with our thumbs up our you-know-what."

"Correct. But I hope you'll express it slightly differently to the chief."

"Ginny, you know not to worry. Why do you think Washington is trying to get me to be our ambassador to the UN? It's clearly my diplomatic skills."

"Not to mention your hallucinations," responded Ginny as they walked back to the chief's office.

The detectives were in and out of the chief's office in less than ten minutes.

"At least he didn't bite our heads off."

"True, but I felt like he was tempted to."

"Joe, are you getting overly sensitive?"

"No. You're right. It was better than the average chief meeting. He was pleased with all the steps we've taken and are taking. But he is concerned — rightly so, I might add — that we still have no idea how we're going to get the warrant to search their property."

"And, surprise, surprise, he reminded us three times in five minutes not to turn this into the next Waco or Ruby Ridge."

"Yeah, he might be a bit paranoid about that. But, on the other hand, that sure wouldn't be the most desirable outcome."

"You said that so nicely, Mr. Future UN Ambassador."

Chapter 16

Ginny and Joe were sitting in the conference room at 12:50 when O'Grady called to announce Kalinski's arrival. Joe went downstairs to meet him, while Ginny went to the coffee area to pour out the half-day-old coffee and make a fresh pot in honor of their visitor.

Back in the conference room, introductions were made. Much to Ginny and Joe's surprise, the chief walked in and introduced himself to Kalinski.

"Despite what my detectives may think, I'm not yet quite so old as to be incapable of learning anything new. This militia stuff has been developing rapidly, and I'm sure I could benefit from a brief refresher and update. Can't stay too long, but I'd like to sit in for a portion of the session."

"Delighted to have you with us," said Kalinski.

Ginny took coffee orders, left the room and was soon back with four mugs of hot, freshly made coffee.

"OK, what say we get started?" said Kalinski. "I suggest I first go through some overall private militia stuff. As the chief said, they've been rapidly growing and expanding their geographical presence, and some of their beliefs and methods have been changing. Then, after that, we can spend a few minutes talking specifically about the Free Republic of American Patriots. They've been far from our biggest worry so far, but we try to keep some level of current intelligence on all the groups out there."

"Go for it," said Ginny as she and Joe took out their notepads and pens.

"Like ice cream at Baskin-Robbins, militia groups come in many flavors. Most of them are anti-government in one way or another, and many are organized much like the military. Most have stockpiles of guns and ammunition, often illegally obtained, and many also buy or build explosive devices. Several engage in various levels of domestic terrorism, some only protest legally and most plan for all sorts of major activities or catastrophes.

"Some of the most common domestic ideologies of these groups are as follows, with many groups simultaneously holding two or more sets of these extremist views.

"Sovereign citizen extremists believe they are separate or sovereign from the United States, not subject to any government authorities or laws. They often target government members, such as police, judges and tax officials.

"Anarchist extremists believe that society should have no government, laws or police. They tend to target capitalist institutions like large corporations, plus government and especially police organizations, and many of these groups see violence as the only viable route to achieving their vision. Some, ironically often calling themselves 'patriots,' believe it's their duty to protect the country from our corrupt government, or our government which has exceeded its constitutional limits, or from various international threats.

"The white supremacist groups hate all other races and religions and, of course, immigrants. They believe that white, Christian citizens are being discriminated against and will be replaced by ethnic and racial minorities — essentially pure racism. Various US-based neo-Nazi groups are increasing in size and number at an alarming pace. Of course, these folks also often call themselves 'patriots,' though they're way more interested in tearing down the government than supporting it.

"The animal rights and environmental groups are fine with using violence to stop activities which they see as hurting animals or the environment.

"No need to spend much time describing the widely known anti-abortion and gun rights groups. Plenty of crossover there with the white supremacists anyways.

"A fairly new category are the involuntary celibates, otherwise known as incels. A loose community of mostly young males, they believe that one's place in society is determined by one's physical characteristics and that women are responsible for this unfair hierarchy. There have been several cases of women being killed as a result."

"Yikes," said Ginny. "You sure were right when you said it was like all the flavors at Baskin-Robbins. The bad-tasting ones, at least."

"Told you. When viewing all these groups, it's important to remember that it's not illegal to hold or express anti-government, hateful, prejudiced or extremist beliefs. It only becomes illegal when someone acts illegally because of these beliefs.

"Many of these groups are big conspiracy theory believers. One biggy is that the UN has the right to use military force anywhere, including within the US, so we'd better prepare for an invasion by them. Others think the federal government will force anyone who refuses a vaccination to be relocated to camps throughout the US, supposedly run by the Federal Emergency Management Agency. You think of anything, and it's likely there's at least one group out there that believes it."

"How do you separate the risky, violent ones from the more peaceful ones that more-or-less legally march, protest and distribute their propaganda?" asked Joe.

"Tough. We can obviously do it based upon their behavior to date, but that doesn't necessarily correlate with what their future behavior will be like. That's why, despite, of course, focusing on the ones known to be violent, we also need to keep our attention on the so-far-nonviolent ones."

"Mel, I don't want to mess your sequence up, but I've got to head out to a meeting shortly. Before I leave, though, I'd love to get a sense of the trends in terms of which groups are growing and what seems to be changing."

"Not a problem, Chief. In fact, that was where I was about to go. Far-right terrorism is much more prevalent than that from far-left groups or individuals inspired by overseas militant Islamic groups. Right-wing extremists have been responsible for more than two-thirds of the attacks and plots in the past few years. Of the groups I mentioned earlier, the anarchist, anti-capitalism, animal rights and environmental groups are mostly left-wing. The others are all right-wing. And, as I said, some groups have a confusing blend, or mish-mash, of often-conflicting leftist and rightist beliefs."

"Can you tell us more about individuals acting alone, rather than as part of a militia or a group?" asked Joe.

"Sure. This is a large and growing problem. Most of these individuals are influenced or indoctrinated, if you will, by some group. But they're usually not members. Rather, they're part of a loose network mostly organized and operated online, which makes it extremely difficult for law enforcement to identify and keep track of potential attackers. Many show early antisocial tendencies, have mental problems, engage in online rantings, and display other personality-based clues, but, all too often, these are recognized as such only after the fact."

"Wow, you do have your hands full. Sorry, but I've got to run now. Ginny and Joe will fill me in later on what I miss. Thanks for coming. I enjoyed meeting you, and learned quite a lot."

The chief left, and Joe suggested, "Let's take a five-minute break — for emptying and refilling. Kidneys and coffee mugs respectively, that is."

Ten minutes later, the three of them were back in the conference room.

"OK," said Kalinski. "Now let's spend a few minutes on the specific group you're interested in. To start with, the Free Republic of American Patriots is one of the many groups with a custom combination of beliefs. They're clearly white supremacists, with their racism, anti-Semitism and anti-immigrant prejudices very obvious. Also anti-abortion and strong gun-rights advocates. In addition, they're very susceptible to believing the conspiracy theory of the moment, which causes their anti-government, anti-police, anti-authority feelings to wax and wane depending on the latest conspiracy theories. Here's what we've got on individual members," Kalinski said as he pulled two typed pages out of his thin leather briefcase and handed them to Ginny. "This is a list of about 30 of their Ohio-based members, out of a total of what we think is about 50 or 60. A lot of these names came from our Salt Lake office. We've also identified some of the leadership roles and personal relationships."

"Let's go to the leadership stuff. We've already developed a fairly large list of members. We can compare our lists, then check our databases for any new names you've provided later on."

"Fair enough. Let me grab my copy."

With Kalinski holding his copy of the sheets in front of him and Joe and Ginny sitting side by side and looking at their copy, Kalinski started in. "Mark Davis, head of the local branch here, is the nephew of Orin Heaton, the head of the main unit in Utah. Davis' first and only legally-married-to wife is Abigail Davis. His two other so-called wives, whom he never legally married in order to skirt the polygamy laws, are Lynn Thatcher and Clara Hansen. The second in command is Aaron Turley. He takes charge whenever Davis is away, which seems to occur for a few days every couple of months. No one admits to knowing where he goes or how he gets there.

"Wallace Rowley is head of the guards around the property; he can often be found personally watching the front gates. Abigail Davis is the unofficial head of all the women, and under her Roslyn Gardner is in charge of caring for the younger children. Lastly, Beckam Kimball is the treasurer who takes care of all their money and spending. Also known are four members who hold normal jobs outside of the group: Jed Farnsworth is an apprentice electrician, Bart Carr an auto dealer service technician, Spencer Ludlow an assembler at a furniture manufacturer and John Zollinger a city bus maintenance worker. That's about it."

"Well, it's a lot more than we knew before this afternoon. Very helpful. Much appreciated," said Ginny.

"My pleasure."

"OK if we call you as questions arise?" asked Joe.

"Definitely. May not have the answers, but I'll do my best."

"Great."

"OK, let me escort you downstairs," said Ginny.

"Enjoy the weekend with the family," said Joe.

"We'll do our best."

Ginny led Kalinski downstairs and then returned to Joe.

"Good guy," said Joe. "Very down to earth, seems to be really trying to help."

"Full agreement. Let's hope that somehow all this info will help us get that damn warrant."

"I'm hoping with all my power, but I fear we may still not be there."

"Me too."

"Let's sneak outta here. I'm totally out of steam."

"Works for me. Let's go. We'll sort through and follow up on Kalinski's info tomorrow. We still have another town to look at on our way home."

Chapter 17

The detectives spent most of the next morning working on the information Kalinski had provided.

"That overview from Kalinski was really interesting — and a little unnerving."

"Yeah. I really had no idea there were so many subsets of militia groups."

"Me neither, Ginny. People sure are weird these days. And getting weirder. I also didn't realize the great majority of violence came from far-right groups. I thought it'd be more equally split between far-right and far-left."

"I did, too. But the data is what it is. Now we oughta shift gears and focus on the info he gave us about our local group."

"Agreed."

The detectives spent more than two hours going through the names Kalinski had given them. All but four were already on the list that Ginny and Joe had. They checked various databases for these four, but found next to nothing. They then began trying to draw an organization chart, based upon the less-than-complete information they had, trying to show the relationships among the various leaders of the group and noting who performed which functions.

Just before 11, the chief yelled for Joe and Ginny to join him in his office.

"I know, Chief. We're overdue on an update about the militia thing, but—"

"Joe, you're doing it again. You're always guessing why I want to talk to you two and, shocking but true, you're almost always totally wrong."

"Chief, I—"

"Dammit, Joe! Ears open, mouth shut. Clear enough?"

With his right hand over his mouth, Joe vigorously nodded his head up and down.

It was a struggle, but Ginny was able to prevent herself from giggling out loud at the sight of Joe.

"What's up, Chief?" asked Ginny.

"Now that's the right way to start off. Ginny, you've got to do a better job of training your partner here."

"Yes, sir. I'll work harder at it," said Ginny with a smile.

"9-1-1 got a call about half an hour ago. From a Lynn Thatcher."

"We know that name. She's one of the wives of the local leader of the militia group."

"'Boing!'" said the chief, mimicking a spring. "And the light bulb lit up."

"She's wife number two of Mark Davis," said Ginny. "To be precise, she's not actually married to Davis. They live as if three women are all his wives, but he never officially married numbers two and three. Lets them avoid any polygamy legal issues."

"In any event, she called about her husband, or make-believe husband. Seems he often mysteriously leaves the place for a few days every couple of months. But this time he's been gone longer than usual, and she's worried something might have happened to him. She said it's been about a week and a half now. No one seems to know anything, or if they do, they're not saying. She wants to file a missing person report, or whatever else is needed to get us to look for him."

"This may be what we've been waiting for," said Ginny. "Sounds like his disappearance happened a few days before that anonymous call about a murder. Maybe there was a murder, and Mark Davis, the group's leader, is the victim."

"Could be," said the chief. "You need to see whether this additional call is enough to get a warrant to search their property and interview some of their members."

"It should be," said Joe, "but the prosecutor's office will make that call. Can we meet with, or at least talk with wife number two to get all the details before trying for that warrant?"

"Check the 9-1-1 call. She's supposedly at a roadside stand off 665 selling vegetables and homemade baked goods until sometime this afternoon. Since you've been seen a few times at their property already, it might be better if Ginny goes by herself. Ginny, get her alone for a few minutes if you can. Ask her about Davis' disappearance while looking like you're discussing the size of the blueberries in the pies."

"Good idea, Chief. Think I'll go shopping now. Don't know how much longer she'll be there today."

"Ginny, all kidding aside. This is serious now. Be sure to buy a few of the pies if they look good," said Joe.

Ginny and Joe went downstairs to listen to the recording of the 9-1-1 call. Joe then went back upstairs while Ginny walked to her car and headed for the fruit stand.

Ginny parked in front of the stand about 20 minutes later. There was one lady in front, in the process of selling some corn and tomatoes to a customer. Ginny saw one other worker, but he was about 25 feet behind the stand, unloading produce and stacking the empty cases. When the customer left, Ginny walked up to the saleslady.

"Good morning. How are you doing? I'm Virginia. I'm interested in some vegetables — and maybe a few of your delicious-looking pies."

"Hi, I'm Lynn. Doing great today. Hard not to, with this fabulous fall weather. Glad to help you. Want to start with the vegetables or pies?"

"Definitely the pies." Then, in an almost-whisper, Ginny added, "I'm with the police department. Could we talk about your call earlier this morning?"

Thatcher's face took on the look of panic. She quickly glanced to the side, relieved that her co-worker wasn't too close. "Oh, my God. OK, but please wait. Tommy will be leaving in a few minutes to go get some more pies. We can talk then. Let's just do the normal shopping stuff 'til he leaves. Please!"

"Sure. No problem."

The two ladies spent the next few minutes looking at and talking about the pies, Ginny indicating she wanted to buy one blueberry and one apple pie. Thatcher put the two pies aside and led Ginny to the vegetable display. As Ginny fussed with the various vegetables and asked several questions, both ladies kept an eye on the co-worker.

Sure enough, after less than five more minutes he yelled, "Lynn, will you be OK? Gonna head back and get another load of pies. Should be back in less than an hour."

"I'll be fine, Tommy. Go for it. Bring mostly apple, that's what we're almost out of."

"Roger that." He threw the empty cases in the back of the pickup, climbed into the cab and was on his way.

"OK," said Ginny. "Let's get right to it. Don't know when another customer will arrive and interrupt us."

"What do you need to know?"

"What led you to call 9-1-1 this morning?"

"I'm married to Mark Davis. He's head of our group here. Like I told the lady on the phone, he fairly often leaves for a few days. We never know in advance, and we never know where he went, or why, or even how he traveled. He doesn't own a vehicle and we're never missing any of the group cars or trucks when he's gone."

"When was the most recent time before now that he went on one of these trips?"

"Not sure of the exact dates, but it was one and a half, maybe two months ago."

"And how long was he gone?"

"I'd need to check. But probably three or four days, five max."

"And no one ever found out where he went or why?"

"That's right. Unless, of course, he told someone or someone somehow found out, but he, or she I guess, has never admitted it."

"What's your best guess as to the where and why of these trips?"

"No idea. Really. Some of us have talked about it, but no one seems to know."

At that point, a customer arrived. The discussion was put on hold while Thatcher helped the customer with various vegetables and Ginny tried to make herself look busy in front of the pies. After what seemed like an eternity, the customer made her purchases and left.

"OK, back to where we were. What's different this time that led you to call 9-1-1? You never called regarding any of his other trips, did you?"

Thatcher looked down as she answered, "No, I didn't. I called this time 'cause I really am worried. He's been gone for well over a week now. Way longer than any of his other little trips."

"Anything else? Can you think of any reason, or anyone who would like him gone?"

"No. I'm just sorta getting spooked. There's all kinds of rumors and whispering about someone being murdered on our property. No specifics. But Mark is the only one not with us, so if somebody got murdered it was either an outsider who snuck onto our property or, God forbid, Mark." Thatcher sniffled a few times and used her hand to wipe at the tears starting to flow down her cheeks. "Please tell me what you know about a murder."

"Why do you think I know anything about one?"

"We know the police came. Twice. They didn't have, or at least didn't give us, any details, but they wanted permission to search our property. We, of course, said no. But their raising the issue, and Mark being missing for so long, has me panicked."

"I understand, Lynn. But let me assure you, we really have no detailed information. We were just following up on an anonymous call saying some unnamed person had been murdered. Could very well have been a crank call for all we know. Do you know anyone who might want your husband dead? Or out of the way?"

"I — no. I — uh, uh, have no idea. Everyone likes Mark."

"Please don't take this the wrong way. Are there any problems in your, ah, unconventional marriage?"

"No more problems than in any other family. You'd be surprised at how normal life in a polygamous unit like ours is."

Ginny raised one eyebrow. "I see."

"What should I do now?"

"As I see it, you've got two choices. And you may not like either of them."

"What are they?"

"The first is to do nothing, keep your eyes and ears open, and just wait."

"And the second one?"

"This would be the more helpful approach, but you may not want to do it."

"What is it?"

"Give us a formal, on-the-record statement repeating what we've been talking about. I'm fairly confident that your statement, along with the anonymous call about a murder, would allow us to get a search warrant for your group's property. That would let us determine whether or not there was a murder, at least one committed on your property."

"If I did that and they found out, I'd be in deep trouble. Kicked out of the group as a minimum, injured or maybe even killed — if there really is a killer in our group."

"That's why I said you might not like either choice."

"Damn! You have no idea how much the police are disliked and distrusted."

"But there might be a way."

Thatcher's face lit up and she stood a little taller. "Oh?"

"We don't need your statement to become public. We just need it recorded on tape, and then handwritten and signed by you and a witness. We'd have to present it to a judge to convince him to sign the warrant, but it could be kept confidential beyond that. As you can imagine, judges and prosecutors are pretty good at keeping things confidential."

"But even if I wanted to do that, how'd I do it without my group knowing about it?"

"We'd need some excuse for you to go someplace alone for an hour or so. Maybe you fake being sick and say you need to see a doctor, or there's some reason you need to go into town alone to do some special shopping. Something like that. We could meet you and get your taped and written statement. You then see one of our cooperative doctors or do your shopping or whatever, then head back home with no one being any wiser."

"Yikes. Scary. Like I'm some kind of undercover secret agent. But I guess it could work. I just need a little time to think about it, and to see what kind of fake reason I can come up with for a trip downtown."

"I understand. Here's my card, with my cellphone

number on it. Call me day or night, whenever you're ready, and we can set things up."

"OK, thanks."

"You're welcome."

"One other question. Do you think Mark's dead?"

"Lynn, I wish I knew. But we really have no idea. That's why this search warrant is so important."

"OK. I'll call as soon as I think all this through."

Ginny paid for her two pies and headed back to the station. Along the way, she pulled into a Burger King drive-thru and picked up lunch for Joe and herself.

Back at the station, Joe and Ginny enjoyed their burgers and fries, after which they shared the two pies with the chief and the detectives who were there. Joe was happy to share, but disappointed that they'd only have about one-quarter of each pie left to take home that evening.

After finishing their late lunch Ginny called APA Larkin, filling her in on Thatcher's call to 9-1-1 and Ginny's visit with her. Larkin confirmed that if Thatcher gave an official statement it probably would be enough to get a warrant, but warned Ginny that they'd only know for sure when they went to a judge and tried. Larkin and Ginny traded cellphone numbers in case things developed in the evening or over the weekend.

Ginny and Joe spent a few minutes with the chief, Ginny summarizing her meeting with Thatcher and Larkin's optimism that a warrant probably could be obtained, and the detectives reminding the chief of Joe's meeting later that day with Patterson's confidential informer inside the militia.

The chief surprised both detectives with his unusually positive attitude, complimenting them on the steps they'd taken and would be taking and also for not causing any standoff-like problems with the militia.

Chapter 18

As they had come to work in one car, the two detectives left the station a little after four so Joe could drop Ginny at home before he headed to meet Patterson and Patterson's CI, Spencer Ludlow.

Joe arrived around 5:15. Patterson had already unlocked the gate. Joe pulled into the parking lot behind the old Hastings plant and parked about ten feet from Patterson's patrol car. Both were parked within an alcove formed by the uneven outline of the building, and neither car could be seen from the street. Patterson got out of his car and joined Joe in his.

Ludlow arrived at 5:25. He parked next to Joe's car, got out of his car and sat in the backseat of Joe's car, behind Patterson. Joe was surprised when he saw Ludlow. *Coulda fooled me. Not at all what I expected. Looks to be late 20s or so, totally clean-shaven with a normal haircut. About five-ten, not especially thin or fat. Could be one of the guys I went to school with and hung out with after graduation. Wonder how the hell he wound up with a bunch of screwball conspiracists. Sure does confirm that "you can't judge a book by its cover."*

Introductions were made, and Patterson got right into it.

"Spencer, thanks for meeting with us. Realize you're allegedly out for a couple of drinks with your co-workers before heading home, so we'll need to keep this short and sweet."

"Appreciate that. Don't want to generate any suspicions."

Joe briefly described the original anonymous 9-1-1 call and their difficulties since in getting access to the property.

"Not surprised. We don't exactly welcome visitors."

"Why's that?"

"General feeling that the government, and probably a lot of the neighbors, would like us to just disappear. The more you and they learn about us, the more you might be able to make that happen."

"Any other reason?" asked Joe.

"Yeah. Some members probably have and do stuff that's not totally legit, and that's stuff we'd like to keep on the Q.T."

"Oh? Like what?" asked Joe.

"Don't want to go into details, but it could, hypothetically so to say, include things like illegal guns or guys with more than one wife. Minor stuff like that."

"Maybe minor, maybe not. But that's not our main concern right now."

"Oh? That'd be a first."

"What's your take on the possibility of a murder having occurred there?"

"Wow! That clearly isn't something minor. I've heard the rumors like everybody else, mostly 'cause of you coming to try and investigate."

"Do you think a murder's possible?"

"Sure. Anything's possible. But I don't know who mighta been killed, much less why, or by who or where the body is."

"Anyone missing from the group?"

"Nope. Don't think so."

"What about your leader, Mark Davis? We heard he's missing."

"He's away, but I wouldn't call it missing. He often leaves for a few days, totally unannounced. We never know where he goes or why. This is probably just another of those trips."

"Just imagine for a minute. If he was murdered, why might someone do it?"

"Damned if I know. But he is in charge, you know. And, in any organization, the top dog always makes some enemies or generates some jealousies."

"Can you be a little more specific?"
"Umm. Let's see. He's the only one with three wives, and he has the largest and nicest living quarters. Plus, he often makes decisions without discussing them with us first. But all big bosses do that."

"Any ongoing arguments or philosophical differences you can think of?"

"The only one I know about is that many of us feel we're not really doing anything. We always talk about the issues we believe in and the changes we want to see, but we never protest or riot or whatever to make any of these things happen. I'm not up there with the big shots, but, from what I hear, Mark's always the one who says no to any proposed actions — even simple, legal things like marching or protesting."

"Has this led to fights?"

"Not physical fights. But several heated arguments. And it doesn't help that Mark isn't shy about reminding everyone that his uncle is head of our main group in Utah."

"Any names jump to mind of those he most often argues with?"

"Not really. But it's always some of the more senior members. Us little guys are more inclined to stay quiet, or maybe just grumble among ourselves."

They spent another ten minutes or so with Ludlow, who provided all the member names he could recall, identifying those in the various leadership positions.

Thanks and good-byes, and all three drove out of the lot, with Patterson stopping on the way out to relock the gate.

Over dinner, Joe replayed the meeting for Ginny.

Chapter 19

Friday seemed to last forever to Ginny and Joe. Other than unsuccessfully trying to come up with a list of next steps, they fiddled with paperwork, waiting for something to develop. Nothing did. The detectives were relieved when it finally became late enough for them to leave and start their weekend.

— — — — — — — —

By contrast, Saturday flew by for Ginny and Joe. A strenuous jog by both detectives before breakfast, checking out two additional towns as possible locations for their purchased-home-to-be, an enjoyable after-lunch and after-lovemaking nap, a trip to the supermarket, and steaks grilled on the barbecue for dinner rounded out their activities for the day.

— — — — — — — —

Ginny's cellphone rang at 7:30 Sunday morning.

Grabbing her phone from her night table, Ginny sat up on the edge of her bed, brushed her hair out of her face with her free hand and said, "Hello?"

"Detective. This is Lynn Thatcher. Sorry to call so early on a Sunday."

"Not a problem. We were already up," lied Ginny, without knowing why she felt compelled to lie. "What's going on?"

"I decided to help you get that search warrant. Mark's still not back, and I'm going crazy with worry."

"I think you've made the right decision. Any idea how you can get downtown alone without raising any suspicions?"

"I'm scheduled to work at the vegetable stand later today. I was thinking I could fake fainting and fall down, then tell them something hurts very badly and that they need to call an ambulance. I'll insist that any co-workers at the stand not come with me in the ambulance because they need to cover the stand. Sundays are usually big sales days for us. If you can arrange things, we could then be alone in the ambulance and, if we need more time, in the hospital before they allow me to have any visitors."

"Sounds like a great idea, Lynn. I can organize the ambulance, as well as coordinate with the folks in the hospital. We have great relationships with several of the EMTs and hospital staff. Since my partner has been seen twice at your compound, and I was seen by at least your one co-worker at the farm stand, let's not take the risk of either of us arriving with the ambulance and being recognized. We'll be waiting for you in your room at the hospital. Just so I can get everything staged, what time would make sense for you to call 9-1-1 for an ambulance?"

"Let's say around two. The farm stand should be pretty busy around then, making it difficult for anyone to accompany me."

"OK, great. I think we have a plan. If you run into any problems, just don't call 9-1-1 to report your fall. If I hit a snag, I'll send you a short text. Any text from me no matter what it says will mean for you to call things off. Got it?"

"Yup."

"OK, good for you, Lynn. See you later."

By then Joe was sitting up in bed, giving Ginny all kinds of quizzical looks while she talked with Lynn. After hanging up, Ginny relayed the conversation to Joe.

"Gotta admit," she concluded, "I was pissed that anyone would call and wake us this early on a Sunday. But I'll make an exception. This was for a worthwhile cause."

"Darn right. Especially if we have a warrant by the end of the day."

"Let's get up and have breakfast, Joe. I want to wait for a more reasonable hour, then we can start calling folks to set things up. I'll call my EMS buddy in the fire department to arrange for the ambulance. I'll also call Larkin to bring her up to date and tell her we should have Thatcher's statement by four or so this afternoon. Hopefully, she can find a judge on Sunday to sign the warrant."

"Good. I'll call dispatch to alert them to look for Thatcher's 9-1-1 call and to notify only the ambulance you specify for that call. I'll also talk to the ER supervisor and arrange for Thatcher to be scooted into a private room where you and I will be waiting for her."

"Sounds like we're all set with our plans."

"Almost. Just one more important plan to finalize."

"Oh? What'd I miss?"

"Two critical things: cream cheese with my bagel and bacon with my eggs."

"Oh, heavens! How could I have forgotten the most important of all our plans?"

"It's OK. I'll forgive you this once, given the excitement of hopefully getting the search warrant this afternoon."

Ginny and Joe arrived at the hospital a little after 1:45. The ER supervisor led them to one of the private treatment rooms in the emergency department. Ginny and Joe sat on the two chairs in the room after the supervisor told them to make themselves comfortable, closing the door on her way out.

About an hour later, two ambulance attendants, one a paramedic and one an EMT, wheeled a gurney into the room. Thatcher was lying on her back, strapped in for the ride. The EMT unstrapped her and helped her get off the gurney and onto the bed. He then helped her remove her outer clothing and put on a hospital gown. Quick hellos and good-byes with Ginny, and the ambulance attendants and their gurney were gone.

Ginny introduced Joe and Thatcher to each other. Ginny turned on the tape recorder she had brought with her, stated the date, the place and the names of those present. With Ginny leading her via a series of questions, Thatcher restated what she had told Ginny when they met on Thursday. Ginny then handed her a pad of paper and a pen, telling Thatcher to write out basically the same info contained in her verbal statement.

While Thatcher was writing, Ginny left the room and returned with the ER supervisor. The supervisor stuck Thatcher a few times in the crook of her arm with an empty syringe, expecting a black and blue mark to form which Thatcher could say came from a saline infusion they'd given her in the emergency room. She could explain that, fortunately, her illness wasn't anything serious. Just dehydration. The infusion, a day or two of rest plus drinking lots of fluids should lead to a quick and complete recovery.

Ginny had the supervisor sign Thatcher's statement as a witness.

Ginny and Joe thanked Thatcher, said they'd be in touch when possible and left with the taped and written statements. As soon as the detectives left, two females from the militia group, who had been out in the waiting room for an hour, were let in the room. They spoke with Thatcher for a few minutes, helped her dress and wheeled her out in a wheelchair to their car. They helped her into the car and drove off, heading to their compound.

From their car in the hospital parking lot, Ginny called Larkin and told her they had Thatcher's recorded and written statements. They agreed to meet in front of the courthouse in half an hour. Once she had the statements, Larkin would fine-tune the search warrant affidavit she had already typed up. As Larkin said, "Nothing like a Sunday evening to go judge hunting."

It was after seven before Ginny heard back from Larkin.

"Jeez, Barb, we were beginning to think you went off on vacation."

"I wish. But I had nothing better to do, so I spent the last few hours hunting for an available judge, specifically one who tends to more readily issue search warrants. To make a long story short, you now have a search warrant signed by the Honorable Edwin Nagler III. And he was fine with its broadness. You've got free rein over the entire property, including all the buildings and vehicles on it. The only thing he didn't approve was searching through the personal belongings of the folks living there, but we shouldn't be surprised about that."

"Super! Many thanks."

"You're welcome. I'll fax the warrant to your office now. OK if I then go enjoy the rest of my weekend?"

"Sure. Knock yourself out. You have our permission." Ginny hung up, then filled Joe in on the details.

"Finally," Joe said, "some progress. We clearly can't search at night, so it'll have to be tomorrow morning. I'm gonna call the chief and let him know. Also see if we can meet him real early tomorrow to get things rolling."

"Good idea, Joe. And pretty sneaky volunteering to talk to him when we finally have some good news and progress to report."

"Yeah, well, he already loves you. I'm the one that needs some relationship building with him."

"No need to tell me all your personal thoughts if it's too embarrassing for you," said Ginny with a grin.

"Very funny. Come on over here to the couch. Let's see if I can help you guess some of my other personal thoughts."

Chapter 20

After gathering the warrant sitting on the fax machine, Ginny and Joe were in the chief's office talking with him at 7:30 the next morning.

"Good work on getting that lady's statement and the search warrant. Great that the warrant is nice and broad."

"Thanks, Chief," said Ginny. "Think they'll honor it?"

"Don't know for sure, but my guess is yes. Not likely they'll ignore a valid search warrant."

"That's good," said Joe.

"But I wouldn't be surprised if they delay you for several hours, discussing things with their lawyers."

"Besides frustrating us just for the fun of it, that would give them time to hide or fix things they don't want us to find. Like illegal guns, and the murder weapon as a couple of examples."

"True, Ginny. But not much we can do about that. Have you guys figured out how you're going to search 600 acres? That's one hell of a lot of real estate."

"We've talked about it some and have two options," said Ginny. "We can do a typical search, but for a property this size, we'll need a very large contingent of law enforcement and firefighter folks."

"And that approach would take days to search everywhere," added Joe.

"So, the second option?" asked the chief.

"Cadaver dogs," said Ginny.

"Exactly what I was thinking," said the chief. "One of those dogs can probably search an area at least as fast as 25 or 30 volunteers."

"OK, then, we're in agreement. Let me make a few calls."

"Just remember, we're assuming, but sure as hell don't know, that the militia group will even let us, much less civilian volunteers with dogs, onto their property. Search warrant or not."

"Believe me, Chief, we haven't forgotten that for a second."

Back at their desks, Ginny scrolled through her Rolodex, found the card she wanted, and dialed the number.

"Good morning. Buckeye Search and Rescue. Amy Valen speaking."

"Good morning, Ms. Valen. My name is Ginny Harris. I'm a detective with the Jasper Creek Police Department, not far from Dayton."

"Pleased to sort of meet you, Detective. What can I do for you?"

Ginny summarized the situation, along with their belief that dogs would be better than dozens of volunteers.

"Detective, have you dealt with cadaver dogs in the past?"

"Yes, some. Although I've dealt more with regular search dogs, when we're looking for a missing child or senior citizen, but those dogs were looking for living persons."

"OK. Glad you've had some experience with what we call scent dogs. Let me tell you a little about our organization."

Ginny put the call on her phone's speaker and introduced Joe and Valen to each other.

"Although Buckeye Rescue's located in Cincinnati, we service the entire state. We're also members of several state and national organizations, so we're often sharing information and providing dogs and handlers to other organizations and, when needed, receiving the same from them. We're a totally volunteer, nonprofit organization. Our handlers and scent dogs are available to help emergency and law enforcement agencies 24/7. When we don't have sufficient resources, we look to our partners for support.

"Most scent dogs, and the ones most familiar to the public, are search & rescue dogs, trained to recognize the various smells of living persons and rapidly search a large area, be it open fields, woodlands or a collapsed building, to locate trapped or lost humans.

"Cadaver, or more officially Human Remains, search dogs are a smaller, less well-known group. They're trained to detect the smells of deceased people, including small traces of their blood or organs or bones, even those buried up to 15 feet underground and, in some cases, up to one hundred feet underwater. Cadaver dogs receive about a thousand hours of training before they're certified. Much of the training is with artificial scents; there are hundreds of different smells that come from decaying bodies or body parts, and these smells change depending on the amount of decomposition and whether the body is underground, underwater or in the open air. These dogs are also trained to differentiate between animal and human remains.

"Search & rescue dogs can't locate cadavers, and cadaver dogs can't locate living persons. The scents from living and dead humans are very different, and each dog is trained to detect one or the other."

"How do we get started?" asked Joe.

"Your partner said that the property was about 600 acres. One of our dogs can cover up to 250 acres per day."

"Wow!" said Ginny.

"The acreage would, of course, be somewhat less if you want to also carefully check out several buildings on the property."

"Which we definitely do," said Ginny.

"OK, so let's conservatively say one dog can cover 200 acres plus a few buildings. That would mean three days or so for one dog."

"Or one day for three dogs," said Joe.

"Very good with the arithmetic, Detective. Let me see who's available starting this afternoon, tomorrow morning at the latest. I'll get back to you within a couple of hours."

"Much appreciated," said Ginny. "Oh! One other thing. Even with the warrant we have, we can't be certain that the militia group will allow entry to their property. We're pretty sure they will, but we won't know for sure until we try."

"Thanks for mentioning that. It's of utmost importance to us that our handlers and dogs are kept free of risk. We need either their honest willingness to have us do our thing, or you need a large enough group of law enforcement folks to guaranty our safety."

"Understood."

"OK, I'll be back at you as soon as I can."

The call ended, and Ginny said to Joe, "She seems to know her stuff, and isn't one to let too much grass grow under her feet."

"Sure sounds that way."

The detectives brought the chief up to date. Joe headed out to bring back lunches for Ginny, two other detectives and himself, while Ginny browsed the Internet researching cadaver dogs in general and the Buckeye Search and Rescue Dogs organization in particular.

Chapter 21

Around two o'clock, Ginny received the return call from Valen.

"Good news and bad news. Any preference for the order?"

"Nope. Gimme it all."

"Can't get started 'til tomorrow morning. It'll be close to dark by the time we get organized and on scene if we tried for today."

"Darn."

"Understand your disappointment, but speed is usually a bit less urgent with cadaver dogs than search & rescue dogs. Not like the cadaver will further die unless we find it quickly."

"Can't argue with that."

"We can leave here real early tomorrow and be wherever you want us by 7:30, which is about when the sun's popping up."

"That'll work. How many dogs can you muster?"

"Definitely two for tomorrow morning, one of which I'm 110% sure of."

"Why so sure?"

"'Cause that one is Major, my German Shepherd."

"You mean you're—"

"Yup, Major and I are one of the volunteer teams. And we're in. There's also a second team who said yes, and he's extremely reliable."

"Two is definitely better than one."

"Also have a third team. But he's worried about safety there. Wants to wait and see how it goes with us first two teams. If all's OK, he said he'd show up by noon."

"OK, then. Seems like with two and a half teams tomorrow, we should be able to wrap it up in one day. One and a half at most."

"Correct. Sundown's not 'til 7:30, so we'll have a nice long 12-hour day. And, if need be, we can leave the buildings until last and do them after sundown."

"Great. Do we have to do anything or prepare anything for you?"

"Nope. We're pretty self-contained and self-sufficient. Give me a few cellphone numbers just in case and tell me where to show up. We'll be there before 7:30."

Ginny gave her the information and ended the call. She filled Joe in, and they both went to update the chief and ask him to again arrange for a bunch of local agencies to lend manpower for the following day, and probably into day two — to show strength in numbers before they entered and then to provide safety for the dogs and their handlers.

"How many?" asked the chief.

"I'd say at least the same as last time. A few more would be even better, with a handful arriving late in the day and planning to patrol the area overnight," said Ginny.

"Shouldn't be a problem."

Ginny told the chief where and when they should all gather in the morning.

"One other thing, Chief," said Joe.

"Uh oh, I knew things were going too well."

"There's no problem. Just want to get your OK for us to buy sandwiches and a lot of water for the troops. Even though there's a chance we won't be let in, we need to buy it all tonight."

"Go for it. Worst case, we'll have one hell of a picnic lunch in here tomorrow."

"Thanks, Chief," said both detectives in unison.

The two detectives returned to their desks and were soon out the door. They stopped at the Subway near their house and ordered a variety of foot-long sandwiches and the same number of bags of potato chips, confirming they'd be back to pick everything up in a couple of hours. They then drove to the supermarket for four large cases of bottled water, after which they stopped for an early dinner at their favorite Indian restaurant. By the time they finished dinner, it was time to pick up the sandwiches and chips. Once home, they put the sandwiches in the refrigerator and left a note on the counter as a reminder to take the sandwiches with them in the morning. They put their two large coolers in the back seat of the car and left the water and potato chips in the trunk. Knowing they had to be up and out early the next morning, they were in bed by nine, with their alarm clock set for five AM.

Chapter 22

Joe and Ginny pulled up at the militia's front gate at 6:45 the next morning. They wanted to address any possible problems before the arrival of the dogs and the other law enforcement personnel. There were two different guards at the gate. *Probably got here before the shift change*, thought Joe as he got out of the car and walked up to one of the guards.

"Morning. I'm Detective McFarland with Jasper Creek PD."

"And?"

"And I'd like to speak with Aaron Turley."

"Sorry, but I'm sure that —"

"Don't be too sure. He and I met a few days ago, and I think you'd better call him."

"But it's—"

"You're right about that. I'm sure it'll be your butt if you don't tell him I'm here and let him, rather than you, decide if he wants to see me."

The guard thought for a moment, then told Joe to wait where he was. He held a brief, whispered conversation with the other guard, then raised his walkie-talkie to his mouth and spoke. Joe couldn't hear what he was saying.

Two minutes later, the guard walked back to Joe. "He sounded pissed and annoyed, but said he'd be down here in ten or 15 minutes."

"I'll go sit in my car and wait for him."

Twenty minutes later, Turley arrived just as before, he alone in a pickup, accompanied by two other vehicles filled with armed men.

Joe casually got out of his car, made a scene of removing his guns and laying them on the car seat, then walked to the gate.

Joe put his hands up and said, "Suppose you want to frisk me."

"Yup. That's what I was told to do." The guard opened the gate, let Joe in, closed the gate and conducted a thorough frisk. He then walked Joe to the passenger side of Turley's pickup, and Joe climbed into the front seat.

"Morning, Aaron. Nice to see you again. Sorry to bother you at such an early hour."

"You can skip all the niceties. Whaddaya want this time?"

"Same thing. Only this time we've got a warrant," said Joe as he pulled the warrant out of his shirt pocket, unfolded it and handed it to Turley.

"What am I supposed to do with this? I can't understand all this legal mumbo-jumbo."

"Suggest you get your lawyer to give it a quick look-see. You probably know enough to realize it's illegal to not honor a valid search warrant."

"How do I know it's valid?"

"Hence my suggestion that you show it to your lawyer."

"Well he's not here. Rarely here, and never this early."

"How about you call him now? I can talk with him, then take a picture of the warrant and text it to him. We'll do all this right here in front of you, so you can see there's no tricks."

"Umm. Lemme call his cell and see if I can get hold of him."

George Peeters, the group's attorney, who lived and had his office in Columbus, groggily answered the call after five rings. Turley described the situation, then put Joe on the phone. Joe introduced himself, described the warrant and reason for it, and offered to immediately get a copy of the warrant to Peeters by either texting a photo of it or by having someone at the station take the copy on Ginny's desk and fax it.

As he wasn't yet in his office, Peeters opted for the text. Joe photographed the five-page warrant, two pages of which were the affidavit requesting the warrant, got the lawyer's cellphone number from Turley and texted the photos.

Ten minutes later, Turley got a call from Peeters. Turley stepped out of the truck and walked far enough away so that Joe couldn't hear him. Another five minutes, and Turley got back in the truck.

"So?" asked Joe.

"He described the warrant to me and confirmed that it seemed valid — all the right language, a judge's signature and everything."

"Good. So, where are you on this? Gonna follow the law or not?"

Turley stared at Joe with his cold blue eyes for a long moment before responding. "Hang on. Lemme call him back and put him on speaker. Sorta like he's sitting here with us."

"Good idea," said Joe.

A few minutes after the call to Peeters was underway,

Turley said, "OK, sounds like the warrant's legit. So we're gonna let you in. I don't like it, and Davis will be pissed when he gets back. But it is what it is."

"Good. A couple of specifics you two should know. Given that we're looking for a body, or at least evidence of a body, and the large size of the property to be searched, we're going to be using cadaver dogs. Two initially, and maybe a third joining later. Each of the dogs, of course, has a handler. Civilian."

Joe spent a few minutes answering Turley's questions about cadaver dogs in general, how long they thought they'd be there, if the dogs would be running around without leashes, if his members were safe from the dogs, and so on. Joe then explained the presence of several law enforcement folks to help with the search and to ensure the dogs and their handlers stayed safe, emphasizing that the officers would remain armed. Joe also indicated they'd want to talk to certain members of the militia, depending on what the search did or didn't turn up.

The phone meeting ended, and Joe indicated he'd be back shortly with all of his colleagues along with the initial two dogs and their handlers. He returned to his car and drove to the start of the gravel road where everyone was gathering.

Chapter 23

Everyone had arrived by 7:20. Joe and Ginny introduced themselves to those they hadn't met before, after which everyone stood in a large circle as each person announced his or her name and organizational affiliation.

"OK. Time to get to work. A few important ground rules. First, we're expecting full cooperation from the militia folks. Not welcoming love but cooperation. Our responsibility is to de-escalate any problems. Force is the very last option. If there's trouble with the militia or any safety problems of any sort, I'm your go-to person. Ginny's my backup if you can't reach me." Joe then gave his and Ginny's cellphone numbers to everyone. "In terms of the actual search, Amy Valen from Buckeye Search and Rescue Dogs is totally in charge. Do what she says and go to her with any search-related questions or, hopefully, findings. We'll be focusing on the outside initially, but at some point, later today or tomorrow, we'll also be searching all the building interiors. It's a large property, so a few of us will try to ensure they don't move anything from spots we haven't yet searched to spots we've already searched and cleared. Amy, why don't you give them your cellphone number?"

Valen told everyone her number.

"Any questions?" asked Joe.

"No questions. OK, then. Follow us in. They'll lead us

to where we park, then we're off and running. One final thing. We've got sandwiches and water for all in our car. After we park, be sure to grab a sandwich for later and three or four bottles of water. Be careful not to let yourselves get dehydrated."

When the caravan of cars reached the gate, there was an old jeep with three heavily-armed militia members and a driver waiting just inside the gate. The gate was opened, and the jeep slowly led them to a grass field behind the main building, indicating that they should all park in that field.

Everyone parked and gathered around Joe's car. Joe opened the trunk and back doors of his car. "Don't forget food and, more importantly, water before you head out. Couple more things before I hand the invisible microphone over to Amy. This car will be our incident command center. Ginny or I, or both of us, will always be here — except for an occasional quick kidney break. Each dog/handler team will be accompanied by two law enforcement officers. I'll make the initial assignments in a minute. We'll rotate these assignments every few hours as we law enforcement folks, at least me, will not be able to keep up with the dogs and their handlers for very long. These teams really know how to cover ground quickly. Each team will have a walkie-talkie to speak with us in case they can't get cell reception. Any problems, issues, suspicions — call us. I'd much rather receive ten useless calls than not receive one important one. That's it for me. Amy, you've got the floor."

Valen walked up to the front of Joe's car and started right in. She had clearly done this several times in the past.

"OK. Thank you all for joining us today. We'll initially have two teams, each with a dog, the dog's handler and two law enforcement officers. Three other officers will be responsible for roaming the property — separately, not all three together — trying to prevent, or at least spot, militia members moving things from not-yet-searched to already-searched areas. As Joe said, we'll be moving rapidly so we're going to rotate you guys around every two hours. We and our dogs are used to running all day; many or most of you likely aren't. Ginny and Joe, before I get into specifics, it might be better for you to make the initial assignments and the schedule of the two-hour rotations, so everyone can focus on what they'll be doing when."

Joe and Ginny made these assignments as Valen had requested.

"When your route takes you to a vehicle, the plan is to examine the vehicle, inside and out. Call Joe or Ginny if you need their help in getting one of the militia folks to unlock the vehicle or trunk. As for buildings, we're leaving the interiors for later. Do check around the outside of each building and the crawlspace under the building, if there is one, but don't worry about the insides for now. OK, here's a copy for each of you of the survey map of this property from the county. On it, I've marked several search grid lines, and in each area I indicated either Team A or B, as well as 1, 2, 3, and so on to indicate the search sequence. Be sure to make notes about anything unusual, as well as which vehicles you searched and which buildings you searched around the outside of."

Joe was impressed. *This lady really knows her stuff. She*

had to have been up half the night putting all this together. I think we've got ourselves a winner here.

"I know the grid areas look like they were drawn by a drunk sailor. But the long, thin rectangles, the squares, the triangles and the irregular shapes represent my best attempt at adjusting our grids to take into account open vs. wooded areas and the property boundary lines. This is how we'll start. I'm sure things will change during the day. Some areas can be searched quicker than others, but you can't always tell from a two-dimensional map. So, almost for sure, I'll be calling some audibles, to borrow from the world of football, as the day goes on.

"One other thing. Despite how cute and friendly they are, please do not pet, play with or feed anything to our dogs. They are here to work, not play, and they get their satisfaction from being successful at their work. Do not distract them. We have our own plastic bowls, pre-measured dry dog food, and treats for rewards for work well done. Thank you."

"Everybody set?" asked Ginny. "Everyone know your first assignment and then at least your second one after we rotate?"

Following a series of head nods and "Yeahs," Valen said, "OK, it's a bit past 8:30 now. Let's get started. We'll make our first set of rotations at 10:30. Grab some water and food and let's get at it. Any issues, get hold of Ginny or Joe, or me if you can't reach either of them. Oh, one other extremely important subject. To periodically relieve your bladder, pick a nice tree in the woods and go at it. For more serious matters, there are several Porta Johns, or Porta Potties if you prefer, spread around the fields for the militia's use while they're farming. Feel free to grab a seat and make yourself comfortable in one of those as the need arises. I hope that's delicate enough while still being clear."

Everyone nodded yes, chuckled or both.

It took a few minutes for each person to properly orient their map, identify where on the map they were currently located and where they had to get for their first assignment. But not long. Ten minutes later, Ginny and Joe were the only two still in the parking area.

"Off to a good start, I think," said Joe. "That Valen is one impressive lady. Seems to have this well under control. So far, at least."

"You should be impressed. I spent a few minutes with her while we were waiting for the others to arrive. She was a firefighter in Cincinnati before she got into this. Not easy breaking into what, back then, was an all-boys club. She participated in several searches in her firefighting days. Retired after she'd put in her twenty. She'd seen rescue dogs working searches, decided to get a dog and have it trained for search & rescue. She did that and still does it. About five years ago she got Major, and decided to train him as a cadaver dog. So, she's got two dogs of her own, one of each type. Husband was a Marine. One of the very few who died in Operation Desert Storm. No kids. She really devotes her time to this kind of thing."

"Sorry about her husband. But she sure is what the doctor ordered for us now."

"Agreed. Now let's hope we get the results we're looking for."

Chapter 24

The day went pretty much as Valen had said it would. Joe and Ginny remained at their car, answering several questions from some of the law enforcement officers. Ginny couldn't have imagined how well things were going. *Wow. She's got this whole thing working like a well-oiled machine. Everyone seems to know what they're doing, and no one's been shy about calling Joe or me if they're not sure. As she predicted, Valen made several changes to the search grid and sequence of areas to be searched, but these were amazingly well-communicated and didn't cause any confusion.*

Several of the militia members strutted around the compound, trying to look tough and in control, while warily keeping their eyes on the search teams, not at all sure of what, except for a dead body, they were looking for and, even more concerning, what they might find. Other than stares and smirks, with occasional head shakes, from both the militia members and the law officers, there were no actual or real threats going in either direction.

Since things appeared to be safe, Hunter, a huge, tan Belgian Malinois, arrived around noon with his handler, Elliott Neely. Joe drove to the front gate to ensure Neely and Hunter were let in without difficulty, escorting them to the parking area.

Valen spoke to Neely, Joe and Ginny through Joe's cellphone speaker. "Elliott, you and Hunter need to start searching the building exteriors and interiors. Ginny and Joe, I'd like you two to alternate roles every two hours, one going with Elliott and Hunter while the other maintaining the Incident Command at Joe's car. I doubt whether you can search all the buildings in half a day. So, one of the other teams will join in if they finish the property search early enough. Otherwise, we'll finish the buildings tomorrow morning."

"We're on it," said Ginny. She grabbed a map from Joe's car, and the three of them laid out an efficient route to cover all the buildings with as little extra walking as possible.

"Ginny, why don't you take the first shift with Neely and Hunter? I want to go see my dear friend, Turley, and let him know we're starting to search inside the buildings. We did discuss it earlier on the phone with his lawyer, but Turley may need a little refresher course on the warrant and what all it allows. In the meantime, why don't you guys grab some lunch and pack a few bottles of water? Don't start your search yet. Hold down the fort here 'til I get back. I'll be back as soon as I can."

Joe walked to the nearby main building and was immediately led into a small office by Turley. Turley's first reaction to the interior searches was, "Hell no." Joe showed him the wording in the warrant specifically listing the building interiors, reminding him of the discussion on this very point which they'd had with Turley's attorney earlier that morning. That did the trick.

Joe returned to his car and gave Ginny and Neely the OK to begin their search. "Just remember, our warrant covers the interiors of the buildings, but not any of their personal possessions. So if it's sitting out in the open, it's fair game. But no opening drawers or closets, not even lifting a shirt off a pile of something on the bed. We gotta be meticulous on this point. One wrong move and everything we do legally find could be tainted and inadmissible."

At the same time, Turley was informing the militia members that the interior search was about to happen, saying they should all just accept it and stay out of the police and search dogs' way.

Although the last to arrive and begin searching, Hunter was the first dog to find something. Behind the second building being searched, the dining hall and social center, was a large concrete firepit, used primarily to burn trash from the dining room. When Ginny caught up with them, Hunter was silently sitting directly in front of the firepit.

"We got something. Hunter's trained to sit and wait wherever he finds a cadaver, or traces of one."

"What did he find?"

"That's for us to determine."

Ginny looked around the ground where Hunter was sitting, then in the firepit, but didn't see anything suspicious.

"Ginny, my guess is that there's some minute trace of a body here. They could have tried real hard to clean it all up, but it's damn near impossible to remove every microscopic bit of evidence. And that's enough for a dog like Hunter."

Using her flashlight despite it still being light outside, Ginny slowly examined the ground and remnant ashes in the firepit. Careful examination revealed a few very small stains on several small pieces of not-totally-burned cloth mixed in with the ashes, but it was impossible to know if the stains were blood, salsa or ice cream. They'd need the forensic folks to make that determination. While Neely gave Hunter a treat and a big hug, Ginny called Joe and brought him up to speed. Joe called the station to request a crime scene team, then called Valen to bring her up to date.

"Thanks for the update, Joe."

"Boy, you weren't kidding. These dogs are amazing. I doubt we ever would have found those traces without the dogs."

"They do have special skills. Don't know, but my guess is that someone tried to burn some clothing with the dead victim's blood on it."

"Very likely. We've got the crime scene folks on their way here, so we should know more after they do their thing."

"Good. Now let's get Hunter back to work."

"Just about to. I'm gonna go with him and Neely for a while, and Ginny will handle the incident command stuff."

"Sounds good."

Ginny went back to the car, got a roll of crime scene tape and blocked off the area around the firepit. She then reassigned one of the police officers to stay there and make sure no one entered the taped-off area.

Just before four that afternoon, a three-person crime-scene team, led by their supervisor, Charlie Evans, arrived at the gate. Ginny switched roles with Joe, and Joe drove to the gate to help the techs gain entry and then led them to the parking area, after which they walked to the crime scene.

The techs carefully inspected the crime scene; they dusted for and found several fingerprints on the firepit wall. More importantly, with two techs holding a blanket above the firepit to block out the sunlight, the third tech used black light to identify what was probably blood tracings and possibly microscopic pieces of skin on the unburned fabric, as well as on the firepit wall. They scraped these up and sealed them in evidence bags. After a discussion with Joe, they decided to head back to their lab to analyze the samples. If something else were found at the compound, it would be easy enough for them to return.

Rudy Musser, the militia member who had been ordered to bury the body and who later placed the anonymous call to 9-1-1, had been on patrol in the general area outside the dining hall and social center. He grew increasingly concerned as he watched the dogs and their handlers start their search of the property. His concern turned to outright fear when he saw one of the dogs find something in or around the firepit. *Oh, my God! Now what do I do? I'm as good as dead. I couldn't tell anyone I was the one who called 9-1-1. Or buried Mark. Now they found it. Damn. They'll be checking for fingerprints and who knows what else. Thought I was so smart burning my jacket after I got those few blood stains on it. Figured it was safe, what with his body lying quite a ways from here. That'll teach me. This can't be good. Don't know if I'm more afraid of the FRAP members or the cops. I'm damned if I say what I know and what I was asked — or more like forced — to do, or if I stay silent and make believe I don't know anything. There's no way out for me. Beat up or killed by the militia. Or accused of murder by the cops. Great choices I have. I better just do or say nothing 'til I figure something out. If I can!*

The dogs didn't find anything else that day. Everyone left except for two uniformed officers who stayed, spending the night to be sure the one crime scene wasn't disturbed. Three additional officers arrived for the night shift, assigned to basically walk around to reduce the chances of anyone relocating any evidence. Joe told Turley about the remaining officers and the plan for everyone else to return in the morning.

Chapter 25

Just as Joe had informed Turley, the search resumed by eight the next morning. The first thing Ginny did was check with the officers who had stayed overnight. She was pleased that no one had attempted to enter the crime scene. She sent the two officers home and assigned the two replacements who arrived to continue protecting the firepit. She was also pleased to learn that no one was seen trying to relocate any evidence overnight.

About 11:30, Ginny got a call from Valen. "Ginny, I think Major found the mother lode."

"Oh?"

"Yeah. He's sitting in front of what looks to be a recently dug and then filled in hole out here in the woods. About the size of a grave, if you're asking me."

"Where are you? I'm on my way."

Valen described her location, and Ginny started walking there, rapidly. While walking, she called Joe. He and a few other officers headed to the location, after first retrieving various shovels and hand-digging tools from the trunks of their cars.

With some vigorous digging, which soon switched to slow and careful earth removal by hand, the body — sloppily rolled up in a blanket — was soon discovered. Work immediately stopped. Joe called for the crime scene group, along with the coroner and his team, to get there as soon as possible. Always practical, Joe asked Charlie Evans, supervisor of the crime scene group, to stop on the way in and bring a dozen or so pizzas for everyone to share. Crime scene tape was strung around the entire area, and everyone stepped outside the tape, waiting for the experts to arrive.

Joe walked back and found Turley.

"Aaron, let's go into your office. Need to discuss something."

"What is it now?" asked Turley, not even trying to hide his annoyance as he gave Joe a sideways glance. He shut the door after he and Joe had entered the small office.

"Let's sit down. This may take a few minutes."

Turley's face and strained neck veins indicated his curiosity, and concern, as he took the chair behind the desk and Joe sat on the chair in front of the desk.

"Those dogs are amazing."

"Yeah, and?"

"They found your leader's body."

Turley's face went from pink to red to pale white in a matter of seconds. "You mean Mark? Mark Davis?"

"He's the only leader you have here that I'm aware of."

"But, but we all thought he was just away on one of his little secret trips again."

"Yeah, well, at least one person, for sure, knew that wasn't the case. We find out who that someone is, we probably got our killer."

"I, uh, I can't believe it."

"If you don't believe it now, you will soon. After the

coroner gets here and lifts the body out of the grave, you and I are going to the gravesite. You can then confirm for me, and for yourself, that it's Mark Davis."

"Do I have to? I'm not comfortable viewing dead people. Especially people I know."

"Afraid so. Also, you need to tell all your people that no one, and I mean no one at all, is to leave or enter the compound without my approval."

Turley continued to appear shocked and upset, but agreed to Joe's rules and request.

It was close to 1:30 by the time everyone arrived. The others enjoyed pizza while the CS team and the coroner and his group worked. The body and blanket were fully exposed. Dozens of photographs were taken, after which the body and blanket were lifted onto level ground and the coroner made a cursory examination.

Joe and the coroner had a brief discussion. "Jeez, Doc, even I can make a pretty accurate determination of the COD."

"Good for you, Joe. I bet the hole in the center of his forehead is a pretty big clue."

"Yup, it definitely is. What can you say about the TOD?"

"Can't be too sure. I'm not an expert on how a body decomposes underground, especially one wrapped in a blanket. But the state of the body leads me to think that two weeks ago or so wouldn't be far off the mark."

"You OK if I bring one of the militia leaders out here to see if he can identify the body?"

"As long as he only looks and doesn't touch anything."

"Deal."

Joe went back to the main building, found Turley still

in his small office and asked Turley to accompany him to the gravesite.

"Shit! How can this be?" Turley quickly took a few steps back from the gravesite and turned his head away to avoid continuing to look at the corpse. He seemed to try to speak a few times, but no sounds exited his mouth.

Joe focused all his attention on Turley's reactions. *He's either truly surprised and shocked, or he missed his real calling as an actor.* "I take it you recognize him," said Joe.

"Yeah. But I can't understand it. It's Mark. Everyone liked, maybe even loved, him. Who would do this? We were starting to get nervous since he's been gone longer than usual, but no one suspected this. Jesus. I have to inform the whole group, especially his wives."

"I don't know, Aaron, but I'd say at least one person didn't love, or even like, him. I want my partner or me to be with you when you inform everyone. Should probably give the wives the courtesy of hearing it first, in private. We'll also want his one truly legal wife to make the formal identification. I trust and believe you, as we would his other so-called wives, but we need the official ID to come from a legal relative — either by blood or marriage or adoption."

"Yeah. OK. Whatever."

"Doc, you OK with us returning with his wife, now widow, for the official ID here? A lot easier than making her travel downtown later."

"Fine with me. Same rule applies — look but don't touch. And bear in mind, the longer we're here the longer the delay in starting the autopsy."

"Understood. We'll be as quick as we can."

Joe called Ginny and had her meet Turley and him back in Turley's office. A few minutes later, one of the other women led Davis' three wives into the small office, after which she left, closing the door behind herself.

Turley introduced Joe and Ginny to the three women and then continued, "Ladies, I'm afraid we have some very bad news."

All three wives simultaneously turned pale, and Lynn Hansen, wife number three, grabbed the edge of the desk to prevent herself from collapsing to the floor.

Abigail Davis, wife number one and the only legally married wife, said, "Spit it out, Aaron. We're not stupid. There's only one reason for you and the cops to have the three of us here. Especially with Mark being gone so long."

"You're right. I'm sorry, but a short while ago Mark's body was found buried in the woods, not far from one of the old logging roads."

"My God," said Davis. "I can't believe it. Who would do this? Why?"

At the same time, Thatcher was crying hysterically while slumped over in a chair and Hansen was sitting on the floor with her head shaking back and forth, her eyes glazed over.

"Ladies," said Ginny, "we're sorry for your loss and offer our sincere condolences. I want to assure you that we will do everything in our power to determine who did this and bring the murderer to justice."

"Thank you," said Davis. "But that, of course, won't bring Mark back to us."

"No, it unfortunately won't."

"How was he killed?" asked Davis.

"A gun shot to his forehead."

"My God," said Thatcher. "At least death was most likely fast for him."

"Yes, it was," said Joe. "Instantaneous. He surely felt no pain."

"Thank heaven for little things," said Thatcher.

"Aaron identified the body as Mark's, but we need a relative to do the official identification. As his only legally recognized wife, that would be you, Ms. Davis. We thought it would be easier for you to do it now, rather than having to come downtown later today or tomorrow. But it's your choice."

"Let's do it now and get it over with."

"OK. You other ladies are welcome to join us or not, as you wish."

Thatcher said she'd join them, but Hansen elected not to, preferring to return to her bedroom.

Ginny went with Turley to inform all the other militia members. Except for the children, two women to care for the children and two guards at each of the gates, everyone squeezed into the dining room to listen to Turley and Ginny.

At the same time, Joe escorted Davis and Thatcher to the gravesite, where, not surprisingly, between heavy crying and sobbing from the two women, Davis officially identified the body as that of her husband.

The coroner informed the women that it would be close to a week before the autopsy was completed and he'd be able to release the body. Davis said she and Turley, and the other two wives, would need to discuss things. They would also inform Mark's uncle in Utah, and work with him regarding the details and location of the funeral.

Joe had one of the uniformed officers escort the two women back to the main building while he wrapped things up with the coroner.

"Thanks, Doc. One more thing, then I think we're done for now. When you get back to the lab, even if you can't start the autopsy immediately, I need you to get the bullet out of his skull and, if it's not totally shattered, let us know the details. We need to search for the murder weapon, but we can't confiscate all their guns. Once we know the caliber we can narrow the search, then have any guns we find tested for a match with the kill bullet."

"Will do. I'll call you as soon as we get it out. Hopefully it's in good enough shape to identify it."

"Thanks."

The coroner and his team left with the body and blanket, heading back to their lab. The crime scene techs spent almost three more hours documenting, photographing and collecting anything that looked like it might have the slightest link with the murder.

Chapter 26

Ginny called Barbara Larkin, the assistant prosecuting attorney she'd been working with on this case. After filling Larkin in on the developments, especially finding the body, she started right in. "Barb, a couple of immediate questions."

"Go for it."

"First, are we correct that the warrant allows us to search for weapons, and to temporarily take them for the BCI to test whether one of them is the murder weapon? Assuming, that is, that the coroner retrieves a usable bullet from the victim."

"Yes, but with a few caveats. First, as you said, if the coroner can get the bullet, if it's still in the body, and if the type of gun used can then be identified, you can search everyplace on site for that type of gun. And yes, you can seize all you find of that type. But only temporarily, and only for as short a period of time as practicable. After you seize them, you need to expeditiously get them to the Bureau of Criminal Investigation lab in London. Fortunately, we're talking about the London halfway between Jasper Creek and Columbus, not the one way across the ocean with that Big Ben clock and a queen. Have the BCI's Firearms Unit do their comparisons and then return all the guns ASAP. If one is identified as the murder weapon, you, of course, do not have to return that one. You need to do all you can, including telling the people there what you're doing and why, to avoid a big Second Amendment howl. Be sure to tell them you're not looking for or interested in illegally owned guns, and, except for the murder weapon, if it's identified, you will return the guns and destroy all records of the tests and of ownership after every gun has been tested."

"But—"

"Ginny, trust me. No buts on this. Not done right, we could have a real mess on our hands."

"OK, you convinced me. One more question."

"OK."

"We'd like to interview everyone here. Someone must know — or have seen or heard — something. Plus, talking with everyone could help us identify the anonymous 9-1-1 caller who first alerted us to this murder."

"And?"

"Does the current warrant cover this, or do we need another warrant that allows us to force everyone to be interviewed? And does it let us record a sample of their voice, which can then be compared to the voice on the recorded 9-1-1 call?"

"No, the current warrant doesn't include that. And we can't get a warrant that would. We might, and I emphasize might, be able to get a warrant for one or two, maybe even three, identified suspects. But that's it. We can't get a warrant for a so-called fishing expedition."

"Damn. Any suggestions?"

"One, but you may not like it."

"Lemme hear it, then I'll decide if I like it or not."

"OK. You need to get the people there to voluntarily agree to be interviewed by you. Note the word interviewed; not interrogated. They're not suspects. You just want to know if anyone saw or heard or knows anything. And, if some decline to talk with you, you can't do anything about it. It would probably help get more of them willing to talk if you assure them, perhaps in writing by, say, your chief, that once the case is solved all recordings and your notes of the interviews will be destroyed — except, of course, for any related to the murder. On the other hand, if one or two are suspects, you can force them into an interrogation, with Miranda rights, an attorney if they want one and so on."

"Tell me more."

"You can record the interviews you do conduct. It's ideal to tell them in advance, in an offhand way, that you'll be recording the interview to help you with your notes, and that they can get a copy of the recording if they want. But you don't have to tell them you're recording the interview. Here in Ohio, any one person taking part in the conversation, in person or by phone, can legally record it without telling the other party or parties in the conversation. But there's one big 'but.'"

"I knew it sounded too good to be true."

"You can have the recordings of your interviews compared with the recording of the 9-1-1 call, but — here it comes — there's a good chance it will be of only limited value at best in court."

"But I thought—"

"Hold on. Let me finish. Assuming you can demonstrate the qualifications and experience of whomever you have in court to explain his or her analyses and comparisons, the court will most likely allow the admission of that evidence. But I'm sure the judge will point out to the jurors that it's totally up to them to fully accept, partially accept or totally disregard the voice matching.

"And defense counsel won't be shy about pointing out the weaknesses of our evidence — the fact that you probably didn't get your interviewees to repeat the exact words used on the 9-1-1 call, differences in the recording qualities because of the different recording devices used by 9-1-1 and by you, background noises, people's attempts to modify their voice either on the 9-1-1 call or during your interview or both, and so on. So, it might help you with your investigation, but probably won't help me with the prosecution."

"Damn. That's a big 'but,' but it's still useful to us."

"It sure can be. If the caller was a member of the militia. And if he voluntarily agrees to talk with you. If only a few refuse to talk with you, you might correctly assume that your suspect is one of those refusing. That is, if the call wasn't made by someone who's not a member of the militia. In any event, I bet you and Joe can significantly shrink the eligible pool on your own. First off, you can eliminate any of the women. Secondly, if you listen to the 9-1-1 recording a few times just before your interviews, you can probably eliminate several whose voices, accents or speech patterns are different than the 9-1-1 caller's."

"Very true. OK, we've got a few things to work on with the guns and the interviews and voice recordings. Thanks for your help, Barb."

"No problem. Keep me informed of your progress."

"Will do."

Ginny filled Joe in on her phone call with Larkin.

"Good you spoke with her. Some good advice. Stuff we might not have thought about so carefully."

"Yeah, she's good. On our side, but knows what lines we shouldn't cross."

"OK, now what?"

"Couple of thoughts. First, we need a large enough team that a few of them can focus on making sure no one is moving or hiding any weapons. Almost impossible to do this one hundred percent, but a few officers just walking around would be a big help. Second, I think we need a signed letter from the chief confirming that all the guns we take for testing will be returned within a couple of days except, of course, for the murder weapon — if we find it. And once this case is over, we will delete all information we have about the guns and their ownership — again, except for info related to the murder weapon."

"Good ideas. The chief's letter should also say that we're not interested in the legality of the guns, we're just trying to identify the murder weapon."

"Agreed, Joe. And the chief's letter should also mention us wanting to briefly talk with everyone here to see if we can unearth any clues about the murder. Although anyone can refuse these voluntary interviews, we'd hope that most want the murderer of their leader to be found and would agree to be interviewed. We plan to record the interviews to help with our note-taking, but once the case is solved, except for any interviews that may have played a role in our solving the case, all recordings and all our notes, including the names of who we spoke with, will be totally destroyed."

"Maybe it should be two letters, one about the guns

and one about the interviews. Otherwise, it'll be one long mother."

"Good point."

"Those letters should, I hope, get us the cooperation we need."

"Should, but only if Turley and the others believe what's in the letters. Maybe we should have Larkin work with their lawyer to get the right wording and, hopefully, get the lawyer to reassure Turley."

"Another good idea, Ginny."

"OK, why don't I call the chief and, assuming he's on board, then call Larkin to get things rolling?"

"Deal. Don't forget to update the chief. We're finally seeing some progress, and I'd hate for him to not be fully aware of it."

"For sure."

"And while you do that, I'll explain everything to Turley and try to get his support, or at least neutrality."

"Sounds good. Let's do it, partner."

Ginny's call to the chief went better than most. Not surprising, since the chief had the same objectives as Ginny and Joe — solve the murder without causing a Waco-kind of standoff. After getting the chief's agreement to sign whatever the lawyers come up with, Ginny called Larkin. Larkin said she would immediately get started on drafts of the two letters and set up a call with the militia's lawyer.

Joe spent his time organizing a few of the law enforcement officers to try to prevent, or at least minimize, the movement of any guns without their approval. He then spent about 15 minutes speaking with Turley. Joe was partially successful, getting Turley to move from, "Hell no!" to, "I still don't like it, but I'll wait to see the letters and hear what our attorney has to say about them."

Joe returned to his car after speaking with Turley. Valen, along with Major, walked up.

"I think we're about done here, Joe. We've pretty much searched the whole grounds, as well as inside and around every building and vehicle. The body, plus the traces in that firepit, ain't too bad for a day's — or actually two days' — work, as they say."

"'Ain't too bad' doesn't cut it. You guys were fantastic. I'm still in awe at how effective your dogs were at successfully searching this huge area so quickly. We'd be nowhere as far along without you guys. Thank you so much. Relay our thanks to your colleagues too — and, of course, to the dogs. Give 'em an extra few treats tonight on our behalf."

"Will do. Pleased how it worked out, and delighted to have played a role. You know where to find us when the need again arises."

"You betcha."

Valen found Ginny, who was still on the phone with Larkin. She interrupted Ginny's call for 30 seconds for a quick good-bye, then the three handlers and their dogs were on their way home.

Darkness was starting to set in. Joe made sure that all the officers were clear about their plans and assignments: some were staying on site until two AM, at which time they'd be relieved by those officers heading home now for a break and a few hours of sleep. Those staying would have to make do with cold, leftover pizza for dinner.

Ginny and Joe headed home, planning to return early the next morning.

During their drive, Ginny brought up an additional suggestion from the chief.

"After he genuinely expressed his satisfaction with our progress so far, he said it's our case and our decision, but, if it were him, he wouldn't rush to have the voice recordings professionally analyzed."

"What? Why not?"

"Two reasons, Joe. First, he already knew and repeated almost verbatim what Larkin said about it most likely being next to worthless during the trial."

"Jeez. What's the chief doing, going to law school at night?"

"Probably not. But he does have a lot more experience, not to mention contacts among law enforcement and lawyers, than we do."

"True."

"His other point was that the few well-recognized qualified experts, whom defense attorneys and prosecutors can't successfully belittle in court, are in high demand. There's a large backlog and long wait for them to do their thing."

"Shit," Joe muttered. "Long waits aren't exactly what we can best afford right now."

"It was like my discussion with Larkin all over again. The chief suggested we try to narrow the list of possible callers down to a few, by you and me comparing the 9-1-1 tape to everyone we interview. Then we can meet again with each person we identify as the possible caller. There shouldn't be too many of them. We take a hard line, telling each one we had the voice on the 9-1-1 call analyzed and we know he's the one who made the call. If we stick to our guns, even as they initially deny it, we might get one to crack and admit he made the call."

"Sneaky, but it might work. Depends how good we are at reducing the list of possibles to just a few."

"True. The chief also added, 'And if that doesn't work, you can still go the expert approach, having added only a day or two more to what will be a long wait anyhow.'"

"Hate to admit it, but he makes some good points."

"Joe, that might be why he's the chief and we're both detectives working for him."

"Think so?"

Chapter 27

Up early the next morning and anxious to get back to the militia compound, Joe got a phone call while he and Ginny were finishing their bagel and cream cheese breakfast, along with their second cups of coffee.

"Morning, Doc. You're up bright and early."

"Well, when you said you needed info on the bullet as quickly as possible, I took you to mean it. But not to the point of calling you at 2:30 this morning when the lab woke me up to tell me they had the bullet."

"Glad you properly calibrated the level of my need for really quick results. What did you find?"

"It's an FN 5.7x28mm. Shouldn't be too many guns for you to collect. Getting more and more popular, but still a lot less common than many other calibers."

"Very true. Who'd ever have thought a round originally developed for NATO to replace the 9mm, now a common military and police round, would become increasingly common among lay folks?"

"Our love of guns, not to mention the courts' interpretation of the Second Amendment, might play a role in all that."

"Right you are. Is it in good enough shape for comparisons?"

"Definitely. The projectile is heavy towards its base, so it tends to tumble upon striking a surface. This leaves a larger wound channel than the small bullet would seem capable of. The good news is, it transfers its kinetic energy by tumbling rather than crimpling up. You find the right weapon and I'm sure the experts can confirm a match."

"We'll first focus on the Belgian FN Five-seveN. I've seen them at the shooting range. Lightweight polymer frames, with a 20-round clip. Could be your militiaman's best friend. Even heard claims that the high velocity lets the bullet penetrate some body armor."

"Good luck. We've got the bullet packaged and labeled, ready to send to the BCI as soon as you have a gun or two to go with it for comparison."

"Thanks, Doc."

The detectives made two stops on their way to the militia site. First stop was the station, where they grabbed a dozen tapes and a second recorder so they could record as many interviews as they could conduct. They then stopped at a Dunkin' Donuts, picking up two dozen assorted donuts and two Boxes O' Joe, each holding about ten cups of coffee, along with cups and packets of cream and sugar.

After arriving at the compound, Ginny and Joe checked with their colleagues. They reported that everything was quiet, and that they'd been told the same by the night crew at two AM. Other than that, there wasn't much to do except wait. They couldn't organize or start either the gun search or interviews until they got the letters from the chief, which they would then need to review with Turley.

The donuts and coffee were attacked by what seemed like a pride of starving lions. Joe and Ginny were glad they had thought to swing by the Dunkin' Donuts on their way in.

Joe decided to call the chief, hoping he could arrange for the Highway Patrol or one of the federal agencies to provide an incident command trailer. Although Ginny and he planned to conduct the interviews in a couple small offices in the main building, Joe wasn't sure how soundproof they were. It was a very brief conversation.

"What, are you crazy? Hell no!"

"But, Chief, why—"

"Because I want my word to continue to mean something. If you expect me to sign a letter saying we're not interested in or looking for illegal guns, the last thing I want are federal agents or other state agencies getting more involved. We have no way to prevent them from jumping all over anything that even smells like an illegal gun. Hell, you might as well send an engraved invitation to the ATF."

"Say no more, Chief. I get it. My mistake. Forget I even suggested it."

"Forgotten. Let me know when you get an update on the status of those letters."

"Will do. Hopefully soon. You'll hear from me or Ginny, or Larkin from the prosecutor's office, as soon as everything's set and agreed to with their lawyer."

"OK. Later." And the chief ended the call.

Chapter 28

Around 12:30, Ginny and Joe went from having little to do to being overloaded with activities. Larkin and the militia's lawyer agreed on the wording of the chief's two letters. Larkin worked with the chief to get the letters printed on police department stationery and signed. Copies were texted to Joe, and a uniformed officer was given the originals and told to immediately drive them to Joe and Ginny.

While waiting for the original letters, Joe forwarded the text copies to Turley as he and Turley sat in Turley's office. Turley spent almost 40 minutes on the phone with his attorney, with Joe leaving and reentering the room several times, participating and explaining where it was helpful but giving Turley and his lawyer privacy whenever they requested it. During the periods of waiting outside Turley's office, Joe was pleased to note he couldn't hear any of the conversation taking place within. This put his mind at ease for the upcoming interviews.

The last time Joe was called back into the office, Turley had already ended the call with his lawyer. "OK, he convinced me that the letters are pretty good. So you can go ahead with searching for the gun. I'll meet with everyone to tell them about the search, and to say we should all be willing to talk with you and your partner. You have no idea how much I hate cooperating at all with cops, but, hell, we all want to find the bastard who killed Mark."

"OK, but I just want to make sure you're clear. Now that we've identified the type of ammo that killed Mr. Davis, our warrant lets us search everyplace for the gun. Our chief's letter about the gun search is merely for purposes of goodwill. With the warrant, we don't need anyone's permission to search them and their belongings. The letter about the interviews is important because we need people to voluntarily agree to speak with us.

Following Turley's presentation to virtually all the members, coupled with personal discussions with the few who had strong doubts, everyone agreed to be interviewed. Turley still had to talk with the women taking care of the children, the guards at the two gates and the few members who worked offsite. He planned to catch these people that evening and assumed he could get them to agree to be interviewed then or early the next day.

Joe called the chief.

"Hi, Joe. What's up?"

"Three things."

"Lemme have 'em."

"First, your letters did the trick. They've agreed to the interviews and the gun search. In fact, Turley didn't even care about the originals of your two letters. He was fine with the copies I texted him — he only cared that his lawyer was satisfied."

"Good. What else?"

"The coroner got the bullet and it's in pretty good shape. It's a FN 5.7x28mm. So, we're gonna first focus on looking for any Belgian FN Five-seveNs. I know there are a few other oddball guns that can shoot these, but the chances are pretty good it's a FN Five-seveN."

"Agreed. That mother has really taken off these past few years. What's your third item?"

"It's really a follow-up point to the gun search. Being realistic, we won't be starting the search until morning. So, I've got a request for more manpower — the more the merrier. We'd like more uniformed folks here this afternoon, overnight and tomorrow. Basically walking around to minimize the chance of anyone trying to hide any guns. Then as many officers as possible to help with the search tomorrow, and possibly into Saturday."

"Man, you don't want much."

"I know, Chief. But this is a huge hunk of land, much of it thickly wooded, plus there's all kinds and sizes of buildings, as well as a dozen or so vehicles."

"I understand. Believe me. Let me see who we can free up from here, and then how much help we can get from our neighbors. Like I told you earlier, I want to avoid the state and federal folks, as they're a lot more likely to be all over the illegal weapons issue."

"I'm with you on that. Anything you can do would be most appreciated."

"OK. Let's hang up so I can start leaning on all my friends."

"Thanks, Chief. Bye."

"Bye."

A few minutes after two, the detectives told Turley they were ready to start interviewing.

"I can't tell you how thrilled I am to hear that," said Turley. "Let me show you where you'll be doing your interviewing."

"We already know," said Ginny. "You mentioned the two empty rooms down the hall from your office."

"Yeah, well there's been a change in plans."

"Oh?" said Joe.

"Turns out we may need them for other things. But it's not a problem. Lawyer said anyplace would work so long as you each have a place with a desk and two seats. Plus, some privacy."

"That's true. So where should we sit?"

"Follow me. Lawyer confirmed to me it doesn't have to be luxurious, so long as it's functional."

Turley led the two detectives outside, past the children's dining area and recreation building, and into a large, dilapidated old barn. Once inside, it was immediately obvious that the building was currently used for storage of everything not being used anymore, but considered too valuable to throw out. Old equipment, piles of broken farm equipment, stacks of damp, half-broken storage boxes and anything else you could think of were everywhere. The lighting was very dim, just bright enough to allow one to avoid walking into things. Turley indicated a small room at each end of the building. The rooms had been outfitted with the required furniture, and a small desk lamp was on each desk.

"Boy, you sure didn't go out of your way to accommodate us," said Joe.

"I think we're providing everything our lawyer said we have to. Oh, and let me show you the waiting room where those about to be interviewed can wait to be called." And with that, Turley led the detectives to an area near the center of the barn where several bales of hay were stacked up. "These bales make great waiting room chairs," said Turley.

"Is this really the best you can provide?" asked Joe.

"Not sure, but it's definitely the best we're gonna provide. And it's only this good 'cause our lawyer said it had to be. Oh, and sorry about the smell. Old, stale and musty. But you'll get used to it after a few minutes."

"Thanks for nothing," said Joe with a snarl.

"Oh, you're most welcome. Let me know when you want me to start sending folks in here."

By 2:40 that afternoon, Ginny and Joe were each seated behind a small desk, each in their own small room. They each listened to a recorded version of the 9-1-1 call a few times, trying to lock the caller's voice and accent into their memories.

Then Turley sent over the first few militia members. Ginny had arranged for one of the uniformed officers to run back and forth between the old barn and Turley's office, telling Turley whenever it was time to send the next few people over for their interviews, and for a second officer to sit with those sitting on the bales of hay waiting to be interviewed. Each session took 10 to 15 minutes, and they all followed a pattern very similar to Ginny's first interview.

"Hi. I'm Detective Ginny Harris, with the Jasper Creek Police Department."

"Hey," the dark-haired woman said, failing to introduce herself.

"First off, we want to offer our sincere condolences on

the loss of your leader. Be assured we're doing everything possible to identify who killed him. In that regard, thank you for agreeing to speak with me for these few minutes."

"OK. But let's get this over with. Aaron said we had to cooperate with this, so here I am."

"I plan to record our discussion," Ginny said as she held up the small recorder in her right hand. "That's just to help me with my note-taking. As Mr. Turley told you, he and your attorney have written assurance from the chief of police that, except for any interviews crucial to our solving and prosecuting the case, all the recordings and all our notes will be destroyed. If you desire, you can get a copy of the recording before we destroy it."

"Sure wish I could believe all that. But, OK, let's get this over with."

"Fine. Let's get started." Ginny turned the recorder on and stated the date, location and her name into the recorder. "Please state your name and how long you've been a member of the Free Republic of American Patriots."

"Paula Simmons. Been a member for, let's see, almost six years now."

"So you originally joined back in Utah?"

"Yeah. My boyfriend back then got interested in it and joined. I sort of tagged along."

"Is your boyfriend here in Ohio now with you?"

"No. We broke up back in Utah. Probably the main reason I came here. He stayed with the group in Utah. I wanted to stay in FRAP, as we call it, but really didn't like seeing him every day at the compound. So, when the opportunity came up a few years ago, I quickly volunteered for here. I could stay in the group and be away from him."

"Makes sense. How well did you know Mark Davis?"

"As well as most everybody else did. I mean, we knew and spoke to each other, but nothing much. He was the big chief, and I wasn't anyone special — just one of the troops."

"Any idea who might want to kill him? Or why?"

"No. Best I could tell, most folks here liked him, even if some got upset about how resources were allocated, or the fact we never did much outside our compound. But malcontents like that usually just leave. I heard rumors over the years that he and some of the other big shots sometimes disagreed and argued about things. But I never heard of anything that could lead to murder."

"Who were some of the people he argued with? And what were the arguments about?"

"No idea. Like I said, these were just rumors I heard from time to time."

"We believe Mr. Davis was killed about two weeks ago. Anyone strike you as acting weird or different these past few weeks? Or, have any new people joined your group here recently?"

"No, don't think so."

"Were you here two weeks ago?"

"Sure. I've been here all the time since I moved from Utah. Mighta gone into town once a month or so, but that's about it."

"Any thoughts or suggestions about where we ought to be looking, or who we should take a more careful look at?"

"What? No. I got no idea. But I sure hope you do. Isn't that your job?"

"We have several leads, but nothing I can divulge at the moment. Thank you for your help today, Paula."

"Sure."

Ginny got up and escorted her out of the office. She then waved to the officer in the waiting area, who told the next waiting person to enter.

And that's how it went for Ginny and Joe for the rest of the afternoon.

Joe took two short breaks between his interviews. One was to receive a call from the chief, who told Joe he had secured seven uniformed officers who should arrive by five, and three more who would arrive around eight that evening. Approximately ten others would be there by eight the next morning. Joe could utilize them however he saw fit, from having them patrol the grounds to actually assisting with the search.

"That's great, Chief. Well done!"

"And they're all local — no state or feds."

Around four o'clock, Joe took his second break. He met with one of the more senior officers on duty and arranged for the officer to welcome the crew arriving at five, also tasking him with making sure they understood their assignments.

Ginny and Joe stopped interviewing at around 7:30, having stayed that late to interview the few FRAP members returning from their off-site day jobs.

They told Turley they'd be back the next day to complete the interviews.

The detectives waited for the final three officers to

arrive at eight so that Joe could explain their assignments to them for the night.

Joe and Ginny then left. On their way home, they stopped at one of their favorite Chinese restaurants, deciding to eat in the restaurant as a change from their normal takeout.

They discussed the day's activities, as well as their plans for the next day, while enjoying wonton soup, egg rolls, Kung Pao beef and orange chicken, complemented by piles of rice and beer, two bottles for Joe and one for Ginny.

"I think the interviews went as well as could be expected. How about you, Joe?"

"Yeah. No new useful information, but three possible 9-1-1 callers."

"I only got one. But that's because Turley sent me mostly women to interview."

"Makes sense. Turley was a pain in the butt though. I was really pissed at the crap house he put us in for the interviews."

"Correct. We need to remember he doesn't exactly love any cops, and that includes us. In any event, we should finish the rest of our interviews by early afternoon tomorrow."

"Yup. And I think we'll also wrap up the gun search by tomorrow evening. Worst case, midday Saturday. Hope we find it."

"Yeah, well, it's a lot of area to search. A bit like looking for a needle in a haystack, to quote a phrase."

"I have to say, the chief was amazing. Not a growl or complaint when I spoke with him, and he really came through big time with resources for tonight, tomorrow and Saturday. Hate to admit it, but I'm impressed."

"Glad to hear it. I also think our guys did a pretty good job of patrolling the area, hopefully keeping the killer from relocating the murder weapon — though, it's impossible to cover every location constantly."

"Not to mention that the killer had two weeks to do whatever he wanted with the gun."

"We tried. But we couldn't do anything until we finally got that damn warrant."

"No need to convince me," Joe said. "We've done our best; even the chief can't find a reason to be unhappy. Just wish it didn't feel like we were already too late somehow. Shot point-blank in the forehead, wrapped in a blanket and dumped in the ground…that's just cold."

The detectives finished their beers while sharing their fortune cookies, and were home and in bed an hour later.

Chapter 29

Joe and Ginny arrived at the compound at 7:30 the next morning, armed again with plenty of donuts and coffee. On the way in, they stopped at a nearby McDonald's and placed a large order of burgers, fries and sodas for lunch. The order was large enough that the McDonald's manager agreed to deliver the order to the compound a little after noon.

The detectives wanted to arrive at the compound well before eight, leaving enough time to get an update on anything that happened overnight before the additional officers arrived. Joe focused on getting the update and then issuing assignments to those not scheduled for relief at eight. Ginny hunted down Turley to inform him that she and Joe would be ready to continue the interviewing process around nine, and that several officers would be starting the gun search that morning.

Joe met with the group of ten officers who would be conducting the search. "OK, let's get started. Those of you who've been here before helping us, thanks and welcome back. Those of you who haven't, welcome to the team. We're now switching from a general search of the grounds and buildings to one specifically aimed at finding the murder weapon. As a result, there's a significant change in how we can and will operate. The search warrant allowed us to search inside the buildings and vehicles, but it specifically excluded all of their personal items. So anything lying out in the open was fair game, but we couldn't open closets or drawers or lift something to look under it. A big change now that we're searching for the murder weapon is that we definitely can and should open everything and look under everything. We need to ignore any illegal stuff we find and concentrate on the type of gun used to kill the victim."

Over coffee and donuts, Joe described the methodology behind the overall search of the buildings, the grounds around each building and the vehicles. He formed five two-person teams and gave specific assignments to each team. "C'mon now, hold it down. This part is important. We're looking for any gun capable of firing 5.7x28mm ammunition. Fortunately, this isn't one of the very common calibers, so we can focus our efforts. Assuming the weapon was a handgun, it'd have to be the Belgian-made FN Five-seveN. I'm sure most of you know it. Pretty easy to spot, as it's all polymer. If it's a rifle, it could be any of the varieties of FN P90s or the Banshee MK47. For every gun you locate, regardless of its caliber, put one of these tags on it, photograph it and its location and describe everything in your notes."

"Do we also body check for concealed?"

"Yes. Even though our warrant allows this, we should try to get them to voluntarily agree to be searched. Doing this with their cooperation will make things go a lot more smoothly. Find Ginny or me if anyone refuses to cooperate. The other important point may be tougher for you. It goes against all our training and experience. We are not looking for or interested in whether a gun, or any weapon, is illegal. We made that commitment to them in exchange for their hopeful cooperation. You can mention in your notes if it appears to be illegal, but that's it."

"Are you really sure about that?"

"Yes. Really and totally. One more thing: if you find a gun we're interested in, don't mess up any possible fingerprints. Put your gloves on and carefully put it in an evidence bag and seal it, being sure to fill out the who-where-when kind of stuff. Be sure you take plenty of photos of the gun where you found it, and then of the gun in the sealed bag. And, to the degree possible without getting into a hassle, try to determine and then document who the gun owner is. Any questions?

"None? OK, let's get to it. We'll have a bunch of burgers here at my car about 12:45 or one o'clock. Be sure to take a couple of bottles of water with you, and be sure to stop back here later for lunch. OK, see ya. Thanks and happy hunting."

Joe watched the teams load up with tags, evidence bags and water, then head off in all different directions. He then assigned one of the officers on patrol to stay at Joe's car, and to come get him in the old barn if anything important came up.

Joe then headed to the same little room as yesterday so he and Ginny could get through the remaining interviews.

By 11:45 Ginny and Joe were finished with what they had started calling the "regular" interviews.

"Whew. Glad that's finally over."

"Me too," said Joe. "It was getting pretty old. Any hot tips or possible 9-1-1 callers?"

"No info. But one possible caller."

"Same for me."

"OK. Let's take a break, go see how the gun search is progressing."

"Works for me. Then we only have Turley and the three wives to interview after lunch."

"Let's head to the car and get ready for our gourmet lunch."

"Right behind you. Just need to make a pit stop along the way."

Just before 12:30, Turley called Joe to tell him the guard at the gate had contacted him, saying some guy was there to make a delivery to Joe.

Joe thanked Turley, drove to the gate, transferred the lunches from the restaurant manager's car to his own and drove back to the parking lot.

Joe was made all the more hungry by the smell of the burgers and fries, but he maintained his willpower and didn't start eating until about ten minutes before one, by which time most of the officers had reassembled around Joe's car.

While handing out lunches and munching on their own, Ginny and Joe were brought up to date about the search. With about two-thirds of it completed, they had found two FN Five-seveN handguns and one FN PS90 50-round semiautomatic rifle. Each had been photographed in place and then carefully bagged and documented. They had the name of the owner for each of the handguns, but no one admitted to owning the rifle, which had been found in the cab of one of the pickup trucks.

"Well done, folks," Joe said. "Don't know about the handguns but, needless to say, the rifle is clearly illegal.

Doesn't take too much quality detective work to reach that conclusion. That model is only legally available for sale to law enforcement, and it'd be more than a stretch to define these militia oddballs as fellow officers of the law. Not surprising no one spoke up as being the owner."

"Though as we said," added Ginny, "our interest is in finding the murder weapon, not acting on illegal guns."

As lunch wound down, Joe said, "OK, guys. Time to get back to the search. We should be done by five or so, I would think. Ginny and I have a few final interviews, after which we'll be hanging out back here. Good luck."

The groups were soon on their way back out to comb the remaining property and those buildings not yet searched.

Ginny and Joe used the speaker on Joe's cellphone to call the chief. They filled him in on the morning's progress and told him they were going to arrange for one of the uniformed officers to take the guns to the BCI. Ginny then called O'Grady at the front desk, asking him to have a uniformed officer pick up the bullet at the coroner's office and then come to the militia compound around 4:30. Ginny and Joe would give the officer the three guns found that morning, plus any more discovered that afternoon. The officer should then deliver everything to the Firearms Unit of the Bureau of Criminal Investigation in London. Joe called the BCI so the receptionist there would know where to take all the evidence, being sure the guns were checked for fingerprints before being turned over to ballistics.

Chapter 30

Joe and Ginny headed back inside to complete their final interviews.

"I think we should do these last few together. We're pretty good at playing off each other."

"Works for me. Joe, let's start with Turley. OK? Then, if you're all right with it, I suggest we talk with all the possible 9-1-1 callers. And then, finally, the three so-called wives. Preferably as a group. Curious to see the dynamics between the three of them. We might learn something, and can always re-interview them one-by-one if need be."

"Wonderful. Heck, me alone in a small room with four females! Sort of like a polygamous interview."

Ginny raised one eyebrow sharply. "Right. Just don't get any ideas beyond interviewing."

"Not to worry. You're more than enough for me to try and keep up with," said Joe with a grin.

"Joe, why don't you tell Turley we're ready to talk with him? While you do that, I'll bring my chair down to your executive office."

"Will do, number-one-wife-to-be."

The interview with Turley took about 30 minutes. He maintained his surprise, almost shock, at Davis' murder. But he didn't have much new information to add. When Joe told him about the guns found and collected that morning, especially the law-enforcement-only rifle, Turley sat still and silent, not giving any hint of what he knew or didn't know about illegal guns on the property. He did confirm that he would probably be the one to replace Davis as the leader, but that the decision would ultimately be up to the leaders of the mother group in Utah.

"But, I assure you, becoming the leader here is no reason for me to kill Mark. He was always good to me, and I viewed him as a straight shooter. We worked for the same causes together."

"Understood," said Joe, "although 'straight shooter' isn't the wisest phrase to be using right now."

"Uh, yeah. But you know what I mean."

"Yes, we do. Aaron, do you own any guns?"

"Sure do. And they're legal, by the way. Got a Glock 19 that I normally carry. But figured it's safer not to be carrying while all you armed officer-types are wandering around. Also have a Remington 870 shotgun that I keep in my room."

"How about Mr. Davis? Did he have any guns?" asked Ginny.

"For sure. He was a bit of a gun nut. Didn't often carry, but he had a collection in his room. Glock 19 and FN Five-seveN handguns, a Mossberg shotgun and an AR-15 hunting rifle."

"Why so many?"

"Probably 'cause he liked guns. Even though he didn't shoot them hardly ever."

"OK. Anything else you can tell us that might help with our investigation?"

"Just that Abigail, Mark's widow that is, spoke with Mr. Heaton, Mark's uncle and our leader in Utah."

"And?"

"He, of course, was very upset about Mark's death. He did say he felt strongly that Mark's funeral should be in Utah, where Mark lived most of his life and where most of his family is. He also said he'd be fine with having Mark cremated here and the remains then brought to Utah for a service and the burial. Mormons discourage but do allow cremations, and Mr. Heaton sees it as the most practical solution to the logistical issues in this case."

"OK, we'll let the coroner know and tell him to contact you when the body is ready for release. Before the body's released, we'll let you know who we will and won't allow to go to Utah for the funeral. Assuming the murderer hasn't yet been found, our list of suspects will be required to stay here. Can't have them running off to Utah, and then what?"

Turley bolted straight up in his chair and glared at the two detectives, first Joe and then Ginny. "But it's for our leader! You can't prevent members from attending his funeral. That's un-American."

"I wouldn't bet too much on that, Aaron. I know for a fact that we can," said Joe. "Hopefully, it'll be a small list of suspects, but it'll be what it'll be."

"Man. And then people don't understand what we hate about our government. But, I do kinda see your point. You don't want the murderer disappearing."

"Glad you can see that. That it?"

"Yup."

"We'll stay in touch, and we may be back with more questions."

"If you have to, you have to."

"Give us about a half hour to review our notes. We'll then probably have a few people we'd like to briefly speak with again. Just to clear up a few details of our interviews with them. And then, after that, please have Mr. Davis' three wives available for us to speak with as a group."

"And, if you play your cards right and are lucky, we should be out of your hair after that," Ginny added.

"Finally. Something to look forward to," said Turley.

After Turley left, Ginny said, "Not the clear confession that would have simplified our lives, but a few useful tidbits."

"Definitely. We now know that we've got to keep looking for Davis' FN Five-seveN, for one. Also, that the funeral and burial will be back in Utah."

"Yeah, I learned something. I'd always thought Mormons were dead set (no pun intended) against cremation, not that they just discouraged it. More importantly, although I've got nothing specific to point to, I'm not convinced becoming leader of the group wouldn't be sufficient motive for murder. Seems like the leader gets to do and have whatever he wants, which is definitely not true for all the others."

"With you on that. At least for the moment, our good friend Aaron is in the lead position in terms of suspects."

"Yup. Let's see what else we learn from our remaining few interviews."

Chapter 31

Ginny and Joe carefully re-listened to the recording of the 9-1-1 call next to recordings of the six interviewees whom they had identified as the possible anonymous caller. With the 9-1-1 call on one recorder and the interview tapes playing on the other, they were able to switch back and forth while comparing voices, speech idiosyncrasies and accents. After about 20 minutes, they had reduced their six possible callers to four.

Joe wrote down their names and went to see Turley. "Aaron, we've got four people we need to talk with again. We'd like you to get the four of them. They can wait together on those bales of hay along with one of our officers, but we'll talk with them individually. After each is done, he's free to go. We just don't want him talking with the others we haven't interviewed yet. Want to avoid any coordination of their answers. OK?"

"Sure. Sounds like you're playing detective games, but that's fine. Gimme their names and I'll round 'em up"

"Good. I'll go grab an officer and explain his babysitting assignment to him."

"What are the four names?"

Joe looked at his notepad and said, "Isaiah Young, David Mecham, Rudy Musser and Holt Olsen."

"OK. I'll get them all to your waiting room in the next ten minutes or so."

Ten minutes later, the interviews began.

"Mr. Young, I'm Detective McFarland. We met yesterday. This is my partner, Detective Harris."

"Hello."

"Mr. Young, why'd you withhold information yesterday?"

"What? What are you talking about?"

"The call to 9-1-1."

"What call to—"

Slapping his palm on the desk, Joe yelled, "You can cut the bull now. We know for a fact that you're the one who made that anonymous 9-1-1 call about Mr. Davis' death."

"No way! You got your facts messed up."

"It's not our facts," said Ginny. "The lab compared the spectrographs from recordings of the 9-1-1 call and our interview yesterday. Bingo, they matched. Sorta like a fingerprint of your voice. They even call it a voiceprint comparison. The system analyzes the frequency, quality, duration, resonance, intensity and pitch of the recording. Almost impossible for two people to have the same voiceprint. That's why these analyses are allowed as evidence in criminal trials."

"I didn't understand most of the technical stuff you just said, but I didn't make that call. I swear on my mother's grave! If I did, I'd tell you." By this time Young was sweating profusely, his face turning bright red.

"Are you saying that we should believe you rather than the scientific evidence?" asked Ginny. "Why?"

"Because I'm telling you the truth, that's why."

Ginny and Joe probed for a few more minutes, then turned Young free.

"Seemed believable to me. Whaddaya think, Joe?"

"I agree. We went at him pretty hard; his reactions and responses seemed like how an innocent person would react."

Ginny left the room and returned with their second interviewee, David Mecham. His interview was almost identical to Young's.

"OK, Ginny. I'll go get number three."

Joe walked out and returned a minute later.

"Ginny, you and Rudy Musser remember each other? You interviewed him yesterday."

Ginny said, "Yes," while Musser nodded affirmatively.

Like the others before him, Musser initially denied making the 9-1-1 call. However, as the detectives kept pushing, he began to get increasingly defensive and nervous.

"There's no way. I don't even have a cellphone. So that's proof I didn't make the call."

"But the scientific evidence can't be wrong."

"Someone must've made a mistake. Maybe the evidence got mixed up with other people's. Or someone imitated my voice to get me in trouble."

"Do people often try to frame you for things you didn't do?"

"No, of course not." Musser continued as his face reddened, "Oh, I mean sometimes. Maybe. I can't be sure. I mean, how can I know? Especially if they're good at it."

"So, are you saying you don't know if you made that call or if someone framed you?"

"Yeah. That's what I think happened."

"Rudy," said Ginny, "let me explain something to you.

Making an anonymous call to 9-1-1, unless it's an intentional crank call, is not a crime."

"It wasn't a crank call. I swear."

"So you did make that call?"

"Uh, I…I—"

"Let me finish my explanation before you answer. Making that call anonymously is not a crime, but then lying to the police about it is. It's called obstruction of justice. Think before you answer. What you say next might have a big influence on your foreseeable future."

"OK. Gimme a minute to think."

"If I say I made the call, I'm in real trouble here. Kicked out at best. Beat up and maybe even murdered at worst. But if I lie to you, I could wind up in jail."

"Couple of things to think about. If you admit it to us, there's a good chance your admission will never be made public. We want to learn everything you can tell us, though it probably wouldn't prove useful in a trial. But if you wind up being arrested and tried for obstruction, everyone will know it was, in fact, you who made the call."

"Damn."

"And, if it came down to it, you leaving the group and relocating, with or without assistance from us, with a new name and identity might be possible."

"OK. OK. Yeah, I made that call. I was trying to do the right thing, without saying who I was. And now look at the mess I'm in."

"Let's not panic yet," said Joe. "Tell us exactly what happened that day."

Musser described how Turley called him into his office

to tell him Davis had been killed. Turley then told Musser where the body was, and that he had to go and bury it.

"Did Turley say he killed Davis?"

"No, not in so many words. But I got that impression. He knew a lot of details about the shot to Mark's head, where the body was and how it was wrapped in a blanket. Also, he seemed — I guess excited is the word. He implied the group would be free now to really do something about our beliefs."

"Did you tell anyone about this?"

"Heck, no. Too scared. And he warned me not to." Musser then described how he worried about it overnight, got his secret burner phone and called 9-1-1 the next day.

"Thank you, Rudy. That was very helpful."

"Yeah, for you. But not so much for me. Now what?"

"We carry on as if nothing has happened and you told us nothing new. If asked, you can tell folks we tried to pressure and bluff you into saying you made that call, but it didn't work. Everyone else we talk with today will have the same story. Now we're going to meet with our last person of interest, Holt Olsen, just so it doesn't look like we learned anything special from you."

"OK."

"We'll be in touch only if there are developments that might directly affect you, or if we have more questions. Ginny will walk you out now. Thanks for your help, and for being a good citizen."

Ginny left with Musser, after agreeing to give Joe ten minutes before she returned with Olsen.

Joe went outside and met with the officers who had

been conducting the gun search. They were finished, having found and collected one additional FN Five-seveN, this one being carried by one of the guards at the back gate. Joe told the officers to do one more search of Davis' apartment and office, as he reportedly owned a similar handgun that hadn't been found.

Joe returned to the interview room, and the two detectives went through a twenty-minute questioning just for show before releasing Olsen.

Following that, Ginny and Joe took a short break for biological reasons.

Back in the small room, Ginny said, "Joe, you are good. You even had me half convinced."

"About what?"

"That we had the voice recordings professionally analyzed. And the indisputable scientific conclusion was that whoever we were meeting with was the anonymous caller. You were so emphatic and convincing. Your lying was Oscar-winning caliber."

"Sure am glad the law allows us to lie to suspects, or even possible suspects. One of the few areas where they haven't tied one hand behind our back — yet."

"Nonetheless, you performed admirably, Joe. Didn't take too long to break Musser."

"The chief was definitely right. Again. A lot quicker and surer. And cheaper than sending the recordings out for professional comparison."

"No question. And Musser's comments did nothing but further increase our interest in Turley. He didn't say Turley killed Davis, but Turley obviously was the first to know about his murder. Plus, he knew where the body was lying, and that it was wrapped in a blanket. As a bare minimum, he was the one who instructed Musser to hide the body."

"Good info to have. Hope we're able to keep Musser's testimony secret. He seems really worried about retaliation, or excommunication or whatever, from the group."

"We'll try. Great if we can. He was trying to be a good citizen. But solving the case and putting the perp away is our first priority."

"For sure."

"Ready to meet with the three wives?"

"Yeah. Just give me a couple of minutes to check again with the guys looking for Davis' gun."

"Go for it."

Chapter 32

At around 4:30, the searching officers reported they had found all of Davis' guns except for his FN Five-seveN. They listed all the places they had searched, and Joe was satisfied they had conducted a thorough search. He collected the three handguns and one rifle to go to the BCI lab, thanked the officers who had worked on the search and sent them home.

At 4:50, the Jasper Creek uniformed officer arrived to pick up the guns. Joe gave him the four guns, and they both signed the chain-of-custody forms. Joe confirmed the officer had the bullet from the coroner's office and gave him instructions regarding who to see when he got to the BCI lab.

By five o'clock the officer was on his way to London. Joe informed Turley they were ready to meet with the three wives. Turley agreed they could use his office, and Joe and Ginny went to Turley's office to await the wives' arrival.

"Hi, ladies," said Joe. "Please grab a seat. Sorry for the tight quarters and the late hour, but it is what it is."

"First of all," said Ginny, "we want to repeat our sincere condolences on the death of your husband."

Mumbled expressions of "thanks" from the three wives.

"Secondly, we want to again assure you that we are and will continue doing everything possible to identify the murderer and bring him, or her, to justice. This, of course, won't bring Mr. Davis back, but it should give you some sense of closure and peace." Ginny continued, "We'd like to start by getting a basic description of how your polygamous family came to be and worked. I have to admit, I know very little about this kind of arrangement. From the perspective of our investigation, it's important that we understand how your relationships worked — especially, and you'll forgive me for saying this, if some aspect of it served as a motivation for Mr. Davis' murder."

"Sure. We're happy to talk about it," said Abigail Davis, Mark's first and only legally married wife. "The more people understand it, the less of a taboo about it there'll be." The other two wives nodded their agreement.

"Why don't I start? You guys chime in whenever you want," said Davis.

"OK," said Thatcher.

"Mark and I were married 23 years ago. It was a traditional, legal marriage. Even before Mark proposed, we had discussed and agreed that Mark would eventually take one or more additional wives. We believe that this is much sounder for the family, especially the children, rather than the man getting bored or restless and starting to cheat on his wife. With the frequent result of a bitter marriage or divorce."

"But," interrupted Ginny, "I thought the Mormon Church outlawed polygamy many years ago?"

"You're right," responded Hansen, "the Church officially prohibited the practice of polygamy way back in 1890. But it still exists in practice today. There are thousands of Mormon fundamentalists who still believe in what the Church calls plural marriage. The Church allows men to form spiritual unions with more than one woman, but they abide by the law in that they prohibit more than one legal wife at any one time. Things are further confused for the general public in that several polygamist groups use the name 'Mormon' in their group's name, even though they're not at all affiliated with The Church of Jesus Christ of Latter-Day Saints."

"Things are never simple," said Joe.

"Anyhow, let me get back to my so-called lecture," said Davis. "After Mark and I were married about three and a half years, he suggested it was time to add a second wife. And I agreed. Mark was so full of love that a second wife wouldn't reduce Mark's love for me. I, in fact, met Lynn first. At a book club that met monthly at the community center near our ranch in Utah. We became good friends and I introduced her to Mark, eventually suggesting to both of them that she join the family. And she did. Although not legally married to Mark, we held a spiritual ceremony, making her every bit as much a member of the family as I am. We love each other and are happy to have each other — to talk with, to share chores with, to support each other and to both provide love and, yes, sex to Mark."

"Wow," said Ginny. "I'm not married, but if I were, I'm not so sure I'd willingly bring in another woman to share my husband."

"I can understand that," said Davis. "But you have to realize that we grew up with this kind of arrangement being normal. We all knew families and had relatives living in polygamous marriages, and openly without feeling the need to hide it. Heck, both Clara and I grew up in these situations. We feel we were lucky to have the love of more than one mother, and to always have had a bunch of sisters and brothers to play with."

"Probably what subconsciously attracted us to have this for ourselves," said Clara, looking down as she said it.

"Probably so. Let me just finish the chronology. I'm almost done. About four years later Clara joined the family. We currently have a total of six children, four boys and two girls, ranging from 18 months to 12 years in age. Plus, Lynn and Clara are both pregnant right now. Our arrangement is a great situation for the children — they always have other children to play with, and they feel like they have three mothers, all of whom love them. Of course, things will be very different now without Mark."

All of a sudden all three wives started crying: Davis softly, Thatcher loudly with her body shaking and Hansen mostly unable to contain a continuous series of sniffles. Joe was glad for Ginny's presence. *Ginny's doing her best to comfort and calm the women down, being very careful with her comments. I have no friggin' idea what to say. I don't know how to handle it when Ginny or any other woman starts to cry. Sure have no idea when it's three of them at the same time.*

After a few minutes, the wives managed to calm down.

"Let me emphasize," said Thatcher, "we're all here because we *want* to be. We each entered this arrangement voluntarily, with two of us having lived in a polygamous family growing up. We're not prisoners here — we're free to leave if and when we ever decide to.

"It's difficult to describe the relationships. We all love Mark. He loved the three of us equally. There is sometimes jealousy among the three of us, but it passes.

Overall, we're good friends, almost sisters. We're happy when everyone else is happy, and sad when there's conflict in the family."

"In fact," added Hansen, "it might be easiest for you to think of us as being sisters. Three adult sisters living in the same house. We share just about everything, including our husband. We love and help and support each other. We're all happy or sad when one of us is happy or sad. And, yes, we sometimes have episodes of jealousy towards one of our sisters. All sisters do. But these episodes pass."

Wow. Amazing how what we grow up with affects what we accept or perceive as normal, Ginny thought to herself. *I can't tell if they've been brainwashed or hypnotized or what. But this sure as hell is not normal. I sure as heck wouldn't share my husband with anyone, especially my sister — if I had one.* Aloud she said, "OK, thanks for filling us in. How do the day-to-day living arrangements work?"

"We pretty much all do everything. It's not like we're each assigned specific responsibilities or tasks," said Davis. "So, typically, we're all involved with cleaning and laundry. And cooking. But, naturally, we each wind up doing more of what we're best at. Or like the most. Fortunately, Clara does most of the cooking. Much better and tastier meals than Lynn or I can make. Think of Clara as the master chef, and Lynn and me as her sous-chefs."

"And let me say, just in case you're avoiding asking," added Clara, "we each have our own bedroom. Mark pretty much spent an equal number of nights with each of us. And we're never all together in bed with him. No weird or kinky stuff, just like you wouldn't have any with your sister or sisters."

"I should point out," said Davis, with a bit of a mischievous smile breaking out, "it wasn't easy on Mark. It takes a lot of understanding and patience to deal with the emotional and physical needs of three wives."

"I can only imagine," said Joe as Ginny gave him a sideways glance.

"You probably think we're a trio of dumb bozos who were taken advantage of by Mark. But it wasn't that way. In fact, Mark was sometimes troubled and worn out by having to keep the three of us satisfied, sexually and otherwise."

"And Mark wasn't a dictator, or the sole decision-maker," said Clara. "Virtually all our family decisions were discussed and made by all of us."

"A good example is the decision to move here three years ago," said Davis. "Mark's uncle, who's in charge of our whole group in Utah, offered Mark the chance to move here, start up and lead the Ohio branch. Mark was very excited about the opportunity, but the four of us spent several hours over about a week's time talking through the possible move, weighing the pros and cons for each of us and for the family; finally, we all agreed that the move would be a good one. It was truly a family decision."

"Even the decision about where to bury Mark was a family decision — of course, without Mark's involvement," said Thatcher sadly. "Abigail and Aaron discussed it with Mark's uncle, but before we fully signed off on the conclusion, we discussed it and the options with Abigail before agreeing that cremation here and burial in Utah made the most sense."

"And what about Dani?" asked Clara. "To me that's the best example of all." The other two wives cast her sideways glances as she spoke. Abigail looked like she wanted to stomp on Clara's foot.

Joe perked up, saying, "Tell us more about this Danny. This is the first we've heard his name. What's his involvement?"

"Dani is a she, not a he. Dani, that's D-A-N-I. Short for Danielle." Clara blushed as she spoke, as if realizing she'd let something slip.

"Sorry, my mistake. Tell us more about her," said Joe.

"Turns out," said Clara, deciding to forge ahead, "that for at least the last 18 months or so, some of Mark's mysterious trips, or maybe all of them, were to visit Dani."

"Oh?"

"Yeah, he apparently met her at a used book sale at the library. They gradually got to know each other better and better. Then, after he returned from his little disappearance in early August, Mark sat the three of us down."

"And?" asked Ginny.

"He said how he had met and gotten to know this wonderful lady. He wanted her to become his fourth wife."

"We, of course, were surprised," Abigail jumped in. "We had had no inkling up until then. The more he described her, the less support he got from us. I mean, we weren't against a fourth wife in principle, she just didn't seem like the right person to be it."

"Oh? Why?" asked Ginny.

"Plenty of reasons," said Lynn tersely. "She never would have fit in with the rest of us."

"Please explain why," said Joe.

"The list is a long one," said Davis. "First off, she's way younger than any of us, only 26. Lynn and Clara are in their mid-30s, and I'm already 43. Second, she's never been in or known anyone in a polygamous marriage. She's not even a Mormon!"

"In fact," added Lynn, "she was married and then divorced from her husband, after they had two children together!"

"She wouldn't fit in with us, and especially wouldn't be happy with our FRAP organization," said Davis. "I'm sure she'd be forced to quit her job as a schoolteacher, once word got out about FRAP or our 'unusual' family structure, or both. And I doubt she'd be able to get a teaching job close to here for the same reasons."

"About the only positive we could come up with was that she'd probably do a good job homeschooling our kids, and perhaps helping others here with their homeschooling. But that's about it."

"So how did Mark take your unanimous 'no'?"

"He wasn't happy at first, but as we talked it through in detail, he came to understand our point of view. Not sure if we totally convinced him we were right, but he did see it would be a long-term stressful situation if he proceeded," said Davis.

"Were you three upset that Mark's secret trips included his cheating on you?" asked Ginny.

"We weren't happy that he didn't let us know much

sooner, but there was no cheating in the way I think you mean it. We're certain that, although Mark courted Dani emotionally, there was no sex involved. Mark would not do that to us. Sexual relations would await their marriage. That's one of the strongest Church teachings."

"Why didn't any of you admit you knew where Mark went on his so-called mysterious trips before now?"

"We assumed he just made a quick stop at Dani's to say his good-byes and then went someplace else, though we didn't know where," said Davis coldly.

"Plus, like it or not, we don't trust the police. Please don't be offended, that was before we got to know you. You two are the first policemen that we ever really knew personally, and you don't fit the terrible image we have," said Clara.

"Don't worry," said Joe. "As cops, we learn not to get offended that easily."

"I hate to admit it," added Lynn, "but we were embarrassed to let anyone know Mark was meeting with this — other woman, and even planning to marry her before us knowing anything about it."

"I get it," said Ginny. "We understand all these reasons, but you three interfered with our investigation. Not telling us didn't contribute to your husband's death, but it definitely has slowed down our hunt for his killer. No idea if this Danielle-whoever has any useful information for us, or maybe even is the murderer, but time only makes our leads colder and harder to follow. At a minimum, you three need to live with the fact that you contributed to a delay in bringing your husband's killer to justice and, although we hope not, maybe to our never finding him."

"You're right," said Davis. "We're sorry and we apologize, but we can't go back in time and redo things."

"No, you can't. OK, back to you three and Mark making decisions together. What did Mark do after you had all your discussions about why you three felt Danielle was not the right person to be wife number four?" asked Ginny.

"He said that on his next visit, he would totally break things off with her."

"And did he?" asked Joe.

"We assume so," answered Lynn. "But that was this last trip. He was either murdered just before the trip or as soon as he returned here. I guess we may never know."

And with that, the three wives started crying in unison. Ginny and Joe silently waited them out.

"OK, we understand, but we aren't happy with your reasons for not telling us sooner about this Dani and your husband's visits to her. What else can you tell us about her that can help us locate her? She's surely someone we want to talk to."

"To start with, we never heard her last name. We've gone through Mark's personal stuff and didn't find her contact information anyplace," said Clara.

"All we really know," said Lynn, "is that her first name is Danielle. She's 26 years old, supposedly very attractive with long red hair. She's an elementary school teacher somewhere in the Columbus area."

Ginny nodded. "Well, that should be enough to give us a pretty good shot at identifying her."

"One other question," said Joe. "Any idea who might want Mark dead?"

The three women all said no, though they admitted tensions occasionally arose within the organization due to Mark's status and actions — or rather lack of them — as leader.

"Who were these tensions most frequent or most strong with?" asked Joe.

"We don't really know any specifics. Just some of the leaders under him."

"Anything else you want to tell us, or should be telling us?" asked Joe. "Remember, we're on the same side here. We all want to find out who killed your husband."

No one had anything further to add. The detectives thanked the ladies, then ended the interview.

Chapter 33

The detectives' last act of the day was to re-interview Turley.

"Aaron," said Joe, "like we told you previously, before Mr. Davis' body is released by the coroner, we'll be deciding who we will and won't prohibit from traveling out of the county — and especially traveling to Utah."

A growl sounded in Turley's throat. "And like I told you before, it's for Mark's funeral. Are you really going to stop some of us from attending? That's not right."

"'Fraid so," said Ginny. "It's more important to keep our prime suspects here locally, where we can easily get our hands on them."

"Typical government power play, if you ask me. Who are your so-called prime suspects right now?"

"Still working on it," said Joe, "but at this moment, you're numero uno."

"What? Are you crazy? Why am I a suspect at all, much less number one?"

"You clearly have the most to gain by his death."

"How?"

"Don't tell us," said Joe, "you don't like all the benees that come with being the top dog."

"Best living accommodations, first pick of food,

clothing and other stuff. Not to mention the only one with three wives. You saying these never entered your mind?" asked Ginny.

"Well, yeah, sure they did. I'm not blind. Or stupid. But they're not worth killing to get them."

"Says you," added Joe. "I'm sure you also think you'd be a much better leader than he was."

"Yeah, I do. And most of the members would agree with that. Mark was way too timid. Heck, if we went and joined one peaceful march a year, that was a lot. We have all these strong, and justified, beliefs, but, with Mark in charge, we couldn't do more than just talk and grumble about them among ourselves. More like a debating club than a militia."

"Like I said," concluded Joe, "you seem to have plenty of motive to see Davis out of the way and you the new big boss."

"Not much point in continuing this. You obviously have your minds made up. So I'll just sit back and wait for you to find out who the actual killer was."

"Not a problem with that," said Joe. "Just remember, it's in your own self-interest to help us find the actual killer. That is, if it's not you."

And that's how the interview ended. Ginny and Joe headed out the door, walked to Joe's car and left. On the way home, the detectives discussed their day.

"Ginny, I can't wait to get home and either stand or lie down. My butt is killing me. I feel like we've been sitting in that damn barn conducting interviews for the past 24 hours."

"Well, you're not off by too much. We did get there almost 12 hours ago."

"At least we accomplished a few things. Found out who made that 9-1-1 call, not to mention Turley emerging, or remaining, as our top suspect du jour."

"And found four possible murder weapons and got them and the bullet from Davis' head off to the BCI."

"Also damned interested in finding that Danielle lady and seeing what we can learn from her."

"Overall, Joe, I think we more than earned our pay today." Ginny shook her head. "Those poor women. To put so much faith in someone who has three wives all essentially being his servants! What's so special about some guy that he deserves three wives, let alone a fourth? If women could take multiple husbands too, maybe it would sort of be equal."

"You're not thinking of having multiple husbands now, are you? Seriously though, seems like there has to be more jealousy than they let on. Possibly even enough to inspire murder."

"I don't get it, Joe. I wasn't sure if I was watching some weird movie or had been transported back in time several hundred years. Can't decide if I dislike or feel sorry for those three women, but I sure don't feel normal about them."

"I can understand that. It sure isn't normal, not in this day and age — or at least this part of the world." Joe yawned and blinked, adjusting his rearview mirror. "OK, we're off duty. My only remaining request is that when we get home you cook something easy that we can eat quickly. I need the recliner or my bed ASAP."

“Aye, aye, sir.”

Eggs, bacon and a toasted bagel, washed down with a beer, and the detectives were soon on the couch, watching two TV shows before dragging themselves off to bed.

Chapter 34

Ginny and Joe took full advantage of it being the weekend. They slept until almost eight o'clock Saturday morning, a rare luxury for them. After lounging around the house for more than an hour, they showered, dressed and headed to the local IHOP restaurant for breakfast. Ginny went with fried eggs and a short stack of pancakes; Joe ordered a cheese and ham omelet, a double order of bacon and a large stack. Orange juice and coffee for both.

"Don't worry, Ginny. I'm going to jog this afternoon and run away from all these calories."

"I sure hope so. It may have to be a pretty long and fast jog, given all you just ordered."

"You gotta have faith."

The detectives spent close to an hour having breakfast, a nice change from their normal five-minute eat-and-run routine.

From IHOP, they drove through a section of one more neighboring town, trying to decide where to focus their house search.

"OK, Joe. That should be it now. The several places we've looked at, coupled with the many areas I'm familiar with from spending my whole life here, should let us pick where we'd like to live, maybe even with a backup choice or two as well."

"Yup. And just in time. I'm getting tired of all these reconnaissance runs anyway."

Back home, the detectives had a salad and some tuna fish for lunch.

Joe did, in fact, then go for a 45-minute jog around the neighborhood. After Joe returned and showered, the two detectives sat together on the living room couch.

"Ginny, we need to pick one or two towns and go find a realtor."

"Joe, I think we should stop now."

"Huh? Why? I feel like we're making good progress."

"We are. In fact, I feel like we're done. I think we should stay in Jasper Creek."

"Oh?"

"Yeah. Several of the other towns we've seen or that I already knew well look nice. But you never really know after just driving around for a few hours. As we looked at each one, I was unconsciously comparing them to here. A few actually were very nice, but so is Jasper Creek. And we know this town pretty well. We're unlikely to get hit with any surprises once we move in. Sorta the devil we know vs. the one we don't."

"It sure would be the best choice from a commuting standpoint."

"Plus, we know all the restaurants, supermarkets and other shops. We have all of our favorites here. As some politician once said, 'If it ain't broken, don't fix it.'"

"I'm OK with that, Ginny. Let's start our house search here. If we find it, great. If not, then we can pick one of the other towns."

"Deal. Now we need to try to define, at least partially, what we're looking for in a house and property. And neighborhood. Then we need to pick a realtor. I assume we'll use the same one to sell this house and help us find and buy a new one."

"I would think so. Would probably make all the timing-coordination issues easier."

"So, how do we move this ahead?"

"What say we spend part of tomorrow trying to define our dream house, and you start looking online for realtors? Just like last time with your condo sale, we probably should meet with three or so, then choose a winner."

"Super. I feel like we're really finally moving this ahead."

"That's 'cause we are."

The detectives spent a good part of Sunday on this. First, they browsed through houses for sale in Jasper Creek to get some ideas of what they liked and didn't like, as well as to familiarize themselves with the general price levels in town. Then Ginny started writing down their likes and dislikes.

"Joe, I definitely don't want a split-level. I prefer a two-story, but even a ranch, with everything on one floor, is better than a split. To me, a split-level feels like you should live upstairs and rent out the downstairs. They're very separated from each other."

"Fine with me. I also want to be in one of the more semi-rural areas. Not way out in no man's land, but definitely not downtown. Want a big enough property, maybe two or three acres, to give us privacy when we're out back. Also don't want to be looking into our neighbor's house every time I look out a window. But I don't want a property so large that maintaining it is a full-time job."

"I agree. I also want the house to be old enough to have some character — don't ask me what that exactly means — but not so old that it's decrepit."

"Yeah. Old enough that it was built when they still put quality into a house, but not so old that most things need to be updated or replaced. And definitely want air conditioning. And, oh yeah, a dishwasher — other than me."

"What about size?"

"I don't know, Ginny. The layout can make a house feel much larger or much smaller than its actual square footage. I also want a basement — for storage as well as a work bench for me. And maybe even an area for exercising."

"Definitely a two-car garage. I've had it with scraping the snow and ice off the windshield in the morning."

"Agreed. And, most importantly, we need five bedrooms."

"What, are you crazy, Joe? Planning to run a hotel or something?"

"We did say we wanted an extra bedroom to use as a home office."

"Right. But that still leaves four."

"Just planning ahead. If I wind up like Mark Davis, with three wives, we'll need one bedroom for each of you. Plus, of course, one for me."

"Actually, we won't need one for you. I will have murdered you by then," said Ginny with a smile.

"Message received. Figured it was worth a try. OK, let's

go with three bedrooms — one for us, one for our office and one guestroom for an occasional guest."

"That's it then. I think we've got a good starting list. I'm sure our realtor will help us refine it. I also think we should hold off on setting a price range. The realtor can help us with what the going prices are, as well as how much we should expect from selling this house. That amount, plus what I got for my condo, should give us quite a bit of flexibility."

"Yup. But we don't have to spend it all. The last thing I want is for us to be house poor, where we have this great, wonderful expensive house and no money left for anything else."

"Full agreement. Why don't you type our list up, while I start searching for realtors on the Internet?"

"You got it."

Two hours later, Ginny had identified six realtors who looked good based on information on the Internet. Ginny planned to do further research during the next week or so, hoping to reduce the list to three or four whom she would then contact and schedule initial interviews with.

Chapter 35

Monday morning, the detectives had a reasonably civil session with the chief — no major criticisms as they brought him up to date on all their interviews late the prior week, resulting in a growing interest in Turley, as well as an effort to identify, locate and speak with a redheaded schoolteacher named Danielle somewhere in the Columbus area. They concluded their update by announcing they expected to get the results of the BCI ballistics comparisons within the next day or two.

The chief also agreed with Ginny's suggestion that they ask the coroner to delay releasing the body for another few days. The coroner could call Turley and inform him about the delay, claiming they were super busy and getting help from the state because of changes to the corpse caused by being buried in a blanket, or something similar.

Back at their desks, Ginny called the coroner with their request, to which he readily agreed. The two detectives then started their hunt for Danielle.

"Joe, why don't you start by calling school systems in and around Columbus? Also the local teachers' union. There can't be too many 26-year-old, redheaded Danielles teaching elementary school in the Columbus area."

"I'm on it."

"I suggest we hold off on private and religious schools for now. Let's focus on the public schools first. We can eventually work on the private schools if we strike out with the public ones. While you're doing that, I'll start searching databases. Glad her name's Danielle and not Mary. Again, there can't be too many Danielles meeting our criteria. I'll try to get into the teachers' union database and will, of course, check our usual criminal and motor vehicle files. I'll also check divorce records, since the wives mentioned she had been divorced."

"Let's hope they got her name right. And that she hasn't moved to California or wherever in the meantime."

An hour and a half later, Ginny said, "Yikes."

"Yikes what?"

"How many Danielles do you think there are in Columbus and its suburbs?"

"Uh, no idea. Maybe 200 or 300?"

"That woulda been about my guess."

"And?"

"We're both dummies. Would you believe three or four times that, close to 1,000?"

"You gotta be kidding."

"I'm not. Scout's honor."

"OK, then. I fully accept and agree with your 'yikes.'"

"Can't do much with her being attractive or red-headed, but her age lets us cut the list way down."

"To what?"

"Assuming she has an Ohio driver's license, using 24 to 28 years old just to be sure, we're down to 124 Danielles. And I've got a last name and address for each one of them."

"That's still a large number. And, like you said, we've got nothing if she doesn't have an Ohio license."

"Very true. But finding her, or exhausting all the names on the list, should be pretty straightforward with the school systems. Having last names makes it a lot easier."

"Sure does. But we're still asking people to search through a list of names to identify any that are teachers in their system. We won't make a lot of friends with that request."

"You're right, Joe. To make matters worse, let me throw one more fly in your soup."

"Lovely image. I think I'm off soup for the next month or two. But go ahead."

"She was divorced. Probably changed her name when she got married, then maybe did and maybe didn't change it back when she got divorced. So, is her driver's license in her single or married name? And does she teach under her single or married name?"

"Damn. Thanks for the complication. But you're definitely right. In terms of our trying to find her, she's like a spy with two different identities. And we don't know either of her last names."

"I see. And you must be Bond. James Bond, that is."

With the help of the wife of one of Jasper Creek's uniformed officers, Ginny was able to greatly simplify her search. The wife, working remotely from home, was one of three database administrators for the state's Ohio Educational Directory System. This online system provided a map and the name and contact information for every school district in the state, as well as for every public and private school within each district. She was able to help

Ginny identify the local districts, then all the schools in and around Columbus. Getting a list of teachers for each school or district would be an easy online search in some cases, but, in others, it unfortunately would require working individually with someone at each school or district.

Getting a list of members of the teachers' union was also not so simple.

"Joe, this is crazy."

"What is?"

"There's no way to get a list of teachers' union members."

"Why not?"

"First off, there are two major unions in the state, and they barely talk with each other. The biggest is the Ohio Education Association, which is affiliated with the National Education Association. It seems to be primarily in smaller cities and towns in the state. But it also includes high schools and colleges, as well as school nurses, librarians and so on — not just teachers. The second large one, but much smaller than the first, is associated with the American Federation of Teachers national union and serves mostly our larger cities. Both have a zillion local chapters, which maintain all their own data — to varying degrees of accuracy and timeliness, as you might imagine. Add in the fact that there are several local unions not affiliated with any big union, and there are many teachers, mostly in private and religious schools, who don't belong to any union."

"So what do we do?"

"I think we use the state directory system to identify

the districts in and around Columbus. Then we go to them, one by one. Hopefully, there won't be too many."

"Hope we can deal with someone at each district and not have to contact every individual school. That could take us until Christmas."

"Agreed. Let's pick the districts of interest. Hopefully, several will list their entire teaching staff online. After we talk with a few we'll know how big the task is, and whether they, rather than we, will actually look for the Danielle we're searching for, or if we have to go to each school. If we have to check each school, we'll need to ask the chief for a small army to help us."

"OK, but first lunch. I'm starving."

The detectives took the short walk around the corner to Sancho's Taco Shop, their go-to lunch spot whenever they were in the area at lunchtime.

Back at their desks, the two detectives developed a list of 12 school districts within 50 miles of Columbus, including the one within Columbus itself. For each of the 12 districts, they identified and wrote down the names and contact information of two or three individuals who, based upon their titles, seemed to be potentially good sources.

"Joe, this may not be as tough a task as we thought."

"Oh?"

"Yeah, assuming she teaches in one of the public schools. If she's in a charter school, or a private or religious school, it might be just as tough as we thought."

"Convinced me. I'll hope and pray for a public school."

"Wisely, I might add. So, counting the city of Columbus,

there are an even dozen school districts within 50 miles of the city center. And these districts vary widely in size. For example, the city has 14 public elementary schools. One of the other districts has 15, believe it or not, and another one has only one. The other districts fall anywhere in between."

"Quite the range, indeed."

"Lucky for us, nine of the 12 have an online search for teachers and staff. You can just put a first name in and search. In some districts you can do one district-wide search, while in others you have to first click on each elementary school and then do the search for that school only. Still, that's one heck of a useful tool for us. We really only have to contact three school systems and ask them to manually search their personnel records for teachers named Danielle — or, if they won't, give us access to their records and let us do the search."

"Very true. And I'm sure they have their lists computerized. Worst case, they give us a payroll report with the pay info blocked out, and we quickly look through the list for Danielles."

"Joe, you're really getting to be such a computer nerd. I'm proud of you. Why don't you start working through the online searches, while I practice my sweet, helpless female voice and then call those three districts? Heck, in the smaller districts whoever I talk to will probably know the names of all their teachers."

"Let's do it. Don't forget to pray with me that she teaches in a public school — and in one of the districts we selected as being 'near Columbus.'"

"The grinding noise you hear is my mind doing just that."

Three hours later, the detectives were done. Joe found two Danielles in his online search. Ginny tried searching for these two names on the Internet, hoping a photo or description could help eliminate either or both of them based on age, but neither name resulted in a "hit."

Ginny got two of the systems to agree to go through their listings and get back to her by nine the next morning. It was only the City of Columbus district that threw up a temporary problem. Both the human resources director and the superintendent were willing to go through their list of employees, but they were unwilling to do so until they spoke with the school system's attorney and got her approval.

"They were fairly certain they'd have their lawyer's answer by sometime tomorrow. They'll call me as soon as they know. If they get the go-ahead, actually scanning through the entire list of employees shouldn't even take half an hour."

"OK," said Joe. "Seems like that's it for now. Guess we should plan on a pleasant drive to the Columbus area tomorrow. Let's fill the chief in. Once we see whether either of my Danielles fits the age category — and we hopefully get a lead or two out of the three systems we can't check online — we'll want to have a friendly visit with each of our Danielles who's the right age. We'll also need to arrange with the appropriate police or sheriff's departments to have one of their uniforms join us. Proper protocol and all that."

Using her best imitation of a British accent, Ginny said, "My goodness. You're getting so bloody proper, Guv."

"No way, ma'am. I'm just a plain old bloke trying to keep the chief off me back."

"That works also. Let's go bring him up to date, then head on home."

"One of your very best ideas."

"Why, thank you, kind sir."

The meeting with the chief was not very uplifting.

"OK. OK. I'll grant you that you've made a little progress. But you have no Plan B if she taught in a private or charter school, or a school further from Columbus. On top of that, you have no idea what her last name is. What if she dyes her hair black or bleaches it blonde, how will you even know it's her? And even if it is her, you really have no damn idea whether she can be of any help with your investigation. Your broad and thorough approach strikes me like someone trying to balance a one-legged stool. At this point, all we can hope for is that you get lucky. Not the soundest strategy for solving a murder case."

"But, Chief—"

"Joe, let's not get into it. Again. I hope you two wind up being lucky tomorrow. Oh, and one positive thing. You did recognize the appropriateness of having a local with you if you wind up interviewing any of your Danielles. Let's just leave it on that positive note for now. Have a good evening. If I don't see you in the morning, I'll assume you're off to a picnic in the Columbus area."

The detectives said good night, gathered the papers they might need in Columbus and were out the door in five minutes.

Chapter 36

The two detectives left home about 8:30 the next morning. With the drive to Columbus taking only about one hour via I-70, and their assuming they probably couldn't reach anyone at the schools or school district offices before nine, they saw little benefit of leaving home super early. Joe drove so that Ginny could work her phone.

Ginny called one of the two districts which Joe had identified as having a teacher named Danielle. Ginny was quickly routed to the Director of Human Resources.

"Yes, Detective, how may I help you?"

"We're trying to identify and speak with an elementary school teacher in the greater Columbus area with the first name of Danielle. We found one such teacher going through your online listing of teachers."

"Oh, my gosh. Is Danielle in any trouble? I can't believe that—"

"No. At this point we believe she may know or have once known someone we have some questions for."

"Whew. That's a relief. How specifically can I help you?"

"About all we know is that she's in her mid-20s and has red hair."

"Well, that's not a lot to go on. But it is enough to eliminate our Danielle."

"Oh?"

"Yes, definitely. Although I hope to look as good as she

does when I reach her age, I really don't think anyone would confuse her with a twenty-something. She's in her 60s, and probably within a year or two of retiring."

"Well, that does make it pretty easy. Sure doesn't sound like who we're looking for. Thank you very much for your help."

"You're most welcome. And good luck with your search."

Ginny filled Joe in as soon as the call ended, although he had understood the gist of the conversation from hearing Ginny's side.

"OK. I'm going to try Upper Arlington now."

"Go for it. And good luck, partner."

Before Ginny could dial the number, she received a call from one of the two districts that promised to get back to her. They had no teachers named Danielle.

Ginny then called the second school district Joe had found employing a teacher named Danielle.

"So sorry, Detective. I'm embarrassed to say that our website overall, including our list of employees, is sadly out of date. The listing is probably almost two years old. I could spend the next fifteen minutes discussing all the reasons why: budgetary cuts and resultant staff reductions; turnover of administrative staff; no one being exclusively assigned responsibility for keeping the list current; some teachers and staff objecting to being on the list for confidentiality or personal safety reasons; and so on. But I assume you don't need to hear all the gory details."

"That's correct. Can you tell me if this teacher named Danielle still works in your school district?"

"No, she doesn't. She resigned effective at the end of the school term, the year before last."

"Retired?"

"No. She was only in her late 40s. Her husband had some technical kind of job. He apparently received a too-good-to-decline job offer from some small, fast-growing startup, and off they went to California. Don't know about the job, but I bet they're loving the winters compared to here."

"That I can fully understand. Thank you for your help."

"No problem. Sorry our outdated website caused you to waste your time."

"Don't worry about it. It was only a few extra minutes."

Ginny filled Joe in.

"Damn. Our list of possibilities is rapidly shrinking."

"Yup. But we're not dead in the water yet. Still waiting to hear from two districts — or only one, if the city district doesn't get their lawyer's OK. If neither of these pan out, then we have the tougher job of identifying and contacting every private, religious and charter school. We might even have to widen the radius around Columbus."

"All that sounds like fun."

Joe and Ginny pulled off the highway, stopping for a cup of coffee and a half-stale, plastic-wrapped pseudo-Danish pastry apiece.

While walking back to Joe's car after finishing their snack, Ginny's phone rang. Ginny assumed it was one of the school districts calling her back, but she was wrong.

"Hey, Ginny. Vern," said Vern Jones, the detective whose desk sat next to Ginny's and Joe's.

"Morning, Vern. What's up?"

“I went to use the fax machine a few minutes ago, and there was a fax on it addressed to you and Joe.”

“Oh, who from?”

“BCI. The Firearms Unit.”

“Oh, great. We’ve been waiting on that. What’s it say?”

“Let me cut through all the legal and bureaucratic BS and summarize it for you.”

“Hang on one sec. I want to put this on speaker so Joe can hear it.”

Ginny put the call on speaker, then Ginny and Joe huddled around Ginny’s phone while standing in front of Joe’s car. Joe and Jones said hello to each other.

“OK,” said Joe, “what’s it say?”

“To make a long story short, none of the guns checked was the one used to shoot your vic.”

“Shit!” yelled Joe as he banged his palm on the hood of his car, loudly enough that half a dozen people in the parking lot jumped and turned to see what was going on.

Jones gave them a few more details from the fax, including that they captured several fingerprints from the guns but, as Joe had instructed, didn’t bother trying to identify the prints since none of the guns were the murder weapon. Joe and Ginny thanked him for calling, and Ginny hung up.

“Damn, Ginny. That means either the murder weapon is still there, and our search missed it, or it’s been long gone, or maybe never was there. We know Davis wasn’t shot where his body was found, so the damned gun could be anyplace.”

“That’s how it goes sometimes.”

"Yeah. We're sure doing a much better job of turning up noes than yeses, or even maybes. Now what?" asked Joe.

"First thing, we need to abide by the chief's letter. I'll call Grady to have one of the uniforms drive to the BCI in London and bring back the guns they tested for us. While I'm doing that, why don't you call the BCI and made arrangements for them to turn over the guns and the original copies of their test reports to the uniformed officer who will get there later this afternoon?"

"Sounds like a plan. We'll at least have them all at the station. We can then bring them back to their owners any time."

The detectives made the calls and set everything up.

While still in the parking lot consoling each other about none of the guns being a match, Ginny's phone rang again. Ginny answered it with the call on speaker.

"Detective Harris."

"Good morning, Detective. Sorry I wasn't able to call you earlier, but it's already been one of those days."

"Who is this, please?"

"Oh, excuse me. I'm so sorry. This is Larry Ingram with the Hilliard School District. We spoke yesterday."

"Uh, yes, of course."

"Turns out we do, or perhaps did is a better term, have an elementary teacher named Danielle. Danielle Brown."

"Why do you say 'did?'"

"Ms. Brown taught here for the past four years. Had been very dependable and reliable. She even had two children while teaching here. Both times, she had her mother move in with her and the husband. Free, full-time baby nurse. It allowed Danielle to get back to work after only a few weeks. But not this time. Just as this school year began, and I mean just, she called to say she had a family emergency and needed a leave of absence."

"Oh? What was the emergency?"

"Don't know. For things like that, the employee speaks with an outside company we keep on retainer. Part of the contract with the teachers' union. Keeps these matters confidential. The company knows our plans and procedures; after speaking with the employee, even arranging medical exams if it's a medical issue, they just report to us to either accept or decline the leave request. In this case they recommended we grant her request, allowing leave up through the holiday recess coming up in December and early January."

"Can you confirm her age?"

"Yes. Hold on one second. Here it is. 26, will turn 27 in June."

"Do you happen to know the color of her hair?"

"Yes. Couldn't miss it. Bright red."

With a bright smile, Ginny asked, "Can you give me her home address?"

"Is she in trouble?"

"Not that we're aware of. We're trying to locate someone we believe she knows, or at least used to know."

"Sure, OK then. It's 62 Circle Drive, here in Hilliard."

"Great. Thanks for your help. Have a good day," said Ginny as she hung up before Ingram could ask any more questions.

"Guess we're off to Circle Drive. Do me a favor, enter it in your GPS."

"Will do. Should I call their PD, have one of their officers meet us there?"

"Let's hold off on that, Ginny. Right now we're just going to talk with her, so I don't think we need a local escort."

"But you assured the chief that—"

"What he doesn't know won't hurt him. If this turns into anything more than a pleasant interview, and perhaps her initial notification of Davis' death, then we can go the local-escort route."

"OK by me."

The detectives pulled up in front of a pleasant, light-blue split-level house about 35 minutes later.

Knocking on the front door and peering through the garage window offered pretty solid evidence that no one was home. As the detectives walked back towards the front door, a neighbor from across the street came over.

"Can I help you?" asked the woman, dressed in old pants and shirt, reflective of her having been working on her front lawn. She was probably in her early 40s, with obviously bleached hair.

"Yes, thank you," said Ginny. "We're looking for Danielle Brown."

"And you are?"

"I'm Virginia Harris, and this is Joe McFarland. We're detectives with the Jasper Creek Police Department."

"Over towards Dayton, if I'm not mistaken. What brings you all this way?"

"We're trying to locate someone, and we think Ms. Brown might know where she is."

"Oh. Well, sorry. She's gone."

"Gone?"

"Yeah. 'Bout three weeks ago. Told me she was going on a trip and was leavin' her two little kids, sweethearts really, with her mother. Gave me her mother's phone number."

"Great. Can you give us her number? And her name and address, of course."

"Yes and no."

"What does that mean?" asked Joe.

"Yes, I can give you the phone number. But I have no idea what her mother's name is or where she lives."

"Well, we'll settle for the phone number then," said Joe.

"Hold on while I go get it."

She crossed the street and entered her house through the garage, returning five minutes later and handing Ginny a small piece of paper with a phone number on it.

Ginny thanked her, asked for her name and phone number and wrote them in her notepad in case they needed to contact her again. Ginny also gave her a card, instructing her to call if she remembered something, or if Danielle returned home. Joe and Ginny were soon in Joe's car, driving just a few blocks away to park in a shopping center parking lot.

Ginny again put her phone on speaker and called the number she had gotten.

"'Lo."

"Is this Danielle Brown's mother?"

"Yes. Who is this?"

"I'm Detective Harris, with the Jasper Creek Police Department."

"My God! What happened? Is she OK? Was she in an accident? Or worse? Please, please tell me."

"No. Relax. As far as we know, she's fine. We're trying to reach her. She may be able to help us locate someone we want to speak with."

"Whew, that's a relief. But no surprise she's hanging out with someone the cops are looking for. She's as bad at pickin' friends as she was at pickin' a husband."

"Is Danielle with you?"

"Nope. Hell, that wouldn't work for more than two hours. At most. But my two grandkids are with me. She asked me to care for 'em 'til she could get back home."

"Do you know where she is?"

"Not for sure. But I'll betcha dollars to donuts she's with her no-good brother, Zach. Jeez, what a pair. They both, sadly, take after my ex, not me."

"By the way, may I please have your name and address? Just in case we need it."

"Sure. I ain't got nuthin' to hide," she said. "Name's Vera Fielding." She then gave Ginny her address.

"Thanks. And how about your son's address?"

"Sure," again. She gave Ginny his address in Ashley, a small town in Delaware County, about 45 minutes north from where Ginny and Joe were in Hilliard.

"One more question. You described your son as no-good. Can you elaborate on that?"

"Nothing too special. I mean, he's not a real criminal, like a murderer or a member of a drug gang. He's always just kinda doing the wrong thing and getting into minor trouble. Even way back in grade school. Danielle, despite her crappy choices in men, made something of herself. Got a college degree and became a teacher. Her brother's more of an expert on collecting unemployment, sometimes disability, plus whatever other systems he can figure out how to scam."

"Understood. Well, thanks for your help."

"When you see her, remind her what a telephone is for and that she's got two little kids here who miss her."

"Will do. Bye for now."

"Well done, Ginny. OK, off to Ashley, Ohio, which, by the way, I never even heard of."

"No reason you should have. It's super small. Probably less than 2000 people live there."

"Makes Jasper Creek seem like the big city."

"Joe, given what her mother said about her brother, I think we should play it by the book and hook up with one of Ashley's finest."

"Yeah, you're probably right. Why don't you try to set it up?"

"On it."

Chapter 37

Ten minutes later, Ginny had spoken with the Ashley Police Department chief and arranged to meet Officer Billy Becker at PD headquarters on Harrison Street at two o'clock. That gave Ginny and Joe enough time to drive to Ashley, stopping someplace along the way for lunch.

"Joe, I'm still going to wait to hear back from the Columbus Schools. Besides being curious whether they get a yes from their lawyer, I don't want to turn them off until we're one hundred percent sure we've got the right Danielle."

"I'm with you on that."

Joe pulled into the Ashley Police Department's parking lot at about 1:50.

After talking with Ginny and Joe for a few minutes, Officer Becker had one of the administrative staff pull a rap sheet on Danielle's brother, Zach. Several minor incidents of fighting, drunk and disorderly and reckless driving, but nothing too serious.

The two detectives joined Becker in his patrol car, and they were off to the brother's house. It was near the edge of town, on Hwy 243, just past the cemetery. A sparsely populated section of a sparsely populated town.

Becker parked along the side of the highway about 100 yards past the house. He, Joe and Ginny got out of the car and started walking up the dirt driveway towards the house.

"House looks pretty small," said Ginny.

"Sure does. Clearly a one-story, probably two bedrooms. Unusual house — half log cabin and half beach bungalow," said Joe.

"A few repairs and a coat of paint wouldn't hurt," said Becker.

"Surrounded by pretty thick woods. If you want privacy, this is where to get it," added Ginny.

"OK, let's be ready for anything. Probably won't be any problem. Hell, all we want at this point is to talk with her. But you never know. Better safe than sorry."

"Can't argue with that," said Becker.

"Billy, why don't you sneak around back? I'm sure there's a back door, most likely off the kitchen. Just in case we get a runner. Ginny and I will politely knock on the front door."

"Will do. Give me five minutes to snake my way through the woods to the back of the house."

"You got it. Go for it, Sneaky."

Ginny and Joe slowly walked to the front door. Since there was no visible button or knocker, Joe inched past Ginny and loudly rapped his knuckles on the door. When no one answered, he knocked again, this time yelling, "Police! Open up."

Thirty seconds later, the door was opened by an attractive woman who looked to be in her mid-20s, with long, flowing bright red hair.

"Ms. Brown? Danielle Brown?"

"Yes. What's this about?"

“May we come—”

“Uh oh! Runner! Ginny, hang onto her, I’m going after him.

“Stop! Stay where you are! This is the police!” yelled Joe as loud as he could, pushing past Danielle and racing towards the kitchen.

Ginny gently took Danielle by her arm and led her out the front door and about three-quarters of the way down the driveway. She wanted to be able to quickly get Danielle into Becker’s patrol car if any problems arose.

Joe was just entering the kitchen when he saw a man, presumably Danielle’s brother, trying to grab some things off the counter and race for the back door.

Joe yelled, “Police! Stop!” As Joe was reaching for his gun, Zach stopped and turned around to face him, accidentally knocking several glass and metal containers off the counter and stove.

Then, **BOOM!!!** The kitchen exploded in a whirlwind of heat, a momentary burst of flame, loud noise and flying debris.

Danielle’s brother, the one closest to the explosion, lay unconscious on the kitchen floor. The explosion ripped open most of his clothing, and he had suffered serious chemical burns and cuts on his face, arms, chest and stomach. Becker, who was positioned outside about ten feet from the kitchen door, was knocked down by the blast, which blew out the windows in the kitchen door. Becker lay on the ground, conscious but temporarily deaf and somewhat disorientated.

Joe lay motionless on the kitchen floor. He’d suffered numerous chemical burns, alongside several cuts and bruises from flying glass and pieces of metal, as well as what, in all probability, was a serious concussion.

Ginny felt a sense of horror when the explosion occurred, but her training and discipline immediately kicked in. She half-led, half-dragged Danielle to Becker's car, sat her in the front passenger's seat and handcuffed her to the B pillar, the vertical post between the front and rear doors. "Stay put! And I mean it. No messing around. You hear me? Just sit here."

"But my brother. He may be hurt. Badly. I need to try and help him."

"Just stay here. I'm calling for medics, then I'll go in and see how he and my partner are doing. I can't also be worrying about you."

"OK. OK. But please hurry. Please!"

Ginny called 9-1-1, identified herself as a police officer and requested fire and EMS assistance. Not yet knowing what was going on inside, she requested three ambulances — needed as quickly as possible. Also, local police for Danielle's brother as well as for controlling the crime scene.

She then ran into the house through the front door, heading immediately to Joe. She saw him lying on the floor, but stopped short. She called Joe's name, but there was no response. By the smell and the cloud of foul smoke hanging in the kitchen, Ginny immediately knew this had been a meth lab explosion. She stepped outside and called 9-1-1 again, stated her findings and requested that a hazmat crew be immediately dispatched to the scene. *Shit. Now what do I do? Do I just wait for the medics and hazmat to arrive? Do I go into the kitchen and try to help*

Joe? Maybe even drag him out of there so he's not breathing the toxic fumes? I could cover my nose and mouth while I do it. But, shit, if his back or neck is injured, I could cause him to be paralyzed. What the hell do I do?

Ginny decided to quickly enter and leave the kitchen. After happily determining that, despite being unconscious, Joe seemed to be breathing OK, she decided to cover most of his face with a crude tent made with a couple of wet bathroom towels, hopefully leaving him enough open space to breathe while reducing the amount of fumes he might be inhaling. She broke the two kitchen windows over the sink, hoping some of the toxic fumes would be replaced by fresh air. She then went outside and ran around back to check on Becker. Fortunately, he was sitting up, dazed but apparently in reasonable shape — other than his difficulty with hearing anything.

Before Ginny had a chance to check on Brown's brother, the first ambulance arrived. The paramedic, wearing a mask, surgical-like gown and gloves, made a quick initial assessment of everyone. Despite Brown's brother appearing to be in worse condition and without Ginny saying a word, the paramedic identified Joe as a police officer and selected him as the one to be transported first. "Taking care of our own," he said to Ginny as he and his partner loaded Joe onto a backboard and into the ambulance.

With lights ablaze and siren screaming, the ambulance raced to the Burn Center of Ohio State University Hospital on West 10th Avenue in downtown Columbus. En route, the paramedic and EMT riding in the rear with Joe followed their standard protocols: they left in place the cervical collar they had put around Joe's neck before they moved him in case of any neck or back damage; applied pressure dressings to stop the bleeding from any non-burn areas; removed or cut away clothing from the burn areas; gently brushed away any dry chemicals; flushed the burn areas, especially Joe's eyes, with bottled water for 20 minutes; covered both eyes with moistened sterile pads and loosely covered the other burns with dry, sterile gauze bandage; elevated Joe's feet; covered him with a blanket to help him retain his body heat; administered high-concentration oxygen and a saline drip; and frequently monitored Joe's pulse and breathing. The ambulance made the 43-mile ride south, almost entirely along I-71, in under 40 minutes.

Just after Joe's ambulance departed the scene, the chief and two additional officers from the Ashley Police Department arrived. They were followed a few minutes later by the arrival of an engine, a rescue truck and a tanker from the local fire department, a small, rural department staffed by paid firefighters and EMTs during the daytime, with volunteers supporting the paid staff on large incidents and providing coverage during the evening and night hours. Immediately realizing it was a meth lab explosion, the fire crew knew to keep their distance until the hazmat crew arrived and cleared the scene. The crew set up the standard hazmat zones and made sure that their vehicles, the police units and eventually the ambulances were all positioned upwind of the house. They did not spray water into the house because of the risk of spreading the toxic chemicals, but they did break several additional windows to further dilute the fumes. They also set up their hose lines in case a fire broke out, while keeping the surrounding grass and trees wet just in case. They got their dry-chemical fire extinguishers ready in case a small fire erupted.

Fifteen minutes later, Brown's brother and Becker were on their way to hospitals in ambulances two and three. Her brother went to the emergency room at Grady Memorial, 11 miles away in Delaware, Ohio, and Becker to Morrow County Hospital, 15 minutes away in Mt. Gilead. Twenty minutes after the third ambulance had departed, the specialty hazardous materials team from the City of Columbus Fire Department arrived.

Ginny turned Danielle over to the police, then learned where Joe had been taken. She was driven back to police headquarters. Once there, she got into Joe's car, put the red light on the dash and turned it on, squealing out of the parking lot as she raced to the hospital in Columbus. *Sure am glad Joe suggested we carry keys for each other's cars. My God, I hope he's going to be all right. I don't know what I'd do without him. Did I screw up? Should I have done more for him instead of just hanging around waiting for others to arrive? Dammit. If Joe comes out of this OK, he and I are going to take a serious refresher course in first aid. I swear!*

Ginny made better time getting to the hospital than Joe's ambulance had.

Chapter 38

Quickly parking and running into the emergency room, Ginny then began the waiting game. It was almost an hour before she was able to learn anything.

"Sorry for the delay, Detective. But your partner was being worked on until a few minutes ago, so we couldn't really get any information."

"And?"

"Seems like he was lucky. Right now he's stable. He might have suffered a concussion, but we won't know for a while."

"Can I see him?"

"Best not until tomorrow. Right now he's out, loaded up with painkillers. He has several first- and second-degree burns, and these can hurt like hell. A short while ago, because of some brain swelling, the doctors placed him in a drug-induced coma. Since you can't speak with him, we'd rather you stay out. No point in unnecessarily risking infection. With all the burns having removed a fair amount of skin, and some underlying tissue and muscle, he's very susceptible to infection. Your skin is protecting you like a big glove and, right now, his glove has a bunch of holes in it."

"Brain swelling? Coma? My God, what are you telling me? Please. I need to know!"

"Believe me, I'm telling you all we know. Time will tell us more."

"How long will he be in a coma? What if it doesn't help or he never wakes up?" asked Ginny, with tears running down her face.

"As I'm sure you know from your police work, even in a car accident we talk about it really being three collisions: the vehicle collision, the human collision into the vehicle — especially if seat belts aren't worn — and then the internal organs collision. In this case there was no vehicle collision, but the explosive force hitting the body isn't much different than a body flying into a suddenly stopped vehicle."

"And?"

"In your partner's case, fortunately there doesn't seem to be any internal bleeding from or around any of his vital organs, and his skull wasn't fractured."

"Thank heaven for little things."

"But his brain is swollen from the equivalent of a blow to his head with a bat. That's how forceful the pressure from an explosion can be. Forcing his brain into a state of rest with drugs will lessen the demand for blood, oxygen and glucose, which in turn should help decrease the swelling and pressure. This may protect the brain from secondary injury."

"How long will he be kept unconscious?"

"Hard to say. I've seen it last for as short as a few hours to as long as a week or ten days. And occasionally longer."

"What if it doesn't work?"

"The doctors have other approaches if need be. I'm sure they'll discuss these with you tomorrow."

"Can I, can I see him in the morning?"

"Depends on his condition. It's the doctor's call. I'd wait until after nine to make sure he's completed his rounds."

Ginny thanked the nurse, provided her cellphone number and asked the nurse to call her should anything change. Ginny then went to the cafeteria and had two cups of coffee while trying to settle down and gather her thoughts. She called the chief at home to bring him up to date. He was very sympathetic, and asked Ginny to call again in the morning after she spoke to the doctor (and hopefully to Joe). He also told her to call him, regardless of the time, if he could do anything to help her.

She then called the Ashley PD and was pleased to learn that Becker's injuries were all minor; they expected the hospital to release him in the morning. A day or two at home, then back at work with a few days of light duty and he should be good as new. Ginny got his cellphone number so she could call him the next day. She also made sure that Danielle was being held overnight, promising to be there at some point the next day to interview her. She was also pleased to learn that Brown's brother would be arrested upon his release from the hospital, where he was currently cuffed to his hospital bed.

Ginny next called Pete Singleton, whom Joe had worked for on his task force assignment with the DEA. She and Singleton had never met, but they both knew a lot about the other from Joe.

Ginny first told Singleton about the explosion and Joe's injuries, then informed him about the meth lab. "Sir, I'm not sure there's anything for you to do. This seemed to be a relatively minor lab, right in the kitchen. But I'm sure Joe would want me to have informed you."

"Thank you, Ginny. Glad you called. And from now on it's 'Pete,' not 'sir.'"

"Yes, si…. err, Pete."

"You're right. Not much for us to do, but it's one more piece of information we can add to our database. Sadly, more and more of the labs are small like this, and the person doing the cooking doesn't know shit from Shinola. That's why there are so many related fires and explosions.

"Unfortunately, the drug can be made from combining ingredients from cold medicine with a variety of hazardous substances, including drain cleaner, battery acid, and antifreeze, obtainable by a trip to the local hardware store. The ingredients are then cooked using common household equipment — stoves, pots and pans, coffee grinders, hand blenders, kitty litter, trash bags, and plastic bottles, jars and tubing. Plus, some easily obtained chemistry equipment like beakers, funnels, flasks and disposable plastic ware.

"Hell, there's even a new method, widely explained on social media, to make meth without any cooking at all. Mix the right ingredients in a soda bottle, close it tight, shake vigorously and you're done."

"Yikes."

"Yikes, indeed. The sad part is, if not done carefully and with the correct proportions, the thing explodes when you open the bottle and the chemicals react with the oxygen in the air."

"Not good."

"No it's not. Buy the good news in this case, if there is any good news, is that the explosion didn't cause a fire. Fires don't always happen, but they're pretty common. And, as you can imagine, who knows what we'd be looking at now if there had been a large fire there with the explosion."

"I guess you're right about it being a bit of good news buried in a bunch of bad news."

"Well said, Ginny. Hey, thank you for the call, and give the big fella my best regards when you see him tomorrow. And remind him, you and he are past due for a trip up here to join us for dinner."

"Will do. Bye now."

Before she could leave the cafeteria, Ginny got a call from Vern Jones, the detective whose desk was next to hers and Joe's.

"Ginny, you doing all right? The chief just called. Anything you need?"

"Thanks, Vern. All I need is to have Joe get better."

"Understood. Well, I'm swinging up there tomorrow to see you and, I hope, Joe. Chief already approved the time."

"Appreciate it, but, Vern, you don't have —"

"Darn right I don't have to, but I want to. I'll see you tomorrow. I'll call to find out where you're hanging out. I assume you'll find some roach motel for the next couple of days."

"Yup. That's next on my list."

"OK. Hang in there, Ginny. We're all with you. And Joe's too tough to let this mess him up. Try to get a halfway decent night's sleep."

"Will do. And thanks, Vern."

"Welcome. See you tomorrow."

Ginny left the hospital, but it took her a while to leave the parking lot. Once she got behind the wheel of Joe's car, she couldn't stop shaking. Tears running down her cheeks, body shivering uncontrollably, she sat there for about ten minutes with the car heater set on maximum. *What if he never wakes up? Or he does and he's a vegetable? Even a minor disability would drive him insane. Will he ever be the same Joe again? He doesn't deserve this. Why'd he have to be the one to race into the kitchen? Why didn't I race in first and leave him to take care of Danielle? It's not fair! Not to Joe, and, I hate to admit it, not to me. If there's no Joe, there's no me!*

After managing to get herself, first her brain and then her body, back under control, Ginny drove out of the hospital lot. She grabbed a quick dinner at a Burger King and went on a wild shopping spree at a nearby Walmart. *Guess buying all these fancy clothes and top-of-the-line cosmetics and toiletries goes quite well with my gourmet dinner.* As did the reservation she made for two nights at the Shady Maple Inn. Much to her surprise, she was fast asleep two minutes after her head hit the pillow.

Chapter 39

Ginny was up early the next morning, but she knew she couldn't do much until the rest of Ohio woke up. Her main interest was getting to Columbus and seeing Joe and his doctor, but that couldn't happen before the doctor finished his rounds.

Just before 7:30, Ginny got a call from the Ashley police chief.

"Good morning, Chief."

"Morning, Detective. Hope you slept OK."

"Better than I thought I would."

"I called to wish you a Merry Christmas."

"Oh?"

"After hazmat cleared us yesterday, we thoroughly searched the house and grounds. And the pickup in the garage."

"And?"

"We found a handgun under the front seat."

"Whose is it?"

"Ms. Brown's, we assume. Perfect fingerprint match."

"Super. Do you know the model?"

"Yup. An FN Five-seveN."

"That's fantastic. Exact type used to kill the leader of our militia group. I'd like to swing by if I may. I'll be heading to Columbus soon to see my partner in the hospital, and I can drop the gun off at the BCI in London. They've been doing bullet comparisons for us, trying to find our murder weapon."

"Sure. Come on by. We've got it nicely packaged in an evidence envelope with all the chain of custody stuff filled out. You'll just need to sign for the transfer and it's yours. Our boy denies knowing anything about it, says it's his sister's truck. His has been in the shop for repairs. Even if it was his, no crime here in Ohio. Even he can own and openly carry. What a crazy world."

"Sure is. But that's a great find for us. I'll be in shortly."

"OK. See you then. We haven't interrogated the Brown woman about the gun or anything else. Figured you'd want in on that from the get-go."

"Thanks. I want to pick up the gun, then head to the hospital in Columbus. I'll swing back later today to interview her."

Ginny stopped at a Dunkin' Donuts for breakfast, picked up the gun at the station and was on her way, first to London, and then Columbus. Despite her being very impatient to see Joe and his doctor, she first dropped the gun off at BCI. She had visions of leaving it in her trunk while she visited Joe and then returning to the car and finding the gun missing. *The sooner I turn it over to BCI, the sooner I can relax — at least about that one item.*

By 9:30, Ginny was sitting in the hospital waiting room, waiting to hopefully be allowed to see Joe and, of course, to talk with his doctor.

At about 9:45, a middle-aged man in a white coat with a stethoscope hanging around his neck walked up to Ginny.

"Good morning, I'm Dr. Amar Bhupathi. You must be Detective McFarland's partner?"

"Yes. Good morning. I'm Detective Ginny Harris, his partner and his fiancée."

"Oh. Congratulations. I didn't know." He looked around the almost-empty waiting room, sat down next to Ginny and said, "It's quiet and empty enough. We can talk here."

"Yes, please. How is he, doctor?"

"He seems to be doing well, the best we can tell. His cuts were all superficial and he suffered no back or neck injuries. Some of his burns are fairly serious, but none of them are third-degree. Breathing, blood oxygen and pulse are all in the normal range. No internal bleeding or skull fracture. Our major concern is his brain swelling."

"Is he still unconscious?"

"Yes, he's still in the medically induced coma we put him in yesterday."

"For how much longer?"

"Wish I could tell you. But we don't know. We're hoping this will reduce the swelling. It could be a few hours or days more, but it could also be weeks, or even months in some cases. The good thing is that the swelling is no longer increasing."

"What if it doesn't reduce it?"

"Let's not jump too far ahead of ourselves. If need be, we'll switch to other options."

"Such as?"

"Most likely medicines, and then if need be, surgery."

"You mean brain surgery?" asked Ginny, her eyes widening in fear.

"It's not as scary as it sounds. We perform what's called

a decompressive craniectomy, during which we remove a section of his skull to give the brain some more room, allowing the swelling to reduce. After recovery, we're usually able to reattach the section that was removed."

"Oh, my God."

"Again, Detective. That would be the very last step, only if all our other options fail."

"Do you think he'll be all right? Please tell me. Don't hold back."

"Let me assure you, we're doing everything we can. We have a top-notch team of doctors assigned to his case, and we're the most advanced trauma center in this entire part of the state."

"Can I at least see him?"

"Yes, for a few minutes. But we'll need to gown you up. No point in risking any infections. Let me just warn you in advance: he looks a lot worse than he is. He's covered with bandages and has tubes and electrical wires running everywhere. He's still in ICU, so we can have nurses keeping their eyes on him around the clock — in addition to all the monitoring equipment he's hooked up to."

"Not a problem. I'm used to seeing these things in my day-to-day work."

"Bet you are. OK, let's turn you over to the floor supervisor. She'll get you suited up and in to see him."

"Thank you, doctor. Should I check back with you about this time tomorrow?"

"Sure, that would be fine."

Ten minutes later, all gowned, masked and gloved, Ginny was led into Joe's room.

"Oh, my God! Joe! Joe!" moaned Ginny as soon as she

saw him. *Seeing a lot worse than this on the job sure is nothing like when it's someone you love. He looks almost dead. I've never seen him this pale. And the bandages are everywhere. Joe, please, please, you've got to get better. I need you. More than you can imagine. If not for yourself, do it for me. Please!!*

A few minutes later, the nurse was ushering Ginny out of the room.

"Thank you. At least I got to see him."

Ginny removed all her protective gear and stuffed it in a disposal bin. She said her good-byes to the nurse, reminding her to call if there was any change and confirming she'd be back again in the morning.

Chapter 40

Finding a strength inside herself that she hadn't thought she possessed, Ginny pulled herself together, got into Joe's car and headed to the Ashley police station. Along the way, she got a call from Jones. He was on his way to Ashley and wanted to know where he could meet up with Ginny. Ginny gave him the police station's address and said she'd wait for him before starting her interrogation of Danielle.

Ginny arrived at the station before Jones. The chief greeted her, helped her get a cup of coffee and told her to feel free to use Becker's desk since he was at home. Ginny gave the Ashley police chief an update on Joe's condition and received, in turn, an update on the medical condition of Brown's brother.

Ginny spent a half hour almost continually on the phone until Jones arrived. She called the chief and Singleton to give them updates on Joe's condition, then called Becker at home to see how he was doing, giving him her best wishes for a quick recovery while also updating him about Joe, Danielle and her brother, Zach.

Ginny got a call from Desk Sergeant O'Grady checking on how she and Joe were doing. This was followed by a call from the Columbus school district saying their attorney approved the checking of their personnel records for any teachers named Danielle. They checked and found one — but she was in her late 50s. Ginny thanked them for their efforts and for getting back to her, explaining that the age of their Danielle excluded her from interest.

At that point, Jones arrived. He and Ginny spoke for about 15 minutes over cups of coffee. Jones indicated that Denny Caruso and Steven Klein, the two other Jasper Creek detectives along with Ginny, Joe and Jones, would be arriving later that afternoon to have dinner with Ginny. Ginny tried to cancel those plans, but gave up when Jones insisted that they truly wanted to, saying they'd be very upset and hurt if she refused. *Sadly, it takes disasters like this to really know who your good friends are.*

Jones drove a few blocks away and returned with a pizza for Ginny and him to share. He agreed to stay while Ginny interrogated Danielle so that, as Ginny felt would be likely, he could take Danielle back to Jasper Creek and book her for Davis' murder.

Feeling better after having eaten, Ginny went into the interview room where Danielle had been sitting for almost an hour. Jones joined her as a witness.

Turning on Jones' recorder, Ginny gave the normal preamble of the who, where and when of the session.

"Good afternoon, Danielle. Sorry I kept you waiting. This is Detective Jones, one of my colleagues from Jasper Creek."

"Hello."

"Before we start, I want to read you your Miranda rights."

"OK."

Ginny took a worn, folded piece of paper out of her notebook, unfolded it and read Danielle her rights.

"Got it. I'm good to go."

"Are you sure you don't want an attorney? You're entitled to one. The state will pay for one if you can't afford it. He or she can be very helpful in advising you, especially regarding what to say or not say. Remember, whatever you do say, we can present it in court."

"Yeah, I know. I knew that even before you read the statement. Like I said, I'm good to go."

"OK, then. Let's get started."

"Can you first just tell me about my brother?"

"Sure, the little I know. He's in one of the local hospitals. Some serious second- and third-degree chemical burns from his waist to his head. Seems like the kitchen counter protected most of his lower body from major burns. Also cuts from broken glass and metal fragments, but none of them seemed to be life-threatening. The burns will leave several mean-looking scars and may have caused permanent nerve and muscle damage, some of which may limit movement of his arms and hands and cause some fine motor skill problems with his hands and fingers. They think he probably has some long-term respiratory issues, from working in his lab for who knows how long, or from the toxic fumes after the explosion, or most likely, from both. The doctors will know more over time. As soon as he's released by the hospital, and I don't know when that might be, he'll be arrested by the Ashley police for his meth lab."

"Figured as much. Just so you know, I had nothing to do with that. Didn't even know it existed 'til I got there."

"That's between you and the Ashley police. The lab was in their territory, so they're totally handling that."

"So what are you two focused on?"

"Murder."

"Murder? Of who? When? Why are you talking to me?"

"Danielle, we can do this the easy way or the hard way. Your choice, but, either way, we're going to do it."

"Do what?"

"Arrest, indict and then convict you."

"Of?"

"Murder. Of Mark Davis."

"Mark?" said Danielle as she leaned towards Ginny with both her palms on the table between them, and her eyes wide open with disbelief. What are you saying? He's dead? Someone killed him? Are you sure?"

"We'll get to that. You do know him, I gather."

"Yeah, sure. Very well. In fact, we almost got married."

"Oh?"

"That's right. We'd been seeing each other for a couple of years. Started off just as friends, then gradually got more serious and romantic-like."

"Please tell us more."

"He lived in Jasper Creek, so we didn't see each other every day, or even every week. After a while, he started staying at my place for a couple of days whenever he could. At first, I had my mom take the two boys when Mark visited. Our relationship got increasingly personal and intimate."

"You mean sex?"

"Yeah, including sex. Hope I'm not embarrassing you. But I am an adult, you know.

"We started talking about our relationship possibly growing into something permanent. He even got to know the boys. He was really good with them, and they loved it. And him. They even started calling him 'Daddy.'"

"How come he didn't spend more time with you and your children? Just short visits every month or so, as I understand it."

"Yeah. That was disappointing. But he lived in Jasper Creek and had other responsibilities there."

"Oh? Do you know what those responsibilities were?"

"If you're tiptoeing around his weird family setup and his being a member, in fact the leader, of a militia group, you don't have to."

"So you know about all that?"

"Yeah. Once we started getting serious, Mark told me everything. At first, I couldn't believe it. Then I went from disbelief to not understanding. I never did get comfortable with the idea of multiple wives sharing him. Any more than I did with what I always considered those militia groups to be — crazy, conspiracy-theory-believing white nationalist racists."

"So how come you were ready to marry him and join the family and the group?"

"Still asking myself the same thing. Blind love, I guess. Or maybe I had some crazy notion that I could save him, or us, from that whole mess."

"So what happened?"

"I still don't know. The last time he visited, almost a month ago, he was different. Cold and reserved. Told me something came up and we would never be able to get married. He never would tell me why, no matter how many times I asked. How could he do that to me? And to the boys? They've already been through so much with my first husband just up and leaving. Never sees them, no child support, no nothing."

"I want to ask you what happened next. But first I need to tell you something important."

"OK. Tell me."

"We found the gun. With your prints all over it. And the state Bureau of Criminal Investigation has confirmed it's the gun that killed Mark Davis. The bullets are a perfect match." *Joe's better at lying to suspects than I am, but I've gotten pretty good at it just by watching him. And it is often damn effective.*

Danielle opened her mouth to protest or argue something, but no sound came out.

"Danielle, the police here thoroughly examined your pickup. They found traces of Mark's blood and other signs of Mark's presence."

"Of course they did. I used to pick Mark up and drop him off. We'd meet along an old logging road near where he lived. Could only drive partway in, it was that overgrown. But at my end, it met up with Hwy 42. Mark didn't have a car, so I drove him to my place and then back home, or actually back to that logging road, each time. I'm sure his fingerprints and DNA are all over inside the truck, and maybe even drops of blood from a shaving cut."

"OK. But back to the gun. Do you admit it's yours?"

"No. Honest. It isn't. It's Mark's gun. He used to take it out of its holster and lay it on the seat between us, so he could sit more comfortably in my truck."

"So what happened?"

"Whaddaya mean?"

"Danielle, don't start playing stupid now. That gun was definitely the one used to kill Mr. Davis. Your fingerprints are all over it. The police found the gun in your truck, along with Mr. Davis' blood. Time to own up to what you did. Lying about it will only make things worse for you."

Danielle defiantly stared silently at Ginny for a minute. Then, all of a sudden, she hunched over and started to cry.

"I don't know. I just lost it. Driving him back home on his last visit, we got into a big row about why he was backing out of us getting married. He wouldn't tell me shit. Without thinking, I pulled over to the side of the road, put it in park, and picked up his gun. The rest is history, as they say."

"So you admit to killing him?"

"Hell, yes. And I'm not sorry. I'd do it again if I had the chance."

"Then what did you do?"

"Drove to our regular meeting spot. Along that logging road, where you couldn't drive any further. I grabbed the blanket I kept in the back seat and laid it on the ground outside his car door. I pulled him out of the truck, which wasn't easy, laid him best I could on the blanket, folded the edges of the blanket over him and then dragged him a short ways into the woods. I was totally exhausted and drenched with sweat by then. I climbed back in the truck and drove home."

"Anything else?"

"Nope."

"One more question. Why'd you leave the gun in your truck? You knew it could prove that you were his killer."

"I planned to wipe it clean and leave it with his body. But I got so rattled pulling his body out of my truck into the woods that I completely forgot. I only realized it was still in the truck when I was about halfway back home. I was afraid to dump it anyplace, so I stuffed it under the front seat. Figured it was safe there until I decided what to do with it."

"That it?"

"Yup, you got the whole story. Hope you're happy now."

"Almost. Just need you to write out what you told us, in as much detail as possible, and sign and date it. Then I'll be happy."

Twenty-five minutes later, Danielle's statement was written, signed and dated, and witnessed by Jones. Ginny officially arrested her, and Jones helped her get into the back seat of his car for the drive to Jasper Creek, where she'd be processed and locked in a cell overnight. Ginny gave the recording and written statement to Jones, asking him to be sure to get it to Larkin in the prosecutor's office.

After Jones left for Jasper Creek, Ginny called Larkin and brought her up to speed. She, of course, sent her best wishes for Joe and promised to get right on Danielle's indictment first thing in the morning.

Ginny headed back to her hotel. She asked about decent local restaurants, then called Caruso and told him she'd meet him and Klein at the Firehouse Tavern, a 15-minute drive away in Sunbury, about 6:30. Ginny then luxuriated in a long, hot shower, despite the fact that the water flow wasn't much more than a steady drip.

Dinner was decent and the company was great. They left the restaurant about 8:30, Ginny going to her hotel room and the two detectives returning to their homes, one in Jasper Creek and the other in a neighboring town.

Chapter 41

Ginny was again up early the next day. Before heading for breakfast and the hospital, she checked out of the hotel. *Enough camping out in this joint. I hope and pray I can go home soon, bringing Joe with me. In the meantime, I'll get a room in Columbus near the hospital. There's nothing to keep me here in Ashley.*

Following the desk clerk's recommendation, Ginny drove to the Dari Barn for breakfast. She hadn't realized how hungry she was until she started digging into her eggs, bacon and pancakes Thursday special.

She then drove to Columbus and checked into the Days Inn on East 17th Avenue, about two miles from the hospital. As her room wouldn't be available until later that morning, Ginny sat in the breakfast area, making a few calls over two cups of hot coffee. *More pleasant waiting here than in the hospital. I mean it's a decent place, but it is a hospital. And one where Joe is lying in a coma.*

Ginny called the Ashley police chief to let him know that she was changing hotels to Columbus. The chief wished her and Joe well and asked Ginny to call their local prosecutor, as he wanted her testimony for the eventual trial of Brown's brother. Ginny said she'd be happy to, writing down the prosecutor's name and phone number. Ginny reminded the chief to send her a copy of any fingerprints and whatever else the crime scene crew found in Danielle's pickup truck.

Ginny then called Becker and was pleased to learn that he'd be heading back into the station later that day, though he would, of course, be limited to light duty probably through the weekend. Best wishes were extended in both directions, and the call ended with promises to stay in touch.

Ginny next called and spoke with the prosecutor in Ashley. She agreed to be in his office at four o'clock that afternoon to discuss what she knew and had seen of the meth lab, forewarning him that she didn't actually see the lab or the defendant operating it as she was still outside when it exploded. The prosecutor wanted to speak with her anyhow, just to make sure he left no hanging loose ends.

It was finally late enough to head to the hospital. Ginny again met with Dr. Bhupathi.

"How is he, doctor? Any improvement?"

"No, not yet. But don't be alarmed. This is often a slow and rather gradual process. The good news is that he's stable, and all his vital signs remain normal."

"But what if—"

"I'll say it again, let's not get ahead of ourselves. During the night, we began also administering Mannitol, a medicine to eliminate some of the fluid building up in his brain."

"Fluid? Is this a new problem?"

"No, it's fairly common among trauma victims. Fluid tends to build up around any injury to the body. His brain fluid wasn't reducing on its own, so we started this. Eliminating some fluid will help reduce the swelling, thereby reducing the pressure the skull exerts on the brain. We're also keeping him under controlled hyperventilation, as the extra oxygen also often helps reduce the swelling."

"But what if none of this works?"

"There are several additional medicines we can try. And, as a last resort, there's still the surgery option. But we're a long way from that."

"How panicked should I be?"

"I'd suggest concern but not panic. He's getting the best care possible. The key right now is to minimize the risk of this leading to a stroke. Or to any permanent brain damage, which could seriously affect things like his memory, speech or motor movements."

"When do you think we'll know more — for better or worse?"

"I wish I could say. It could be a day or a week. Sometimes, it's months. But I don't think that will be the case here. To you, his condition must seem horrendous. But let me assure you, we've seen many, many worse cases, with a large portion of them eventually resulting in full or virtually full recovery."

"I guess for now, we just wait. Until you say otherwise, I'll be back here every morning."

"That'd be fine. But, if you prefer, you could just check in by phone every day until something changes."

"Thank you. But no. I feel like I have to be here every day."

"That's not a problem. As you wish."

Back in the car, Ginny started weeping, her whole body trembling. *He said Joe could be like this forever. Or maybe even worse, awake but like a zombie. He couldn't even guess when we'd see any improvement. Is this going to be Joe's and my life? For how long? Forever? Wonder if Joe knows what's going on, or if he's just lying there like a lifeless pile of skin and bones and stuff. Sure hope he doesn't know anything. That'd be enough to kill him. I now know what they mean when they say, 'A single moment can dramatically change your whole life.'*

It took almost ten minutes until Ginny cried herself dry and got herself under control. She started the car and headed for Jasper Creek, knowing she had to be back in Ashley at four to meet with the prosecutor.

About one-third of the way to Jasper Creek, Ginny got a call from the coroner. After asking about Joe and offering his best wishes, he told Ginny that Davis' body was ready for release, but he wanted to check with Ginny before releasing it. At Ginny and Joe's request, he had intentionally delayed completing the autopsy as long as he could. But it was starting to get awkward and obvious. Ginny thanked him for checking, then explained that, since they had a signed confession from the murderer, the body could be released. The coroner said he'd call Turley and make the necessary arrangements.

Ginny's first stop was Joe's house, where she enjoyed a long, hot shower, picked a change of clothes and packed enough clothes to be able to spend up to a week in Columbus. After hesitating, not knowing whether it would bring good luck or be a jinx, she also packed a full set of clothes for Joe, hoping it would be what he'd wear when he soon came home. *Please, God, let it be soon and let him be totally recovered.* She parked Joe's car in the garage and left in hers.

Chapter 42

While driving to the station, Ginny called Larkin in the prosecutor's office. After a few minutes talking about how Joe was doing and how Ginny was holding up, Larkin agreed to see Ginny right away to take her statement and talk through the next steps with Danielle. Ginny parked in the PD parking lot and walked over to Larkin's office.

"Well done with the confession, Ginny. Seems to cover all the bases and follow all the procedures."

"Thanks. So, what's next?"

"That confession makes things a lot simpler and faster."

"That's good."

"First thing, when we're done, you should formally charge her with murder. We'll fill out your official complaint before you go, and I'll immediately file it with the court. I can schedule the initial hearing quickly, probably for some time tomorrow. The indictment will come right after that, followed pretty quickly by her arraignment, hopefully early next week. That's when she'll be assigned a court-appointed attorney — unless she has or wants to hire her own."

"Then the real fun begins."

"Correct. You and I should meet with her and her attorney to share evidence with each other. We don't need much more than her confession. They can try to argue she gave it while confused and over-stressed, didn't yet have an attorney, and so on. But we're on reasonably solid ground there."

"One thing I should mention, Barbara. I don't think it's a problem, but I don't want you to get hit with any surprises. While I was interrogating her and getting her confession, I lied to her. Told her BCI checked the gun that was covered with her fingerprints and confirmed it was the murder weapon. Also told her we found fingerprints and traces of the vic's blood in her pickup truck."

"Not a problem. As you well know, lying to a suspect during an interrogation is legal. And you presumably did it while the tape was running, so you clearly weren't trying to hide it."

"Correct."

"Question is, do we want to offer a deal to make this quick, cheap and risk-free?"

"I don't know. What're the options?"

"I need to clear it with the prosecutor, but he should be fine with it. If they plead not guilty, she's looking at 15 to life. If she pleads guilty, I'd be willing to drop the charges to voluntary manslaughter, you know, committed under sudden passion or fit of rage. That would lower the prison term to something in the eight-to-15-year time frame, with early parole for good behavior possible."

"Man, she'd be nuts not to plead."

"That's my intent. But don't be surprised if she pleads not guilty. I've seen plenty of nuts in my time on this job."

"More for the sake of her kids than anything else, I hope she's not stupid. They've already had their father desert them and then the victim, who was about to be dad number two, back out. They don't need to lose their mother forever also."

"That'll be her call. Gimme a couple of minutes to get Charles' blessing, then we can put your complaint together."

Larkin left her office and was back in ten minutes. As she walked back in, she gave Ginny a thumbs up and a big smile. "All set. Porter's on board with the plea offer."

Larkin typed up Ginny's complaint, and Ginny — plus a witness from the prosecutor's office — signed it. Larkin left to file it with the court and Ginny walked back to the station.

Ginny spent a few minutes with the chief, bringing him up to date on the case and talking about Joe.

"Don't even think about it, Ginny. You take as much time as you need. I fully understand you wanting to be at the hospital every day, and it's crazy to do the daily commute from here. Let's hope Joe improves soon so you can get him back home."

"Thanks for your understanding and support, Chief. Also, want you to know the whole department's been fantastic."

"I know it, and wouldn't expect anything less."

"OK. Off to say hello to everyone. Then time to charge Danielle. Then I've got to scoot back to Ashley for a session with the prosecutor there. Wants my statement about the brother and his meth lab, even though I didn't actually see anything. He just wants to be super thorough."

"Go for it. And don't forget to take care of yourself as you go through all this."

"Will do. Thanks, Chief."

Ginny spent a few minutes in the bullpen, chatting with everyone, answering their questions and getting their best wishes for Joe's recovery.

She then briefly met with Danielle in one of the interrogation rooms. Jones was with Ginny, as he'd be acting as Ginny's assistant here in Jasper Creek when things needed to be done and she was in Columbus.

Ginny told Danielle she was being charged with the murder of Mark Davis, and that she would be processed and kept locked up at least until her initial court hearing. Danielle had no response, except for saying, "I guess so," when Ginny asked if she wanted the court to appoint a lawyer.

As Ginny was wrapping up, Danielle asked, "May I ask one question and one favor?"

"Sure. But I need to hear each before deciding whether to answer or do either."

"The question is about my brother. How's he doing, and what will happen to him?"

"I know he's still in the hospital. He's off the critical list, but has severe burns and will have some permanent scarring. I don't know much about the criminal case 'cause that's being handled in Ashley, but I'm sure he's looking at several years in prison. Operating a meth lab is pretty big stuff."

"Stupid bastard. I told him to stop soon as I got there and saw it in the kitchen.

The favor is to call my mother. Tell her what's going on with my brother and with me. Tell her she'll need to keep the kids for now — and she should tell them I love them."

"Yes, I can do that. I've got her number from before. I'll call her while I'm driving back to Ashley."

"Thank you."

Ginny headed back to the car and left for Ashley. Jones led Danielle to be processed, then returned her to her cell.

On the way back to Ashley, Ginny spoke with Danielle's mother. She had heard about the explosion and spoken with her son's lawyer, but she was still having trouble getting much information about her daughter. Ginny filled her in without going into much detail and relayed her daughter's message. Her mother, of course, was terribly upset when she heard about the murder accusation, but she thanked Ginny for calling her.

Ginny then tried to call Turley at the militia compound to talk about the release of Davis' body, her desire to attend the local memorial service and to give Turley permission for him and any in his group to return to Utah for the funeral and burial. All she got was no answer and no chance to leave a message. She waited 15 minutes and tried again, but got the same result.

Ginny realized she hadn't had lunch. She was starving, but there was no way she could stop for even a drive-thru burger without being late for her four o'clock appointment.

Ginny made it to the prosecutor's office with a full five minutes to spare.

The meeting lasted about a half hour. Ginny described how she was outside until after the explosion. She then went in, saw the smashed glass containers and other equipment and supplies, as well as Joe and Brown's brother, Zach Fielding, lying on the floor. She immediately knew it was a meth lab, but she didn't actually see it being used. She explained how her priority was the people, especially Joe. They agreed Joe probably saw a lot more than Ginny did, and that he would be the preferred witness —assuming, of course, that he recovered sufficiently in time for the trial and hadn't blocked the whole episode out of his mind. *Jesus, can you be any less caring or sympathetic? This is my partner and my fiancée. He's not just some random witness off the street. Hate to burst your bubble, but I care a hell of a lot more about Joe than I do about your damn trial.*

Ginny agreed to return if needed for a deposition, or as a witness at the trial. She couldn't wait to get out of there.

She left, drove to Columbus, settled into her room at the Days Inn, showered and went for dinner at Yin Yue, a Chinese restaurant a few miles away that the hotel desk clerk had recommended. Ginny found the food tasty and the bottle of Tsingtao beer refreshing. She was back in her hotel room before eight. Waking up at two AM with the TV still on, she turned off the TV, rolled over and was immediately back asleep.

Chapter 43

The next morning, Ginny was back at the hospital a little before nine.

It turned out to be Dr. Bhupathi's day off, so Ginny met with one of his colleagues. The doctor indicated there was still no change in Joe's swelling, but the burns were healing nicely.

"It will be Dr. Bhupathi's call, but I plan to recommend to him that we get a bit more aggressive with the treatment."

With a tremor in her voice, Ginny asked, "Are you talking surgery?"

"No, not at this point. I plan to recommend a second medicine, as well as a series of hyperbaric treatments."

"You mean like they give divers suffering from the bends?"

"It's the same equipment, but the treatment is in short bursts, nothing like what a diver who rose to the surface too quickly has to go through. There's significant evidence, although it's still considered somewhat experimental, that the extra oxygen absorption helps reduce the swelling. Coincidentally, oxygen will also help with the healing of his burns."

"Is it, is it dangerous?"

"No, not so long as we properly control the pressure and time. Which we, of course, will do."

"How quickly would you expect to see improvement? If there is any."

"Hard to say. Probably a few days, but, almost surely, within a week."

"I hope Dr. Bhupathi takes your recommendations."

"I'm pretty sure he will. We've taken similar actions in other cases, and have already talked about these things informally in regard to this situation."

"Well, thank you, doctor. You've given me a few things to help me be hopeful."

"Good. At his point, there's no reason for you to not be hopeful."

With the doctor's permission, after again donning gown, mask and gloves, Ginny spent about 15 minutes in Joe's room, sitting next to the bed without touching him and talking to him as if he were just lying down to rest. She brought him up to date on the case, told him about her move to a nearby hotel, let him know how supportive the whole department had been and, of course, how badly she needed him to recover.

With little to do except wait for the next morning to speak with Dr. Bhupathi, Ginny returned to her hotel room and made a few phone calls.

She called Detective Jones to tell him and, through him, the whole department about Joe's current condition and the probable additional treatments.

"That's encouraging news. Thanks for letting me know. I'll share it with the troops. I was about to call you anyhow. Joe got another fax from the BCI."

"And?"

"That last gun you gave them definitely is the murder weapon. Virtually one hundred percent perfect match. They also pulled several prints off the gun. From two people. Their report contains a link to their database with the prints."

"Super. Please send a copy of the fax to Barbara Larkin and put the original in the inbox on my desk. Unless Danielle tries to deny her confession, we shouldn't need this confirmation. But it's worth having just in case she gets some aggressive, foolish lawyer who convinces her to switch her plea to not guilty. Since I already told Danielle the gun matched when I lied to her during the interrogation, it's nice that my lie actually came true. I need to call Larkin today anyhow, so I'll close the loop with her about the fax. Thanks."

A few more minutes talking about Joe, with Jones again offering to help Ginny any way possible, and the call ended.

Just as Ginny was getting ready to call Larkin, the Ashley PD Chief called. After asking how Joe and Ginny were doing and telling Ginny that Becker was back in the station on light duty and seemed to be doing fine, he got to the real purpose of his call.

"Finally got the report from the crime scene folks here. Turns out her pickup was a goldmine. They got all kinds of fingerprints and some blood. Their report took an extra day, as they coordinated their findings with your techies to compare to your victim's fingerprints and DNA. And they got matches on both."

"That's good news. Please be sure to send me a copy of their written report and whatever you find from the prints. We've got her confession, but this is good to have in case she changes her plea."

The chief agreed and the call ended.

Unbelievable. Joe would get a real kick out of this. How often are we trying to get strong, tangible evidence from forensics, and we either have to wait forever for it or we never get it? Now it's raining down on us — the ballistics and the blood in the truck — and we may never need it if she's smart enough to stick with her guilty plea. Go figger!

Ginny took an hour or so to walk around a little bit of Columbus. It was chilly and windy, but the fresh air made her feel better, and just looking around helped her take her mind off Joe for a few minutes. She found a café with a delightful fruit and salad buffet. Ginny loaded her plate, topped it with oil, vinegar and crumbled blue cheese, and was overjoyed to have an enjoyable and healthy lunch for a change.

Back in her hotel room just before 1:30, she called Larkin in the prosecutor's office.

They first spoke about Joe, then the BCI gun and Ashley crime scene reports.

"One more thing, Barbara."

"Go for it."

"The vic's body is being released to his widow, or to the militia or whatever. They're planning to have him cremated and hold a local memorial service here. Then it goes to Utah, where the group is headquartered, for a full-blown Mormon funeral and burial."

"Sounds fine to me."

"Couple of things."

"Oh?"

"We haven't talked about it, but should we consider obstruction of justice charges against Aaron Turley, the acting leader of the group? He's the one who found the body and ordered one of the militia members to secretly bury it without telling anyone. Then he lied to Joe and me, saying he didn't know where Davis had gone."

"Definitely sounds like obstruction."

"With Brown's confession, I was ready to tell Turley he was free to go to Utah for the funeral. But given his obstruction, should we and can we prevent him from going there? Or arrest him and get heavy bail set? Or extradite him back here if he does go and doesn't return?"

"Hold on, Ginny. You do know we're only talking a second-degree misdemeanor. Probably 90 days. At most. A lot of trouble for that. As for a possible extradition, we'd never pay to transport him back here for something like that, even if Utah would agree to extradite for a lousy misdemeanor."

"Damn."

"Guess I should be saying something like 'we have to pick our battles,' but I totally understand how you feel."

"One more thing, then I'll let you go. Same goes for his three wives. They're not suspects in this, but if you want their official statements about how they changed Davis' mind about marrying the defendant, we should get them before they head for Utah. Just in case they decide not to return here."

"Good point. Why don't you see if you can set it up? We should interview them as soon as we can, depending on when they might head to Utah. I could even join you this weekend if need be."

"OK, I'll see what I can do. If I can't reach Turley by phone today, I'll be at their front gate tomorrow morning. I'll let you know what I learn."

"Sounds like a plan. Speak soon."

"Bye."

Ginny tried Turley's phone again, but got no answer. She decided to head over to the group's compound in the morning, right after her hospital visit.

Chapter 44

Ginny was pleased by her morning talk with Dr. Bhupathi. Although there was no observable change in Joe's condition, her hopes increased when Bhupathi indicated he was going to institute the second medication and the hyperbaric sessions.

After a quick hello to the still-unconscious Joe, Ginny was on her way to the FRAP compound in Jasper Creek. Although a few miles out of the way, she first went to the station and took all the guns that had been picked up at the BCI to her car. Davis' gun, the murder weapon, was the only one still at the BCI.

Ginny drove directly to the militia compound gate. "I don't give a damn how busy he is," said Ginny to the guard at the gate. "Tell him he's got ten minutes to see me, here or in his office, or I'll have him so legally tied in knots that he won't be able to make it to Salt Lake to attend Mr. Davis' funeral. And tell him I really mean it."

Ten minutes later, Ginny was escorted into Turley's office, where Turley sat glowering behind his desk.

"Didn't expect to see you. Where's your partner? I mostly dealt directly with him."

"He's tied up elsewhere. I'm who you get."

"OK, what's this about?"

"Few things. First, here are the guns we had collected. As promised, we're returning all that we collected here."

She had Turley sign a receipt for the guns, which she then turned over to him. "Secondly, I want to meet with you and Mr. Davis' three wives together. Bring you all up to date on the case, and I don't want to have to say it more than once. Then, I'll be joined by the assistant prosecutor on this case. We'll want to speak with each of the women separately, then with you."

"Prosecuting att—"

"Don't worry. She's here as a witness, and to be sure I do everything correctly and properly. At this point, she's not here to be prosecuting any of you."

"OK. Let's get this over with. We've got lots to do, what with Mark's body finally being released to us."

"Let's go then. I'm not holding you up."

While Turley went to get the three widows, Ginny called Larkin and told her to head right out for the compound. She gave her directions and told her use Turley's name and then wait outside their gate until she was invited in.

"Wow, you didn't waste much time. I'm on my way in five minutes. Never would have guessed I'd be spending one of my Saturdays inside a militia compound."

Ginny was soon talking to Turley and the three widows. "Want to bring you all up to date. We've made some excellent progress on the case. In fact, we have a signed confession."

"Fantastic," said Abigail Davis. "Who's the bastard who killed Mark?"

"Let me preface this by pointing out that the person is a defendant and is innocent until found guilty in court. Even though we have a confession. Defendants often change their plea from guilty to not guilty. We don't expect that here, but you never know. The other thing is that the 'bastard' is a 'bitch.'"

"Huh?" said almost everyone in the room.

"The alleged, sorry but I have to say alleged for now, murderer is Danielle, the lady who almost became wife number four."

Surprise was evident on everyone's face, and questions started flying at Ginny. "Are you sure?" "Why?" "When?"

"I'd rather not get into all those details now. What I do want, however, is to have one of our prosecutors and me meet with you three, one at a time, and get detailed statements about Mr. Davis being ready to marry her until you three changed his mind."

"Are we somehow suspects?"

"No, not at all. We believe his breaking off their planned marriage was her motivation. We want to have your official statements just in case she decides to retract her confession and plead not guilty."

"Makes sense," said Lynn Thatcher, wife number two.

"Our prosecutor, name of Barbara Larkin, should be here within the hour. Mr. Turley, would you please arrange for your guards to let her in and lead her here when she arrives?"

"Sure. And you can use this office for the one-on-ones."

"Thank you. And when we're finished, we'd like to spend a few minutes with you."

"Whatever," said Turley as he stood up and left the room, as did the three women a minute later.

Larkin walked into the office about 40 minutes later. She and Ginny interviewed each of the three wives, one at a time, capturing the entire process on tape. All three women gave almost identical stories as to how they learned about — and then changed Davis' mind about — adding Danielle to the family. In addition, Davis and Thatcher indicated they planned to briefly return to Utah for the funeral, but Hansen, wife number three, planned to remain in Ohio to take care of all their children.

Other than obstruction by withholding what they knew of Davis' final visit to Danielle, these women did nothing illegal. I sure don't agree with their lifestyle choices, but that's neither here nor there. Nonetheless, they should know, contrary to what they believe, that Davis was having sex with Danielle. Might help wake them up to the true nature of their "blissful" polygamous marriage arrangement.

Ginny had the three women brought back in for a few minutes. "Thank you for your statements. There is one other thing that you should know."

"Oh?" said two of the wives simultaneously.

"Despite you being sure that Mr. Davis would not have had sexual relations outside of marriage, you need to know that he and Danielle were having sex together for several months — most likely, in fact, for more than a year."

"No, I don't believe it. It can't be," said Abigail. "How do you know?"

"Danielle told us, as part of her confession. And she'd have no reason to lie about this."

"But—"

"Let's not get into a debate about this. It's true. If nothing else, knowing this might help you ladies open your eyes and evaluate your relationships more clearly. They're not all perfect, utopian situations. I urge all three of you to spend some serious time really thinking this through."

Ginny could feel her thoughts switching to her own pain and Joe's condition, but she quickly cut off that train of thought before she started tearing up in front of everyone.

The women left and Ginny and Larkin then spent a few minutes with Turley. He confirmed that they were not allowing any non-militia members at the local memorial service, but Ginny and Joe could, if they wished, attend the funeral in Utah, as that was going to be held in a Mormon chapel off the militia's property and would be open to non-militia members as well as non-Mormons. Ginny thanked him, but indicated it was unlikely that either she or Joe would travel to Utah for that.

"One other thing, Mr. Turley," said Ginny.

"Yes?"

"We want you to know that you will be charged with obstruction of justice in the murder of Mark Davis."

"Huh? What are you talking about?"

"You knew about Mr. Davis' murder and you lied to us, saying you had no idea where he was, leaving everyone to think he was still on one of his mysterious trips."

"What? How'd you…"

"You were the first one to know about him. You knew where his body was and that he was shot in the head. And wrapped in a blanket. And you ordered him to be buried out there."

"Jesus, you got it all wrong."

"You do admit you knew he was dead while playing

dumb to all your fellow militia members, not to mention to the police?"

"Yeah, but that was 'cause I sorta froze. And I didn't want to panic anybody."

"How'd you become the first to know?"

"I was back in that area hunting deer. Every year I usually snag a few, and we get a lot of good eating out of that. So I was walking back there, looking for deer tracks when I came across Mark's body. In fact, I damn near tripped over it."

"Why didn't you report it?"

Turley's jaw clenched, then released. "Dunno. Just didn't know what to do, so I didn't do anything. I'm sure not in the habit of reporting stuff to the police."

"I also suspect," said Ginny, "that you didn't report it so you could remain the acting leader. Once they knew Davis was dead, they would have been likely to send a new leader here from Utah."

"That never would.... Oh, never mind."

"Mr. Turley," asked Larkin, "am I correct in assuming you'll be going to Utah for the funeral?"

"Yes, of course. Mark was my friend. And I need to represent this whole group at the funeral."

"How can we be sure you'll return to face the charges?"

"'Cause I will. I have responsibilities to the group here."

"Let me leave you with something to think about. These charges are relatively minor in the scheme of things and carry a very light sentence. And, if you're thinking it, you're right — Ohio would never pay to have you extradited back here from Utah for such minor charges. But we do still have a way to ensure your return."

"OK?"

"Just imagine if Davis' uncle, the big chief, were to learn how you kept his nephew's death a secret and that you were the one responsible for him being buried in the ground like you might bury your pet parakeet."

"You wouldn't."

"I strongly suggest you might not want to test that theory."

She's pretty damn quick on her feet, thought Ginny. *Good for her, giving him that warning about Davis' uncle. Probably put the fear of God in him.*

"That's it, Mr. Turley. We're on our way. Have a nice day," said Ginny.

Ginny and Larkin drove out of the gate, then stopped to talk. They agreed to meet downtown, a late lunch for Ginny and an afternoon snack and drink for Larkin.

While enjoying their social hour, Ginny received a phone call. After the short call, she turned to Larkin. "OK, one more nail in the coffin. The prints on Davis' gun that were found in Danielle's truck turned out to be Davis' and, no surprise, Danielle's. Man, I hope you have a filing cabinet for all the great evidence we're giving you," said Ginny with a smile.

"Don't worry, I'll make room," said Larkin as she signaled the waitress for another round of drinks.

Chapter 45

Ginny was back at the hospital Sunday morning. *Just like cops, this is a seven-day-a-week operation. No such thing as weekends and holidays. Damn good thing — don't think I'd make it through a day without checking in on Joe. Just wish we'd see some damn progress already. These new therapies better work. Please, God.*

Dr. Bhupathi didn't seem discouraged by the lack of progress. He said they had to give the new therapies a few days to see if they helped. That made Ginny feel only slightly better.

Back in her hotel room, reading the local Sunday paper over a cup of coffee, Ginny got a call from the Jasper Creek dispatcher.

"Ginny, got a call from a Rudy Musser. Sounded very agitated. Said he needed to talk to Joe or you immediately. Wouldn't tell me what it was about. I took his number and said I'd get the message to you."

"That's it?"

"Yup, that's it."

"OK, I'll call him. I know who he is. Give me the number he left."

Ginny got the number, hung up and called Musser.

"Good morning, Mr. Musser. This is Detective Harris. Understand you want to talk to my partner or me."

"Damn right. What did you tell him?"

"Hold on. Slow down. Who do you think we told anything to?"

"Turley. He came barging in here last night and dragged me outside for a 'little talk.' Said I told you about him having me bury Mark, and that I'd live to regret having done that. You said you'd try to keep it secret."

"We didn't mention you at all to Turley. I did tell him he's going to be charged for obstruction of justice for lying about not knowing where Mr. Davis was, and for arranging for him to be secretly buried. He must of figured out that information could only have come from you."

"Shit. Whatcha expect? Now what do I do?"

"That's up to you. We could warn him to leave you alone. We could even provide you with protection for a while, but not forever. To be perfectly honest, it depends on how wedded you are to the militia way of life. Clearly the safest thing would be to just disappear, move someplace far from here and turn your back on it all. Doubt they'd spend too much time searching all over the country for you."

"Yeah. That's what I've been thinking all night."

"Good. Not only would that be the safest course for you, it's also the one that would let you get back to living a normal life. You really don't need all that militia BS and conspiracy craziness. I've got contacts with lawyers and psychologists who've helped others make moves like that. Pro bono, at no charge. Please call me whenever you'd like me to put you in touch with them. They're very good at what they do."

"Well, OK. Thanks."

"Can I ask you, before you leave, to give us a formal statement about what Turley had you do?"

"That some kind of sick joke? You gotta be kidding. You can ask all you want, but I'm not saying anything else. And I'm sure as hell not hanging around waiting for you."

"Mr. Musser, I really...."

Ginny stopped talking when she heard the dial tone kick in.

Can't really blame him. He's panicked. I could stop him from leaving or find him if he does, but I'm not going to. Even though I didn't give Turley his name, I might as well have. Wouldn't have taken a genius to figure out it had to be Musser who told us. No point risking his life to get Turley on a misdemeanor. Good luck, Rudy. Vaya con Dios!

Chapter 46

The next three months were not Ginny's best. Her mood fluctuated from sadness bordering on depression to worry to numbness, all of which were exacerbated by lack of sleep. Not a night went by in which Ginny wasn't awake and tossing and turning for at least a couple of hours, worrying about Joe and the rest of their lives together.

The holiday season was extremely painful for Ginny. *Damn, this holiday season is worse than I thought it would be. Although we always had Thanksgiving dinner at home with just the two of us, we really enjoyed the day. Watching the parade on TV, followed by tons of football and then a huge dinner of turkey with all the trimmings. We always ate way too much, then swore to never again eat that much. A solid week of leftovers extended Thanksgiving Day into Thanksgiving Week. We also enjoyed Christmas, and the days leading up to it. Our decorations consisted of only a small artificial tree, but we enjoyed looking at the decorations on all the other houses and the stores downtown. It always seemed like such a joyous time of year. But not this year. I had to repeatedly force myself not to be jealous and get upset with everyone being thankful for everything and so full of joy. Hell, what happened to Joe wasn't their fault.*

New Years was also weird. Joe and I were never big on celebrating — the sudden happiness of everyone as the clock struck midnight seemed totally artificial to both of us.

But I did surprise myself this year. Who would of thought that a confirmed atheist like me would pray that the new year bring a speedy recovery for Joe and let us get our lives together back on track? Heck, I've been praying an awful lot lately. What kind of a lousy atheist am I?

Her discussions with Joe's doctors became more and more stale. "We're not seeing any change yet. But that's not unusual. Time is the best medicine we have, but it's impossible to predict either the final outcome or the amount of time required to see real improvement." Twice, Dr. Bhupathi suggested it might be more convenient for Ginny if Joe were transferred to the hospital in Jasper Creek. But Ginny refused both times. *Besides Columbus being the much more technically equipped hospital, they have significantly more specialists on staff here than in Jasper Creek. Moving Joe there would seem like giving up — almost like relocating him to a hospice to await the end. No way!*

As the message never seemed to change, Ginny gradually reduced her hospital visits from every day to two or three times per week. They all had her phone number if something changed. After a month or so, Ginny checked out of the hotel and moved back to Jasper Creek. She'd rather live at home than in a hotel room, especially with nothing to do for the majority of each day. The commute from Jasper Creek wasn't too large a price to pay, especially as the frequency of her hospital visits had decreased.

Ginny gradually started doing some police work again. Mostly petty stuff or assisting some of the other detectives. She didn't have her heart in it, but she was glad to have something to do to help pass the time and take her mind off Joe for a couple of hours at a time. The chief and other detectives were very understanding and supportive, but there really wasn't much they could actually do to help her. Or Joe. Ginny periodically checked in with Larkin and with the Ashley prosecutor, but her interest in the cases was more pro forma than sincerely felt. She was truly in a deep and dark place. She barely noticed as fall transitioned into winter.

I can't believe it. I'm reorganizing my closet again. Joe was definitely right. I do have OCD tendencies. Whenever I feel like I'm not in control of everything, I revert back to repeatedly cleaning and reorganizing my closet. That's something I can totally control, and that makes me feel a bit more in control of everything. I know Joe never went to medical school, so he must have learned all this with his psychiatry merit badge. Nothing I'd love more than to have him here teasing me about this. Like he always did. Shit — I meant "does" not "did."

— — — — — — — —

Then, three months after the Sunday morning she spoke with Musser, at 4:00 AM on a Wednesday in mid-January, Ginny was awakened by her phone.

Uh, oh. A four AM call is never good. "Uh, hello?"

"Detective Harris?"

"Yes."

"This is Rhoda Phillips, the night nursing supervisor here at the university hospital in Columbus."

"Oh, my God! No, no! How could this happen? The doctors kept saying that he could—"

"Detective. Detective, listen. I'm calling you with good news."

"You're what?"

"Yes, you heard me correctly. Good news. Your partner is awake. And he's asking for you."

Ginny started shaking so hard, she had to struggle to keep the phone close enough to her ear to hear anything. Tears of joy and relief were pouring down her cheeks, but she didn't even notice.

"Is he really awake? And OK?"

"Yes, he's really awake. Seems to be normal, but the doctors will, of course, want to run several tests to be sure."

"Can I see him? Please!"

"Yes, whenever you get here. I'll leave word at reception for them to let you right up. No need to wait for normal visiting hours."

"Thank you. Thank you. I'm on my way. Tell Joe I'm coming."

Ginny grabbed whatever clothing she saw first, got dressed and was in her car pulling out of the driveway within five minutes.

She tried to control her speeding on the way to Columbus, but she was not very successful. Driving with her eyes full of tears, she was fortunate that the roads were close to deserted at four in the morning.

An hour later, she was at the nursing station down the hall from Joe's room.

"Yes, you can see him now. I'll take you in. But I want to warn you. Don't be shocked. You know he's lost a lot of weight. Now that he's awake, you'll see for the first time how weak he is and how quickly he tires. His voice is also very soft and crackly. Yours would be too if you hadn't spoken for more than three months."

"I understand. Please, I want to see him now."

The nurse walked Ginny into Joe's room. Light shone from one small fixture hanging in the corner. Joe's eyes were extremely sensitive to bright light.

"Ginny. Hi. How're you doing?" said Joe in the weak, crackly voice the nurse had described to Ginny.

"Oh, my God, Joe. I'm doing better than I've ever been. I've been so, so worried about you."

"No need. You know I'm tough," said Joe with a half-smile.

Ginny looked to the nurse for approval, then ran over and gave Joe a light kiss and an exceptionally soft hug. She was afraid that he was so fragile a tight hug would break him in half. "You're so skinny. I know you wanted to lose a few pounds, but you overdid it."

"Not sure how not to lose weight with only raspberry Jell-O served through an IV tube."

"Very funny. I can't wait to get you back home and fatten you up a bit."

The nurse left and the detectives spent the next 15 minutes talking about everything and nothing: how Joe felt, what Ginny did and felt during the previous several months, not being able to wait until Joe could go home, what Joe wanted for each meal on his first day home, and so on.

"OK, folks," said the nurse as she re-entered the room. "Time to break up the party. My patient needs his rest. You'll have plenty of time to chat in the days ahead."

Ginny gave Joe another soft kiss, said she'd see him later and left the room. Joe was back asleep by the time Ginny reached the door.

Fortunately, the hospital cafeteria was open 24/7. Ginny spent the next four hours there, having three cups of coffee and breakfast, waiting until she could talk with the doctor.

Finally, at 9:15, she went to meet with the doctor, this time in his small office on the far side of the hospital building.

Ginny couldn't stop thanking him.

"Wasn't me. As I told you, time would do it. With a big assist, of course, from the willpower of your partner. He was going to get better no matter what."

With tears again flowing, Ginny asked, "What's next?"

"We'll want to do several tests over the next few days. That's the only way to determine if he's had any lasting neurological damage. Based on that and testing his motor skills, we'll devise a fairly aggressive program of physical rehab. At a minimum, he'll need to build his muscles back up. As you can imagine, they atrophied quite a bit after months of lying in bed. Not sure what else he may need — relearning certain physical things like eating and dressing, and so on. But we'll know more shortly. From a quick look this morning, I don't expect too many problems."

"Thank God. And thank you."

"There's a good chance you'll be able to take him

home soon. There are dozens of therapy organizations throughout the state that are fully capable of administering whatever program we specify."

Ginny didn't even try to hide her weeping. She was so happy, and needed this release badly.

Chapter 47

Ginny checked back into the hotel in downtown Columbus. She drove back to Jasper Creek to pack some clothes, then stopped at the station to give everyone the good news. They were all delighted for Joe and her, and the chief relieved Ginny of all her responsibilities for the next week, or longer if she needed it.

Ginny spent most of every day in the hospital. She never knew when Joe would be pulled away for another measurement or test, or for a physical therapy session, but she and Joe were able to spend at least a few hours together each day. Ginny was pleased to see how Joe was regaining some strength, and how the nurses were gradually weaning him back to a normal diet.

And as Joe got stronger, their conversations got longer.

"Ginny, where are we on Davis' murder? Did ballistics identify the gun yet?"

Joe was amazed at how much he had missed, and was pleased and proud of Ginny when she described all she had accomplished, including Danielle's confession.

"Fortunately, even her lawyer was impressed enough with Larkin's plea bargain offer that they retained her guilty plea. With the confession and plea, things went quickly. She's already started her ten-to-15-year term at the state Reformatory for Women. The good news is that it's only about 40 miles from Columbus, so her mother, who'll be bringing up her boys, can visit her if she wants to. The only ones I feel bad about are her two kids."

The discussion went a bit differently when Ginny started describing the trial of Brown's brother. Joe basically drew a blank. His memory of most things seemed fine, except he had no recollection of the explosion.

"So I've been told. But I don't really remember anything of it. I remember you and me knocking on the front door of her brother's house, while that officer from Ashley, I can't remember his name, went around to cover the back door. Next thing, I'm waking up here a few days ago."

"Joe, we shouldn't worry about that. Dr. Bhupathi told me it's perfectly normal. The brain often totally blocks traumatic events from our memory. Sort of a self-preservation kind of thing."

"I know, but it's still kind of weird. When I hear what happened, it's like a story I'm being told about someone else. He also said some or all of the memory may or may not eventually return."

"Joe, if that's the only lingering problem you have, we're in great shape."

"Can't agree more. By the way, how is that Ashley uniform who helped us?"

"Fine. Name's Billy Becker. Was home a few days, then on light duty and now fully back at work."

"That's good. Yeah, that was his name. So what's the deal with the brother?"

"Unbeknownst to us, he was running that meth lab in his kitchen. When we knocked on the front door, Brown, Danielle's her first name, opened it, and you saw her brother, named Zach Fielding, in the kitchen getting ready to flee out the back door. While you charged into the house, you had me keep Danielle out front. As the brother turned to run, he accidentally dropped or crashed into some of his equipment and chemicals. Then BOOM! You were just entering the kitchen. The blast left you unconscious, with a zillion cuts from flying glass, burns and a wicked concussion from either the explosion or when you hit the floor. Ambulance to here, and then a lifetime of fear and worry."

Joe took Ginny's hand in his and said, "All's well that ends well. By the way, I've been told that you probably saved my life."

"Oh, it was nothing," said Ginny with a false exaggerated wave of her free hand.

"Not the way I heard it."

"Seriously though, I was winging it. I really didn't know what to do with all the burns and cuts, you being unconscious and the toxic fumes floating throughout the kitchen."

"I can only imagine."

"At that moment, I made a commitment — for both of us — that as soon as things got back to normal we'd both attend an EMT course, so we'd know what to do in the future."

"Good idea. We've both had CPR and basic first aid training, but we should have more. Even what I learned long ago as a uniform, I've mostly forgotten. We got to use that information more often than I liked while on patrol, but we don't get to use it hardly at all as detectives."

"Yup, use it or lose it. I sorta knew the basics, but not stuff like toxic fumes."

"Understood. Like many other departments, we have policies about refresher courses, but, more often than not, they rarely or never happen."

"Right you are. Crime seems to always stick its head in the way."

"In any event, Ginny, I'm in. You can sign us up."

"Will do"

"So where's the case against the brother stand?"

"I checked the other day. He's pleading not guilty to the lab, but the prosecutor is confident he's got him good. No one saw the brother in the kitchen with the drug stuff, except you, and you can't remember. But it was his house, and his fingerprints were all over the glassware, other equipment and containers of chemicals. No way he can wiggle out of that. And his multiple scars from second- and third-degree chemical burns sure are strong circumstantial evidence. Still creeping through the courts, but the prosecutor is confident of a guilty verdict, with a probable eight to 12, most likely in Mansfield, about 50 miles north of Ashley."

"Can't say I feel too badly for him. Drugs in general, meth in particular and the explosion as a special extra gift just for me."

"Understood."

In between time with Joe and drinking coffee, Ginny called the chief, the other detectives in Jasper Creek, O'Grady at the front desk, Singleton at the DEA, Larkin in the Jasper Creek prosecutor's office, Becker and the police chief in Ashley, the Ashley prosecutor and most anyone else she could think of to share the good news of Joe's recovery.

Chapter 48

Tuesday was a big day. Dr. Bhupathi met with Ginny and Joe in Joe's room.

"I know you'll be very disappointed, Joe, but we're kicking you out of here today."

"You mean—"

"Sure do. Yes, you're being discharged this morning. They're doing all the paperwork as we speak."

"Wow. That's fantastic," said Ginny with a big, wide grin.

"We completed all our tests and evaluations and we couldn't be more pleased. Doesn't seem to be any neuro damage, and all of your cuts have healed. Our chief plastic surgeon checked your burns. They've all healed well. Most won't even be visible a year from now. A few of the larger burns on your upper torso will create permanent scars. But over time, the color will fade, the ridges will diminish and they'll look a lot less aggressive. At some point down the road, you'll have the option to have a few skin grafts if you want. They'd reopen the burn sites, harvest skin, most likely from your buttocks, and transplant it over the burn sites. I want to emphasize that all of your burns have closed from a functional standpoint. Any grafts you elect will be purely for aesthetical reasons."

"Well, we'll see," said Joe. "I may have them done if the scars start interfering with my leading-man movie career."

“What’s next, doctor?” asked Ginny.

The doctor addressed his answers to his patient. “The key is physical therapy. We’ve written out a definitive set of exercises, as well as the names and addresses of four therapy groups in the Jasper Creek area whom we’ve worked with and been happy with in the past. You need to select one and start the program as soon as possible. It’s a three-day-per-week regimen for three months, and it’s important you stick to it diligently. Most of it is to rebuild your muscles, but certain exercises also deal with common repetitive motions to get your body and brain refamiliarized with them. And I’ll want to see you monthly during the three-month period to gauge your progress and see if we need to make small changes in the regime.”

“Not a problem. I’m committed to giving it my all. Can I eat everything? Can I drive? Can I go back to work?”

“Seems like someone’s been planning his questions for today. Yes, you can eat anything, but I’d go a bit easy on very spicy foods for a few more weeks. Driving and work is up to you. As long as you feel strong enough, like to suddenly turn the steering wheel all the way around, and rested enough to be sure you won’t doze off at the wrong time, go for it. More from the viewpoint of avoiding any possible legal liability than for any medical reason, if it were me, I’d leave my gun in the drawer for the first month or so back at work.”

“Great. Thanks for everything, doctor.”

“You’re most welcome. And don’t forget to make your one-month appointment on your way out.”

With tears in her eyes, Ginny surprised herself by

giving Dr. Bhupathi a big hug and whispering, "Thank you so, so much!" in his ear.

Despite Joe's resistance, the nurse wheeled Joe to Ginny's car and helped him get in.

A little over an hour later, Ginny pulled into their driveway, and they both walked into the house. Ginny was overjoyed to have Joe home after almost four months, most of which were full of her contemplating the very worst possible outcomes. Joe was pleased to be home, but it didn't feel that monumental to him. To him it felt like he was away for less than a week, not for a third of a year.

Ginny and Joe had lunch, after which they researched the different therapists on Dr. Bhupathi's list, called their first choice and made an appointment for three o'clock the next afternoon.

Joe took a 90-minute nap and felt much rested when he awoke. Ginny wasn't more than two feet from his side the remainder of that day and evening.

"Ginny, now I believe you must have really been worried about me."

"Huh? Of course I was. What do you mean?"

"Judging by how neat your closet is, with your pants lined up by color, you must have really needed your OCD to kick in, giving you something fully under your control."

"Well, thank you very much, Dr. Freud. Anyhow, I'm glad you didn't lose your sense of humor while you were in the hospital."

Chapter 49

After breakfast the next morning, Joe asked Ginny to fill him in about all that happened with the militia and their compound. With several interrupting questions by Joe, it took Ginny almost an hour to get through everything.

"Ginny, I'm not surprised that once Turley was confronted, he pretty quickly figured out it was Rudy Musser who had called 9-1-1. Not sure if Musser overreacted or not, but glad he scooted. Seemed like a good kid. Hope he's done with the militia life."

"No idea where he went. But I had the sense that his militia days were behind him."

Ginny then mentioned Davis' cremation and memorial service, to which she was clearly not invited. "His ashes then went to Utah, for a traditional Mormon funeral and burial. Several of the folks from here went to Utah for that. Most came back, but several didn't. Most interesting is Turley, who went for the service but didn't return. Before Turley left, Larkin and I warned him he was going to be charged with obstruction — for having the body secretly buried, and for lying to us about where Davis might be. As Larkin pointed out to him, we'd most likely not even try to extradite him back here. But if he didn't return, we'd be very tempted to tell Davis' uncle, the head honcho, how Turley kept things a secret and had his nephew unceremoniously buried. So, what's your thinking? Tell the uncle or not?"

"Hmm. Good question. I'd say no. In the scheme of things, his obstruction didn't really mess us up that much. Not to mention, not saying anything now gives us something to hold over his head if we ever need anything from him."

"Well, I'm glad to see your injuries didn't damage your slyness at all."

"That's me, still a sly, old fox."

"I should mention that Davis' wives numbers one and two also decided to stay in Utah. Number three, Clara Hansen, stayed here with all their children. In the end, she decided to leave the group and go live with her sister in Lincoln, Nebraska. She took the others' children back to them in Utah, and plans to stay in touch with her so-called sister-wives. Especially as all the kids are half-siblings with each other."

"Interesting."

"Also should mention that wives two and three, both of whom were pregnant, gave birth. Both had girls."

"Probably future militia members and polygamist wives."

"Could be, though I sure hope not. Who knows?"

"Anything else?"

"Another handful of members decided to leave the group. They moved to various locations all over the eastern half of the country."

"What about the group remaining here — and their compound?"

"Disbanded. The folks that matter in Utah decided to call off their geographic expansion, at least for the time being. I haven't driven out there, but apparently everything of value is back in Utah. A wealthy land speculator in Columbus supposedly bought the 600 acres for pennies on the dollar. With very minimal property taxes, he figures he can be patient for years until the land prices rise enough."

"Quite the story."

"Yup. I always said I'd like a nice piece of property for us, but 600 acres out in the middle of nowhere is a bit much. Even for me."

"Me, too. That reminds me. Where are we on looking for a house? Last I recall, you were going to schedule a few realtors to be interviewed."

"Yes, I was. But a minor explosion and a mere almost four-month death-like experience for my fiancé seems to have put that on hold. Let's get you at least partway through this period of therapy so you're stronger, then we can pick up where we left off."

"Works for me. By the way, one more question. We, which really means you in this case, ever figure out the details of Mark's secret little trips?"

"Only in part. Don't, and probably never will, know about his early trips — where he went or how he traveled, but once he met Danielle, she was his destination. He'd walk toward the end of that old logging road, past where he was later buried, and she'd pick him up in her truck and drive to her house. She then brought him back to the same place. He always left his cell in the compound so his location couldn't be tracked, and he always carried his gun, the murder weapon as it turned out, with him."

"OK. I think I'm fully up to date on everything. Now what?"

"I've got a special treat for you. But first, it's still early enough. Let's swing by the station and let everyone greet you in the flesh."

"Sure, so long as they don't start fussing over me."

"Don't you worry, they definitely will."

And they did. Everyone was thrilled to see Joe, and especially thrilled at how well he looked. Other than his loss of weight and tired appearance, he looked much more like the old Joe than they had expected. The welcome, best wishes and, of course, well-meaning jokes were all par for the course. Ginny and Joe then spent a few minutes with the chief, talking about Joe and his planned return to work, after which Ginny updated the chief on the various aspects of the cases she hadn't yet told him about.

"Well done, Ginny. Especially with you having to do the work of two while this guy was relaxing in that luxury spa in Columbus," said the chief with a chuckle.

Back in the bullpen, Ginny said, "OK. Time for your surprise." Ginny stood in the middle of the large room and yelled, "Who's with us for lunch at Sancho's? My treat."

Almost the entire department joined them. A good time was had by all, even Joe — despite the few times Ginny had to redirect him to the milder food choices.

Ginny pulled into the parking lot of Partners in Physiotherapy at 2:45. They spent about 30 minutes with two therapists reviewing the program put together by Dr. Bhupathi. They set up standing appointments for Joe for every Monday, Wednesday and Friday at 1:15. Each session would last one hour, and Joe should expect to receive various homework exercises each week. The first real session would begin on Friday.

Chapter 50

The next three months flew by. Joe was diligent with his therapy appointments and exercise homework. He also began weightlifting and jogging as his strength returned. He was soon driving and back at work full-time, carrying his handgun once again.

The monthly visits with Dr. Bhupathi were positive, the doctor pleased by each month's progress. At the third and final meeting, the three of them celebrated Joe's so-called graduation with burned coffee and stale Danish in the hospital cafeteria. But it tasted like a gourmet meal to Ginny and Joe.

As Ginny had committed to, they both signed up for an EMT course, given at the community college three nights a week plus one Saturday a month for 15 weeks. They learned a great deal and passed the final written and practical exams with flying colors. They were proud to have become state- and nationally-certified EMTs, despite having no interest in switching careers.

Ginny also spent additional time researching real estate agents on the Internet. She reviewed her findings with Joe, and they agreed upon the three agents they would schedule initial meetings with. These three meetings took place over a one-week period in April.

After the interviews, each of the three candidates returned with their proposed action plan and whatever additional information Joe and Ginny had asked for. The detectives selected Laura Gibson of Horizon Realty. Once Ginny told Gibson she had been selected, she returned and walked through the house with Ginny and Joe, offering several tips on how to make the house look more appealing and larger to prospective buyers. Both detectives were impressed, and agreed to start the process in earnest as soon as Joe regained a bit more strength and they had a chance to refine their house preferences and budgetary limitations.

Chapter 51

After breakfast on Sunday morning, Joe said, "Ginny, grab your coffee and let's head for the living room. We gotta talk a few things through."

"Uh, oh. That never sounds good. What's up?"

"It's more than a two-minuter. Let's go sit on the couch."

"OK. Give me your cup. I'll freshen us both up."

Two minutes later, the two detectives were sitting side by side on the living room couch.

"OK, Joe. Let me have it."

"We should slow down the realtor before she gets all cranked up."

"Think we should focus on selling your house before we start looking for our new house? Afraid of legally committing to buy a house and then having trouble selling this one quickly enough?"

"Yeah. But that's not it."

"Better spell it out for me."

"We should turn her off for now on both the selling and the buying."

"But.... Why? What changed?"

"A whole bunch of stuff."

"Joe, have your feelings about me changed? You can be honest. Just tell me."

"Hell, no, Ginny. It's not that at all. In fact, I think I love you more now than ever."

"Whew. Well, that's a relief. So what is it?"

"I think it all grew out of the explosion. I could be dead now. Or seriously handicapped. And all you had to go through while I was in that coma."

"All true. But how does all that lead to stopping the house sale and purchase effort?"

"How 'bout five ways?"

"Let's hear them."

"I'm not sure I want to keep doing this detective stuff. I was pretty damn lucky with that explosion. For all I know, I may have used up all my good luck. Next time could be a permanent disaster."

"Joe, I—"

"Let me finish, Ginny. We can discuss everything after I get all my thoughts out."

"OK. Go for it."

"Number two, although I was unconscious through it all, I can picture the hell you went through for all those months. Now I can picture you worrying yourself sick whenever I'm out doing something and I'm five minutes late getting back. Even worse, I fear that we're going to start subconsciously protecting each other whenever we're doing something dangerous together. That's not only unsafe for us, but it really increases the risk for anyone working with us."

"All right. I'll hold my comments until you get through your list."

"Thanks. Don't worry, the next three are less gloomy than the first two."

"Well, that's a relief."

"OK. Number three is children. We've done a good job of avoiding this subject forever. But I know that you'd love to have a kid or two. I know you feel your biological clock is getting pretty late, yet you don't want to push me 'cause I already had Adam. I appreciate that, but I don't want you to miss out on being a parent. And I know you'd be a great one. If we have a kid, or two or three, should we really both be on the job, especially working together and facing the same risks at the same time?"

"I appreciate that, Joe."

"Hang on. I'm on a roll now. We keep talking about retiring to Florida or one of the Caribbean islands. Half in jest, but also half seriously. Maybe we're getting close. Counting my years with Chicago PD, I've now been on the job just shy of 19 years. And you, 12 years, 17 if you include your initial time as a clerk with the PD. We should check out the Caribbean to see if it's our cup of tea. Or coffee.

"And, last but not least, we still need to get our wedding plans set and finally get married already."

"Jeez, Joe, you make getting married sound like a chore similar to washing the floor."

"Well, that's not what I mean. And you know it."

"I do. Just teasing you."

"OK, so here's my proposal from all of this. We put the house stuff on hold. All of it. We set our wedding date and make all the plans, including time off for a honeymoon. We get married and take a Caribbean cruise. That'll let us check out several of the islands, in between, of course, the normal honeymoon stuff."

"Yikes, your brain must have been working overtime while you were in that coma. You sure came up with a plan, along with all the supporting arguments."

"Ginny, there's one other very important detail."

"Oh? What is it?"

"Buried within all my points and conclusions was my proposal that we actually get married — the sooner the better. Aren't you supposed to answer when someone proposes to you?"

"Yeah, I think so. At least that's what always happens in the movies."

"So?"

"Hell, yes, you big dummy. Was there ever any doubt in your mind?"

And so, Ginny put the realtor on a temporary hold, refocusing her attention on comparing what seemed like dozens of different Caribbean cruise options, selecting the desired cruise and resultant wedding date, finding a wedding venue, finalizing the list of invitees and requesting vacation time from the chief.

STUART SAFFT

Born in Brooklyn, NY, Stuart has lived in 7 states and 4 European countries. He and his wife now live in the foothills of the Blue Ridge Mountains. Stuart earned an engineering degree from Swarthmore College and an MBA from Harvard University. His career has included work for large multinational firms, small startups and management consulting firms. Stuart and his wife are instrument-rated private pilots and Stuart is a volunteer firefighter & EMT and a Red Cross Disaster Responder.

See Stuart Safft on Facebook.

Other Books from Stuart Safft

Where's Ellen?
A Joe McFarland / Ginny Harris Mystery

Body in the Warehouse
A Joe McFarland / Ginny Harris Mystery

Killed at Home
A Joe McFarland / Ginny Harris Mystery

Cold Cargo
A Joe McFarland / Ginny Harris Mystery

Missing from Pond View
A Joe McFarland / Ginny Harris Mystery

Killed, But Why?
A Joe McFarland / Ginny Harris Mystery

www.ingramcontent.com/pod-product-compliance
Lightning Source LLC
LaVergne TN
LVHW010053110826
845155LV00028B/315